Praise for

THE HOLLOW GIRL

"A riveting tale of pain and revenge, Hillary Monahan's *The Hollow Girl* hits the horrifying notes—dread and darkness and grisly ends— yet somehow still feels full of heart. There is magic here, and power, and Monahan's Romani background shines in every detail. I couldn't tear my eyes away."   —**Kendare Blake**, *New York Times* bestselling author of *Three Dark Crowns*

"A richly woven tapestry of magic, betrayal, and revenge told by a strong, spirited heroine who won my heart, broke it to pieces, and then healed it anew. Brava!"   —**Dawn Kurtagich**, award-winning author of *The Dead House*

"A dark tale of revenge and justice in which fighting back means pushing the boundaries of what it can mean to be female."
     —**Mindy McGinnis**, Edgar Award–winning author of *The Female of the Species*

"Hillary Monahan's *The Hollow Girl* is tense and raw, an excellent novel of pain and intimate magic. There is ugly human darkness here, but there is also hope and love and family. Monahan is a natural-born storyteller whose words kept me reading long into the night. Terrific!"
     —**Christopher Golden**, *New York Times* bestselling author of *Ararat* and *Snowblind*

"*The Hollow Girl* is required reading: a tour de force of female power, craft, and emotion."   —**Sarah Gailey**, author of *River of Teeth*

THE
HOLLOW
GIRL

HILLARY MONAHAN

DELACORTE PRESS

Delacorte Press is a registered trademark and the colophon is a trademark of Penguin Random House LLC.

Visit us on the Web! randomhouseteens.com

Educators and librarians, for a variety of teaching tools, visit us at RHTeachersLibrarians.com

Library of Congress Cataloging-in-Publication Data
Names: Monahan, Hillary, author.
Title: The hollow girl / Hillary Monahan.
Description: First edition. | New York : Delacorte Press, [2017]
Summary: Bethan, apprentice to a Welsh Roma witch, is harassed by the son of the clan's chieftan and then, after a brutal assault against her and a friend, must collect grisly objects to save her friend's life.
Identifiers: LCCN 2016049837 (print) | LCCN 2017022964 (ebook) |
ISBN 978-1-5247-0187-1 (el) | ISBN 978-1-5247-0186-4 (hc)
Subjects: | CYAC: Apprentices—Fiction. | Witchcraft—Fiction. | Magic—Fiction. |
Romanies—Fiction. | Disfigured persons—Fiction. | Friendship—Fiction.
Classification: LCC PZ7.M73655 (ebook) | LCC PZ7.M73655 Hol 2017 (print) |
DDC [Fic]—dc23

The text of this book is set in 12-point Garamond 3.
Interior design by Ken Crossland

Printed in the United States of America
10 9 8 7 6 5 4 3 2 1
First Edition

FOR MY GRANDMOTHER,

WHO SHOULD HAVE

BEEN HERE TO SEE THIS

ΛUTHOR'S FOREWORD

Ten years ago, I sat in my grandmother's basement listening to her talk about a story she intended to write. She was a wordsmith by trade, wrote with Charles Schulz (of Peanuts fame), and was one of the original writers of the Maxine cards for Hallmark. The story she'd crafted was of two Romani sisters, one who left her family's caravan after her marriage and struggled to acclimate to a gadjo world. The other sister stayed with the caravan, on the moors of Wales, and studied under her sorceress grandmother.

My grandmother never said she was Romani, but she had stories to tell, about her father from Pontypridd, her childhood, and her aunt Maude. The details of those stories have left far more questions than answers about customs, identity, and assimilation. I was too young and ignorant to know what to ask her about her people but hindsight is always twenty-twenty. I wish I knew then what I know now, etc., etc.

My grandmother died unexpectedly not long after she told me about her Romani sisters. I started writing after that, as a therapy exercise to combat my grief, and came to find out I was the one in the family to take after her. I was the Other Writer. I simply didn't acknowledge that until later. I published some horror and wrote some comedy, and I realized I wanted to write a story that was honorific of my grandmother—the woman who meant so much to me, who was my best friend, who told such amazing tales. The obvious choice was her Romani sisters story, but I didn't feel comfortable tackling the oppression of the Romani in the first scenario, the outsider in a gadjo world. I didn't live it, wasn't close enough to people who did, and my grandmother's stories were incomplete at best. Reading about a subject is different from experiencing it firsthand. There's a delicacy to stories of oppression, and I didn't trust myself to do hers justice.

The second sister, though, the witch—that was something I felt more comfortable playing with, though it, too, gave me some pause. Everyone has heard the trope of the Romani fortune-teller (usually called gypsies, but that word is problematic from a gadjo, and I discourage anyone from using it), but the reality was, among the Kale in particular, some people made their livings through curatives, portents, and spell work. Knowing that, I felt that my challenge was to craft a story that twisted the problematic trope into a story of empowerment while also being honorific of the Romani culture *and* my grandmother's vision. I also wanted to make it my own story in some way, and I did that by incorporating the difficult subject of sexual assault from a survivor's perspective. People should know before going into this book that a rape does happen and is a major plot point. It takes place "off-camera," but it is there, and I wouldn't spring that on anyone without fair warning.

The Hollow Girl is a book close to my heart, not only because of my grandmother, but because it tackles subjects I've struggled with for a long time. Despite its dark points, I consider it a story of survival, and strength, and familial bonds—of women overcoming obstacles. It's about a Romani girl coping with a taboo subject in a traditionally modest society. It's about the choices we make and how they change us, for better and for worse, and I hope you can find some enjoyment in the reading.

I also hope I've done my grandmother, wherever she may be, proud.

HJM
October 2016

CHAPTER ONE

My chin rested in my palm. My eyelids were heavy. Gran's arm
darted out, her liver-spotted hand whacking the inside of my
elbow to knock it off the table. It pulled me out of my stupor,
but almost cost me my teeth.

"I am not saying this twice." She reached for a cluster of
herbs hanging from a hook in the ceiling and snapped off two
sprigs of green with dusky-purple flowers. "Dwayberry."

"Nightshade," I said, fairly certain I had it right.

She flipped over the stems, showing the shiny, dark berries
on the underside. They were beautiful, fat and juicy, like they
belonged in a pie. Gran jiggled them in front of my nose and
they made a *rustle, rustle, rustle.* "Small doses numb pain, larger
cause hallucinations. More than that is the pretty poison—it is
sweet to the taste, so they smile before they die. Seven to kill a
child, twenty to kill a man. Do you understand?"

"Yes."

" 'Yes' what?"

"Yes, Gran. I understand."

Her left eye swept over my face, the pupil milky white and covered by what she called her ghost shroud. It was not a source of power, she told me once, even if people assumed otherwise.

"My gift of sight has nothing to do with my blindness, nor does it have anything to do with our Romani blood," she'd said. "I was born with a caul upon my face. Lifting it lifted the veil between worlds, sometimes allowing me glimpses of what will be. The eye is a theater prop—nothing more."

Her sight must not have shown her much at that moment, though, as she turned her head to set her brown eye upon me, searching for cheekiness I didn't wear. I'd learned at a young age never to sass *my* grandmother. Other children had their hands slapped or their bottoms paddled when they were ill-mannered. I'd once lost the ability to speak for two days. Another time, she'd bound me to a chair for three hours without ever touching me with rope.

"I've been studying herbs for five years." I kept my voice even, neutral, so she wouldn't accuse me of whining. Gran always punished whining with the worst chores, like gathering stinkgrass by the bucketful. "I'd like to study magic. You said anyone can do it with training."

She talked about it sometimes, about the hearth witches of Ireland granting powerful blessings and casting terrible curses. The English witches could hear the wind's whispered secrets and control the weather. The Scottish witches had mastered fire and water, just as our Welsh kinsfolk could influence dreams.

The magic Gran claimed—that I would one day claim—was vast and varied, picked up over generations of traveling.

I hung from every story Gran told about it, mostly because she was never forthcoming with details about the spellcraft, always exiling me from the vardo when there was witchwork to do. My education was her rare offered snippet or fireside story hours with the other children.

Both left me with more questions than answers.

Gran snorted and tossed her head, locks of gray hair slithering past her shoulders. It had started off in a tight bun beneath her red scarf, but the hours had disintegrated it to a stringy, sloppy mess. "You barely pay attention to herbcraft."

"Because I know much of it already. I want to learn something new!" I'd already learned how herbal tonics saved lives under the best conditions, and under the worst, ended them. *That* was the part that interested me. She'd lost me when she droned on about the responsibilities of herbcraft.

"I will be the one to determine when you are ready." She pushed herself from the table, her back hunched as she hobbled through the vardo, past the window, and toward the cot in the corner. She reached for a basket of curatives and charm bags, riffling through the sacks to ensure everything was accounted for. The cures were real enough: some for sour stomach, others for a pained head or aching bones. I knew which was which by the colored yarns tied around the pouch tops. The charm bags sold better, but they were novelties—usually the refuse of the plants we'd used for the medicines. Gran would throw an animal bone or a shiny bead inside to make them look more legitimate, but there was no magic there. It was a pretend solution for a bargain price.

She slid the basket my way. "Do not come back from town until you have coin in your pocket. And wear your scarf over your face. We do not want trouble." I flinched at the reminder, but she ignored me, pulling a silky black scarf off her mirror, her fingers sliding along the silver-threaded edges. "Wear this one. It is pretty."

I took it with a muttered "thank you," winding the scarf over my head and tucking it around my nose and mouth, over my birthmark. I'd been born with half my body painted wine, the other half so pale one wondered if I'd ever seen the sun. Gran called me her eclipse. I was dark on the left, light on the right, and some people—outsiders, the *gadjos*—recoiled, claiming I'd been touched by evil while in my mother's womb. When I'd gone into Anwen's Crossing for the first time the week before, a woman screeched at me, insisting I renounce the devil. I'd assured her that I and my people were Christians like her, but it hadn't mattered. Only the pity of a local priest had kept her and her friends from jabbing me with pitchforks and flaming torches.

I'd never been so afraid in my life. I'd run all the way back to the caravan, a mile from town, breathless and trembling and half expecting the angry faces to haunt my shadow. Gran had listened to my babbled excuses, nodded, and squeezed my shoulder in sympathy, but she wasn't happy. We depended on the income from market sales, and now we'd need to make two weeks' worth of sales instead of one to recover our losses.

Gran peered at me a moment before tugging my braid from under the fabric, the dark coil interwoven with pretty ribbons.

"Such beautiful hair." She smiled faintly, letting me know

4

she cared for me even if she was as demonstrative as stone. "Keep your wits about you. Stay sharp."

"I will. I'll be home before dark."

"Of course you will. With coin in hand this time, no doubt."

"Yes, Gran."

"Good. Now shut your mouth and go."

As soon as I was out the door, I wished Gran were going in my stead. Until last season, I'd been the one assembling the herb bags while she hawked our goods at open market, but her legs had worsened over the winter. She needed a cane more often than not, and walking to town would cripple her. As I was a healthy young woman in her prime, it only made sense to have me take over sales duty.

The real money was in spellcraft, of course, but Gran was very particular about who she'd work with. The gifts most outsiders expected of her were as shallow as their opinions of our people, so that was all she was willing to provide them—shallow magic. Fortune-telling and false charms, empty predictions about lackluster love lives. Gran used their biases against them—a blind eye that sometimes made her stumble on uneven ground or bump into furniture became a gateway to another world, granting her visions of what had been and what would be.

But those who respected her and her craft—usually Roma and friends of Roma—could buy true magic in all its wonders and horrors. Saving a life, changing a fate, blessings, and scrying to see the future.

As we'd only been parked in the area a week, no one had come looking for spellwork yet. Until they did, I would persevere and cover my face in hopes that it would keep me safe from superstitious ignorance. Maybe the priest would be there to help if things got out of hand again. And if not, I had strong legs. I could run like a colt if the need arose.

I rounded the last of our vardos and tents and passed our grazing horses to approach the road, my eyes skipping to the great fire at the center of our caravan town. It was the designated meeting place for my people to talk, cook, and conduct business throughout the day. Everyone gathered there after hours, when the coffee flowed like water and fiddles and harps wailed their songs. I smiled, hoping I might get back in time to dance before bed, but then I caught sight of Silas and his band of horrible friends standing near the cookpots, and my smile went to the wind. I put my head down and walked faster, my fingers tugging the scarf higher on my face. Maybe it was enough of a disguise to keep me beneath his notice. Maybe he'd dismiss me as some other girl.

Most of my clansmen treated me with respect. I was the adopted daughter of Drina—Gran—our wisewoman, who'd left her own caravan to stay with us after the last *drabarni* died birthing me. All I knew about my birth mother was that she'd been called Eira and had been as lovely as a rose bloom, with silky hair and fine teeth. My gadjo father abandoned me upon her death, too distraught to handle the loss of his beloved, and too afraid of his "strange-looking" daughter to raise her, and so I was given into Drina's care.

Silas Roberts never minded the birthmark that had scared off my own father. He even went so far as to give me special attention, propositioning me whenever Gran wasn't nearby. It was the ultimate disrespect. He knew that our clan girls went to their wedding beds pure lest they be ostracized, yet

6

he shrugged off propriety and chased me anyway. Perhaps he thought I would be grateful for his advances because I looked different, and other men might not want me. Neither of us had a marriage set up, so perhaps he thought we'd make a suitable pair. It was rare for young adults to not have an arrangement in place, but Silas's intended had died when he was eleven, and Gran would not give me over to a betrothal knowing I was to be her heir.

That alone should have stopped his pursuit—my relationship to Gran. Gran often said the chieftain was the mind of our people but the drabarni was the heart. She was trusted implicitly with our welfare and, as our healer, was the only one among us who wouldn't be sullied by touching people's most personal, impure fluids. Our kin honored her and her wisdoms and turned to her in their darkest hours.

Yet Silas was ambivalent to her station. He lived as if free of consequence, which I supposed wasn't completely untrue. The chieftain had a soft spot for his youngest child and rarely punished him. Once, after Silas had been caught closing in on another girl in the caravan, the chieftain called him "an unbridled stallion ready for a filly," dismissing his wickedness as "boyish exuberance."

I had no interest in such *boys*.

Seeing him standing there with his hands buried in his pockets and a lopsided sneer on his face, my gripes about going to town disappeared, and I lifted my skirt a few inches to walk faster. As I ducked behind one of the vardos, there was a shrill whistle, followed by a chorus of masculine laughter. When Silas laughed, his friends laughed, like a pack of jackals. They did everything together and had since they were babies, all born within two years of each other, the oldest then eighteen, the youngest sixteen. They were so inseparable, I'd mused before that the five of them shared a single twisted mind.

"Bethan, why so fast? Slow down and say hello. It's a beautiful day."

I disagreed; the morning air carried a chill that shredded through my clothes, but saying so would engage him in conversation, and that was akin to letting the devil into one's home. Instead, I made for the road at almost a trot, the basket swinging by my side. I had a ways to go. Our camp bordered fields of barley and wheat, and the local farmers had built crude wooden fences to mark property lines. The only way to get around them was to walk until there was a break.

I contemplated vaulting the pasture fence by my side, but our customs dictated that I comport myself as a lady at all times, never showing anything above the ankle to a man other than my husband, and leaping a fence would lift my skirt past my knees. If Silas followed me, he might interpret the gesture as an invitation, and he was handsy enough already.

I heard footsteps approaching as someone—a few someones—trailed me: two behind, two alongside, and one at the front. I spotted a break in the fence ten yards ahead, and I darted for it, but Silas leaped out from behind one of the goods wagons to block my path. I stumbled back, my heart pounding, but a pair of hands pressed against my shoulders to shove me forward again. I spun my head to see who was there. Mander and Cam stood shoulder to shoulder behind me, a wall preventing my retreat.

Mander was tall and thin with dark hair worn to his shoulders, his cheek bulging with the tobacco he always chewed.

Cam was bigger, broader, and fairer of skin, with dark hair shorn short and gray eyes he'd inherited from his *diddicoy* mother.

If I peeked around the vardo to my left, I was sure I'd see skinny, befreckled Tomašis and stout, dark Brishen, both jackals awaiting Silas's instructions. Growing up, they hadn't been bad boys, but as Silas poisoned the well, they drank from his waters until they, too, were sick.

"I was *talking* to you." Silas closed the gap between us. He dipped his head to look at me from beneath the dark arches of his brows. To most girls he was handsome, with hair so black it shined blue in the sun; a long, hooked nose; wide lips; and high-sculpted cheekbones, but my distaste for him made me think of a crow, his hair too glossy, his eyes too dark, his chin too pointed. Crows were eaters of death. I could not and would not like anything of their ilk.

I hoisted the basket in his direction, counting on the woven reeds to keep a respectful distance between our bodies. "I have to get to town. The market day is starting soon, and Gran wants . . ."

"Soon. Relax. Be sweet for me."

When Silas stepped forward, I took another step back, and the other boys tittered with sinister joy. Mander pushed me straight at Silas and Silas batted the basket aside, his arm looping around my waist to pull me close, until I was pressed against him. Some of my poultices spilled onto the grass below, and he stepped on them, oblivious to their importance, his hand stroking my back in far too intimate a gesture.

"Smile for me. You're so pretty when you smile."

I slapped at his hands with my free one, a wail bubbling in my throat. I was afraid, but not in the same way I'd been at market. In town, I feared for my person at the hands of an angry mob, feared physical blows that would bruise or bleed. In camp, I dreaded the disdain of my people. I dreaded someone discovering Silas's hands below my waist, or my skirt touching his legs. I did not want to go before the council. I did not want to pay reparations for deeds that were not my choice, or to bring shame or annoyance to Gran's doorstep.

"Let me go. I'll tell Gran, and you'll wish I hadn't."

"And I'll tell my father that you propositioned me. Who do you think the chieftain will believe? His son and four witnesses? Or a single girl with no one to stand for her?" His face shifted from smiling prankster to vile predator before he reached up and jerked the scarf away from my face.

My breakfast churned in my guts, leaving me faint and nauseated. Calling for help could paint me a harlot, especially with Silas's band willing to side against me. I had to think of a way to extricate myself before the matter worsened.

Only one thing I knew scared outsiders and Roma alike.

Gran.

I had to invoke Gran.

"*Loma greeeecia tana faroo!*" I shouted in his face, wadding a ball of spit and lobbing it at his cheek. This was how all of Gran's magic ended—with spit and some loud, declarative words in a language I didn't understand—so I did the same, except my words were nonsense and made of desperation, while hers were a true other tongue.

The spit was real enough, though. It dribbled down Silas's cheek to pool onto his white shirt.

Silas staggered away from me to slap his cheek, eyes wide.

"What did you do to me, Witch? What did you do? I burn. I burn!"

I glowered at him, my fingers tightening on the handle of the basket so he wouldn't see how badly they trembled. I'd never confess to Silas that I knew no curses. If my spit burned, it was because he imagined it. The only power I could claim was the knowledge that I was far cleverer than the chieftain's son. "What do you think I did, Silas?"

No answer. He scampered away from me so quickly he skidded over the dew-laden grass, landing on his knees and then his bottom before running toward the great fire. His friends followed, their boots pounding the earth. I wasted no time gathering my dropped poultices and returning them to my basket. I tugged the scarf back into place and jogged for the road, casting cursory glances over my shoulder every few feet to ensure I wasn't being followed.

It wasn't until the caravan was a tiny speck on the horizon that I relaxed, turning my attention to the market and the coin I must make, for myself and for Gran. Our people took care of our own, and our kin had been more than happy to provide for us, but we always settled our debts.

CHAPTER TWO

Anwen's Crossing was unlike other towns in that the gadjos welcomed all manner of tradesmen, homegrown and outside alike, and provided them with ample room to conduct their business. Vendors who made money in Anwen's Crossing were more apt to spend it there, after all, and such a philosophy had turned an inconsequential port town into a bustling hub of commerce my people visited for two months every autumn.

People started their setups early so they could claim the most prominent positions near the front and back entrances and directly across from the well. Thanks to Silas's nonsense, I arrived in town later than the other vendors, so I was relegated to leftover space. The previous week, I'd been positioned next to the well—everyone had to pass me to get somewhere else. If I'd been allowed to see my day through, I'd have sold out in a matter of hours. That day I found a small table tucked between two larger stands at the back of the square. It would be slow going, but at least I ran a smaller risk of being spotted by the Crossing's henchmen. There was also shade beneath the brightly colored awnings along the perimeter, so when the sun burned hot at midday, I'd be comfortable.

I laid out the herb bags, displaying them in neat, appealing rows. When other vendors strolled by to inspect the competition's wares, I shook my sleeve down so no one spied the dappled, freckly effect my birthmark had on my fingers. Silas once commented that it reminded him of mud splatters on the side of a vardo after heavy rains.

But that hadn't stopped him from holding my hand against my will, had it?

I'd just gotten the love charms lined up beside the hex charms when I heard the hissing. I glanced up to see a grimy-looking man staring at me from the market path. He was as old as the dirt beneath his boots. He wore big clothes over lean bones, and his face was worn with wrinkles, his cheeks riddled with red spots and a few days' worth of unshaved grizzle. Crusts of dried food soiled the deep crevices near his mouth.

"You must be the witchling. I heard you wear devil's stain." He tottered toward me, one of his calloused fingers motioning at my face. His nearness clearly unnerved me, yet closer he came, smelling of sweat and liquor and manure.

I glanced around, uneasy. Had other people heard him? This was how last week had started, too. One woman had seen my markings and told two others, who then told two others. Before long, there had been a dozen gadjos all poking and jeering at me like they wanted to string me up and burn me in the middle of the square.

I fidgeted with the scarf, winding it tighter around my neck so it wouldn't shift out of place. My stomach flipped like a fish washed ashore, and I squeezed the handle of my basket so hard, the dried reeds crackled in my grasp.

Deep breaths helped quell my rabbit-beating heart. Channeling Gran did, too. "Do not borrow problems, idiot child," she'd say. "Some will be ignorant of our ways and distrustful of things they do not bother to understand, but most will appreciate the jingle of your coin." If my birthmark was offensive, Gran's ghost eye surely was, and she'd survived ignorant villagers for more summers than I could count. Of course, she'd had the benefit of her frightening scowl to ward off people—she looked every part the storybook witch with her wrinkles, straight teeth, and toe-curling grimaces. I was a normal girl so I couldn't inspire the same kind of fear. Still, I set my jaw and looked the man in the eye.

"I want to do my business. I'm no affront to you," I said.

"Let me see it. Let me see your sin." He leaned over the table, swiping at me. His fist found my shirtsleeve and gave it a solid tug, and I felt his fingers pinching my skin through the thin fabric. I skittered back until the wooden fence pressed against my back, but it wasn't far enough. I tried to squirm away so he wouldn't touch me with his unclean hands.

"Garth! Leave the girl alone or I'll call the constable." A voice boomed from the farm stand beside me.

I looked over, my heart in my throat. A broad-shouldered young man with yellow hair and blue eyes stood behind the counter, an apple clenched in one big hand, a stack of thick paper with a crude sketch of the square in the other. His fingers

14

were dusted with charcoal, his nails stained black from drawing. "Are you in your cups again, old man?"

Garth's nostrils flared. "Haven't touched a bottle since last night."

"Well, that's a first. Leave her alone. She's trying to sell medicine. Maybe if you stopped being an arsehole, she'd give you something for your gout."

"Or maybe she'll turn me into a toad! Witches can do that sort of thing, I heard!" Garth squinted at me as if he could ascertain my toad-turning ability simply by staring hard enough. I jerked my arm away from him and patted at my sleeve, my teeth biting the sides of my tongue so my jaw wouldn't shudder. I was scared, but I didn't want to show it; once a bully smelled fear, he kept dipping into the pool for more.

"I know no magic. These are cures and charms my grandmother made, nothing more," I snapped.

Garth bounced in his boots and flattened his hand on top of his head as if holding it were the only way to keep it attached to his scrawny neck. "You heard her! Her grandmother made mystical charms. She's got witch blood!"

"And you've got idiot blood." The blond man with the big voice let out a shrill whistle that shredded the din of chattering vendors and early shoppers. Faces turned his way, some curious, some concerned. The blond scanned them all, I assumed to search for the aforementioned constable.

Which wasn't good for me.

"Don't," I said. "Please. Just make him go away."

I wouldn't explain myself to him, but law enforcement

rarely treated my people fairly, and I didn't trust that Garth's pestering wouldn't somehow be twisted into *my* wrongdoing.

The young man nodded despite his obvious confusion. "As you like. You heard her, Garth. Go home to sleep it off."

"Fine, fine. I'm going, but if I get boils, I'm coming back for her, Woodard."

The blond smirked. "If you get boils, it's from the dock whores. Leave before the constable patrols this way. He's due any minute now."

Garth's head swiveled and his lean shoulders hunched in an effort to make himself appear smaller. He scuttled off into the market, weaving his way through the manmade alleyways of carts, tables, and stands to disappear from view.

I glanced at the young man with the apple and the sketch pad. He smiled at me, his teeth a line of white against sun-kissed skin. He was a full head taller than me and built like a bull, with a straw-colored shirt that stretched across a work-thick chest and dark-blue trousers held up by black suspenders.

"I'm Martyn Woodard. A pleasure," he said, tipping an imaginary hat. "Sorry about Garth. He haunts these parts after dawn. Spends his nights drinking and then stumbles through town to get home, drunk as a skunk. He's usually harmless. I don't know what got into him today."

I walked back to the table to rearrange my bags. Garth had knocked half of them askew with his fumbling, and I wanted them neat for my shoppers. "Thank you for the help," I murmured. "I've had trouble here."

"You're the girl from last week? Mrs. Hughes was going on about it at Sunday service. We all damn near wanted to drown her in the baptismal water." He dropped his papers onto the counter and put a crate atop them to keep them from blowing away. I glanced over, but seeing him still smiling at me while tossing the apple back and forth between his palms, I jerked my face away. "Are you living in Cotter's Field for the season?"

I didn't answer.

"You are, aren't you? I saw your wagons pull in. Our farm backs up to the field you're in. That big barn at the back that some of you are sleeping in is our old one. My father likes that you come at harvest time, says your people do good work in the fields."

I smiled politely but said nothing. I tended not to engage outsiders unless absolutely necessary; too many near misses with my birthmark and too many people prejudiced against Roma made me shy of them.

"At night I can hear your music. It's good. Festive. I keep hoping your fiddlers will make their way over to the pub soon. Better than anything we've got local, I'll tell you that. Angus is a terror on his pipe whistle."

Had Martyn been a customer, I'd have managed pleasantries because his coin purse was full—but beyond that, no. The blond had helped me, but I'd thanked him already. My social obligation was fulfilled. I continued to arrange my goods in silence.

Either Martyn was obtuse or he was annoyingly persistent, because he leaned over his counter to offer me the apple. It was shiny and red, a good bloodred, with a twisty stem and a too-green leaf drooping to the side. "It's from my father's orchard. Take it. Consider it a welcome to Anwen's Crossing."

I eyed the fruit, my mouth watering for a bite. I'd had breakfast, but the apple looked crisp and fresh and all things an apple ought to be. That didn't stop me from shaking my head and shuffling behind my table, though, my gaze fixed on the market square. For one, Martyn's hands were dirty, and for another, I didn't want to encourage his attentions. Gift giving could be considered courtship.

Martyn let himself out of his stand and came to stand before my table anyway, studying my bags with that same bright smile stretching across his mouth.

"How much?"

"For what?"

"Anything."

I tapped the nearest charm bags with my fingertip. "A halfpenny, unless you want the bags for sour stomach. Those are a full penny. Fennel is rare and we grow our own."

He looked where I pointed, his lips pursed in thought. As his brow furrowed, his bangs cascaded over his forehead, the wispy ends brushing the tips of his lashes when he blinked. "They'll sell quick enough." Before I could object, he deposited the apple onto the edge of my table and returned to his stand, his hands sinking deep into his pockets. The swinging half door closed behind him and he leaned against a stack of potato crates, his right leg crossed over his left while he surveyed the townscape, his eyes narrowed against the sun.

"I'm sorry you've had a hard time. People lose their heads about the stupidest things around here, pretty girls in particular."

My eyes widened at the gadjo's gall. Ignoring caution, I tore the scarf away so he could see my birthmark, thinking perhaps he wouldn't find me so very pretty when presented with my half-face. Maybe it would be as effective a deterrent as Gran's scowl. "I don't want your apple or your compliments, gadjo. I'm here to do business, not make conversation."

"What's a gadjo?" he asked, looking my way. "I've heard my mother say it before."

The question—the way he asked it, the curious tone and the tilt of his head, his disinterest in my birthmark—robbed me of my fire. I slumped onto my stool, tugging the scarf back over my nose. "A gadjo is an outsider—a man not of my people."

"Oh, so a non-gypsy."

I hissed and shook my head. We Roma could refer to ourselves as such, but from the mouths of outsiders it was a slur. It was a caricature of our truths—dancing women in revealing outfits or our men seducing innocent gadjos. It meant liars and vagrants and stealers of babies. Uneducated, unwashed, *lesser.* We were a strong, moral people. Just like any people, we had bad individuals—Silas and his band came to mind—but they were the exception, not the rule. Yet we endured persecution and hardship. Our people had to behave *that much* better so we wouldn't be punished *that much* worse for the simple crime of existing.

Martyn must have realized his gaffe, because he stopped leaning against his potatoes and stood up straight, his hands smoothing the wrinkles in his shirt. His red cheeks matched the apple gleaming on the edge of my table. "I'm sorry. I didn't know that was offensive. I'm sorry."

I didn't say a word, but swept the fruit off my table to send it rolling under a nearby jewelry cart. He uttered a third apology just as a cluster of buyers tromped our way. Anything else he might have said was lost to the clamor. I was grateful for the reprieve . . . until every one of those shoppers passed me by, going straight to his farm stand and rooting around in his bins like swine hunting truffles.

It infuriated me that the insulting gadjo drew crowds while I sat there with a table full of respectable goods being passed over, but then the strangest thing happened. A woman walked over from Martyn's stand with a squash in hand, exhibiting it like a pear-shaped trophy.

"A halfpenny a bag, he said?"

I started to nod, but then stopped, looking from the squash to the woman, and then over to the farm stand. I couldn't see the blond man thanks to the people flocking at his counter, but I knew he was back there somewhere.

"Which *'he'*?" I asked, knowing the answer.

"Martyn Woodard. He's giving a free squash to anyone who purchases from you. What do the bags with the red string do?"

I was so surprised that Martyn would help sell my goods that I didn't answer her, but stood gawking at the gadjo's bustling stand. My customer didn't notice. She nudged the satchel toward me and poked at the ones tied with green as if she could glean their purpose by touch. Watching her paw through my neat lines broke me from my stupor, and I cleared my throat, picking up a bag and displaying it against my palm. "This one's a love charm. Sleep with it by your pillow and think of your love, and he will come in a dream. Dream often enough, and he will be yours forever."

"Perfect. I'll take one home to my daughter. She's ugly like her father. Any help is a blessing." She slid the halfpenny across the table and snatched the bag from my grasp, only to slide it into her blouse and between her ample bosoms. I stared, incredulous, but then an elderly gentleman came over with a squash in hand and asked about stomach curatives. I helped him with a bag just as a pair of young women lined up behind him, leaning to the side to see what I had to hawk.

It went on like that for hours. People bought from Martyn Woodard before presenting me with their golden squashes. It pricked my pride some; I didn't need anyone to do my business for me, especially not rude farmer boys who were too loose with their tongues, but my annoyance dwindled in the face of so many customers.

By midafternoon, all I had left were a few hex charms. I squeezed my full coin pouch and found a smile. Despite Silas's impropriety, the drunken ramblings of a superstitious idiot, and Martyn's boldness, the day was won. I glanced at the farm stand. Martyn was still there, though his stock looked like it had been picked over by locusts. He was working on consolidating his remaining vegetables, and seeing that he had my attention, he winked at me. As if that wasn't bad enough, when another worker stepped behind the counter to take over for him, Martyn dunked a basket of berries into a barrel of water behind him and brought it, still dripping, to my table before sneaking back to his stand. I would have demanded he take them back, but I had a customer, and playing the shrew in public was bad business practice.

I accepted the woman's halfpenny with murmured thanks. As soon as she waddled off, I ogled the berries. My stomach mewled like a kitten—I'd last eaten at sunrise, having missed lunch in the face of needy customers. I debated with myself for a solid minute before plucking the juiciest fruit from the pile and stuffing it into my mouth. I was reaching for another berry when Martyn returned, two cups full of water in his hands, his smile ever present. I looked around the square, desperate for a customer to call away my attention, but without Martyn's free squash offer, I was the tiny, ignorable table sandwiched between two prominent vendors.

"I'll grovel for forgiveness, if need be." He slid one wooden cup my way, his hand hovering to catch it in case I thrust it away. "I'm truly sorry. My grandmother's Welsh Kale, from Aberhosan. She doesn't talk about it at all, says she wants an easier life for her family than she had, so I'm ignorant about most of it, I'll admit."

"You're diddicoy," I said. His willingness to defend me from the town drunk made more sense knowing he was part Romani. Such kindness from a gadjo wasn't unheard of, but it wasn't typical either.

"What does that mean?"

"You have Romani blood. I'm diddicoy, too. My father was a gadjo."

"Oh! Yes, I'm that. My grandmother's father was a professional harp player from the Wood family. Perhaps you've heard of them?"

I smirked. Every Romani knew of the Wood family. They were one of the largest families traveling Wales and were *at least* distantly related to most of us.

"Yes, I know who they are." I peered at him, looking to see if his humility was a facade, but there was an honesty to his face that suggested perhaps he truly wanted to make amends for unintentional slights.

I looked from the berries to the cup and up to Martyn's face. His eyebrows lifted, his smile stretched even wider, and my resolve waivered.

"Fine. I forgive you if it means you'll stop being so . . . so . . ."

"Apologetic?"

"Yes. That." I lowered my scarf so I could sip, my lips never touching the diddicoy's cup because I did not know how he cared for his dishes. The water was cool and refreshing despite being out in a sun-warmed barrel all morning. I nodded at him like I'd seen Gran do whenever she was particularly pleased with someone.

He drained his own cup and reached for mine when I'd emptied it. "Good. Then we have a deal. Well, we almost have a deal," he said.

I frowned. "What deal? There is no deal here. I agreed to nothing."

"Sit here again tomorrow. I'll send more business your way. My father's produce is the best, so we get long lines at harvest time. People want fresh vegetables before they can't get them anymore. The imports are never as good." He picked up one of the bags from my table, turning it over in his palm and sniffing it. He reared back as if he'd been struck. "What *is* this? It smells awful."

The hex bags were filled with stinkgrass.

He tossed the bag between his palms much the way he had with the apple. A childish part of me wanted to see if I could use the diddicoy's ignorance against him—I was feeling mischievous after such a good sales day. "It's a hex bag. It brings ill will to those possessing it." I leaned forward, dropping my voice so it sounded like I was sharing dark secrets. "There are stories. One girl grew whiskers on her chin like a porcupine, and a boy from Abertawe shrank to half his height."

Martyn eyed me and then the bag. He maintained his smile, but he *did* drop it back onto the table, as if touching it for too long could afflict him with a terrible malady. "Are you a witch, then?"

I shrugged, letting him draw his own conclusions. As Gran said, a little fear went a long way.

"I don't believe it," Martyn announced, stealing a berry from the basket he'd given me. He chewed slowly, as if mulling over a topic of great importance. "Everyone knows witches have warts on their chins."

"Gran has warts. Big ones with hairs growing out of them."

"You're such a good witch that you make a defenseless old woman grow your hairy warts for you?"

I snickered because I couldn't help it. Oh, the things Gran would say to him for casting her as a defenseless old woman! But before I could relay them, a gentleman stopped by to browse my leftover goods. I tugged up my scarf so it wouldn't slip past my mouth, while Martyn quietly slipped back behind the counter of his own stand.

I didn't like the diddicoy, but perhaps our acquaintance wouldn't be so fraught after all.

CHAPTER THREE

I sold my last bags an hour later. There was little point to sitting behind an empty table, so I packed my things and headed toward the back gate of the market square. Before leaving, I glanced back at the farm stand, offering Martyn a wave to let him know I appreciated his help. When he winked back, my cheeks flushed and I dropped my gaze to the ground. Behind my scarf, though, I started to smile before I caught myself.

True, Martyn was handsome, and pleasant in disposition. He was also forbidden. A man in my caravan could marry a woman from the outside. If his new wife adopted our ways—proving that she understood the delicate balance of purity and impurity and assimilating with her new family—she was eventually welcomed.

The reverse, however, was not true. The women carried on our line, our blood, and if they polluted their wombs with outsider seed, they could be cast out. Banishment was a rare thing—we didn't like to lose our own—but it sometimes happened, and this was one reason for it.

Martyn wasn't exactly a gadjo, but his Romani blood was thin. I assumed he was not for me.

Gran would not allow me to wed in any case.

My empty basket swung by my side as I walked. Gran would be suspicious of such an early homecoming, but my full pocket would tell my story. It would please her, and I wanted her in good spirits when I explained what happened with Silas. Despite its nefarious reputation, witchwork kept us safe when others would do us harm, and selling the service provided income that put food in our bellies. That didn't mean Gran and I were above reproach, though. Knowing Silas, he'd already run to his father and told him all manner of lies about that morning, and I'd be painted a power-swollen trollop. Gran would tell them the right of it—that the curse was false and I could claim no magic—but then I'd be reprimanded for making a fool of the chieftain's son.

My enthusiasm for showing Gran my jingling profits faded, and I dragged my feet to make the walk last longer. Fluffy clouds floated across a perfect fall sky, though the storm-tinged ones to the east spoke of evening rains. There were crop fields to either side of me now, which meant I was far enough away from town that I could safely remove my scarf. I unwound it from my head and looped it around my waist, then tugged my braid over my shoulder.

I followed the road, my fingertips gliding over the bumpy wooden boards of the fence at my side. There was no break in it as far as I could see, and after a quick look around to make sure

I had no witnesses, I vaulted over the top rung to land in the soft, ankle-high grass of Cotter's Field.

I was about to head home when I spotted the scarecrow across the way. Normally a scarecrow wouldn't call my attention, but this one was more unsettling than most. It was enormous—at least seven feet tall—and was tied to wooden beams by crisscrossing ropes and a pair of rusty hooks beneath its arms. It had a droopy red hat, a burlap sack head, and overalls riddled with faded patches. Straw poked out of its neck and wrists, with more clumps bursting through the seams at its sides. Someone had taken the time to give the thing a false face. Craggy red yarn formed a vicious smile, and its eyes were black cloth ovals. Each had a white X stitched through the middle.

Looking at it too long gave me the shivers, and I hurried through the field toward our camp to put it behind me, glad the sun still shone. How terrifying the scarecrow must be by moonlight!

Gran's vardo was situated in the westernmost cluster of tents. We were fortunate to have a vardo at all, as they were something of a luxury, but her craft required storage space and shelter, and she'd earned the money to buy her own. I made my way to it quickly, hiking up my skirt so I could tromp through knee-high grass without trouble. I hung my head low to discourage conversation.

Our vardo was parked at the back, farthest away from the camp, because our trade could be grisly. Gran's contact with blood was minimal, but we had our traditions, and keeping away from others avoided spreading contamination. We cleaned fastidiously to keep our space welcoming and healthy.

Gran had thrust open the shutters and propped open the door to invite the fresh air in. I was near enough that I heard her snort in derision. A man was speaking to her, his voice low and gravelly and familiar to me—the chieftain. I squatted in the grass beside the vardo to avoid detection, unhappy that he'd beaten me to my own explanation. Gran had the sight, but that didn't mean she knew all things all the time. The sight was a fickle mistress, and wont to tell her not what she wanted to see, but what it wanted her to see. Now she was being fed Silas's skewed version of the truth.

Gran knows me and my truths. She'll know lies when she hears them. She trusts me.

I hope.

"My son says she has been acting lovesick, and he believes she cursed him. . . ."

"*Pretended* to curse him," Gran interjected. "There is a distinct difference between afflicting someone with the Evil Eye and actually giving it, Wen."

My brows shot to my hairline at Gran's familiar use of the chieftain's first name. It was a privilege reserved for immediate family and his closest advisers, all of whom were men, by our particular family's tradition. Either Gran ignored the rules, or the drabarni had more freedoms than I'd realized.

"It is the lesser point here. I understand she's your apprentice, but if she's so desperate for male attention . . ."

"I do not believe she propositioned Silas any more than you do," Gran spat. "I would not allow a strumpet to succeed me as drabarni. That boy of yours should be married off, and soon. His friends will be matched in the spring, and when he is bored, what will he do with so much free time? Do not look at me like that. You know I speak wisdom."

The chieftain's sigh was weary. "Perhaps you are right. Perhaps I ought to see about finding him a wife to end this nonsense. Would Bethan be . . . ?"

"No. He is not in her stars. A foolish man makes for a foolish wife, and I will spare my girl such a fate."

"I see."

"No, you do not, because you are blinded by love for your son." I heard Gran shuffling around inside the vardo before her voice burst from the window above my head. I huddled closer to the wheel, holding my breath in hopes she wouldn't sense me. "I will talk to her about what happened and I trust you'll talk to Silas. Do I have your assurance he will leave her alone?"

"Yes."

"Good, because if you do not handle it, I will. I am not so blinded by love."

I winced, hoping the chieftain didn't take her to task for the threat, but he simply sighed again and stomped down the narrow steps. "I understand, Drina. No need for anything drastic." Again I found myself perplexed by the nature of their familiarity. Gran had consulted with the chieftain over the years, but they'd always maintained their propriety during those meetings. Not once had I heard them use familiar names.

"I would not see the past repeat itself."

The chieftain paused to look behind him at my grandmother still inside the vardo, and I could see him clearly from my crouched position. He wore his usual forest-green jacket over a white button-down shirt, suspenders to hold up charcoal woolen pants, and a black hat with a short brim to cover his graying head. Only the expression on his face was out of character. It was taut with strain, and he looked uneasy. He reached up to worry at the pale pink scar that started at his eye and curved down to his neck. He'd had it for as long as I could remember, the reminder of an injury stark against his ruddy skin. When I'd asked him about it as a child, he told me he'd wrestled a bear to prove his strength to his people. I'd believed him then.

I was not so gullible anymore.

"I have heard you. I will talk to the boy and hope he is not so arrogant as to dismiss his father."

"I fear it is a wasted hope. You are lucky with your other sons—they are good boys—but that one has darkness inside of him. God bless you, Wen. You will need it talking to that child."

The chieftain had no reply to that. I stayed low, tracking his retreating boots until he turned the corner that would lead him back to the great fire. As soon as he disappeared, I slumped in the grass, relieved that he hadn't caught me spying.

Gran, however, returned to the window above and promptly emptied the tea kettle on my head, dousing me in tepid water.

I squawked and she quietly chuckled.

"Get in here," she said, her voice laced with humor. "But wring yourself out first."

After squeezing excess water from my hair, my shirt, and the hem of my skirt, I climbed the steps with the basket clutched to my chest. Gran sat at the table waiting, her sharp fingernails drumming against the wood. I hefted the empty basket at her, attempting a happy, carefree smile, but all she did was arch a brow and motion for me to return it to the shelf.

Her seriousness was back in place. That boded poorly.

"I didn't know what to do. You were talking to the chieftain and . . ."

"I do not care. Sit down." Her tone stood for no argument, and I slid into the chair across from her.

"I meant no disrespect." A breeze swept in through the open window, and I squirmed when the damp cloth of my shirt glued itself to my back. "May I ask about the conversation with the chieftain?"

"No, you may not. Tell me about Silas."

I reached into my pocket for the coins from market, offering them like they'd buy me an ounce of benevolence, but she waved them away. I shriveled in my seat, the coins squeezed so tightly in my palm, they dented the meat.

"He cornered me this morning," I said. "His friends flanked me so I couldn't escape. I was afraid if I called for help, they'd say I'd invited it, so I mumbled nonsense words and spat to make him believe I'd cursed him." I lowered my gaze to the table and examined the knots and swirls riddling the wood. What had seemed so clever hours ago no longer held its shine. "It won't happen again. I'm sorry."

Gran said nothing. My face burned with shame, and I wrapped my arms around my stomach—it roiled so much, I was afraid it would fall out of my body and plummet to the floor. Still she didn't speak, not even when she got up to rummage through the cabinet beside her cot. I watched without a word. She pulled out a few jars, a black figurine, and a piece of leather rolled like a scroll and bound with twine. There were feathers and rocks and other things I couldn't identify upon first glance. She collected it all in her apron, holding the sides together to form a carrying pouch as she returned to the table and arranged the miscellanea in a tidy line.

"Look," she commanded, and I did, trying to make heads or tails of it. She pushed a wooden fetish carved like a cat my way. It was no bigger than my pointer finger and painted black, some of the paint missing at the tips of the ears and tail, exposing the gold wood underneath. "Do you know why I allow no cats near me?"

"Because they are unclean?" Anything from the waist down on people was unclean, and the same applied to the beasts. Creatures that groomed their lower halves with their mouths were particularly vulgar. We never allowed them inside our homes, nor did they make suitable food. If a dog or cat licked a plate or dish, it was contaminated and had to be thrown away.

Gran grunted and shook her head. "Partially, yes, but also because a cat will perch upon your chest and steal your breath. I cannot abide the thought of it. A breath is a powerful thing— the first and last the most powerful—and yet a filthy cat would claim them? No. I am old now. I will not risk my most powerful breath going to an animal that will not know what to do with it."

I nodded, licking my lips and reaching for the figurine. She allowed me to take it, and I held it upright in the palm of my hand. It peered at me with its painted yellow eyes.

"A baby's scream, a death rattle. One gives you power over life, the other over death. A cat can be sent to collect those things for you, but if you take them yourself, they are much more potent. Do you understand?"

"Yes."

" '*Yes*' what?"

"Yes, Gran, I understand."

She pushed the second item at me, the leathery scroll tied off at the middle. This one worried me; I didn't read well. I'd attended school at points over the years, but the teachers were impatient with my language gap and believed me to be stupid, despite my knowledge of Kååle, Welsh, and English. It was the same for most of my people. The prejudice was too much to overcome, so we received a homegrown education of oral histories. The chieftain, in particular, was a great storyteller, and he'd often say there was no better way to learn than to hear the accounts of our ancestors who had eyes to bear witness to events as they unfolded.

Gran agreed to a point, but she said there were gaps in our education, too. She'd learned to read and write as a girl, and she'd tried to teach me the alphabet a few years ago, but I'd grown fidgety and bored, so she'd said she'd wait until I could better appreciate the gift she was offering.

I wondered if the scroll indicated it was that time.

"Unroll it," she said.

I put the cat figurine aside and reached for the scroll, tugged off the string. When the scroll unfurled, it was not what I'd expected. The puckered leather was a pair of bat wings sewn together with yellowing twine. There were no letters or symbols; this was another sort of education—one that began with the pale, emaciated remnants of an animal that had died long ago. Horrified by the tacky texture, I almost dropped the wings on the table, but I saw Gran's mouth twitch and thought better of it.

She didn't appreciate my disdain for the unsavory part of her craft, but then, as the chieftain once said, a fox doesn't smell its own hole. She *wouldn't* find the tools of her trade unsavory.

"A bat that circles a house three times invites Death. To curse another, you write his or her true name upon a paper and wrap it in the wings. I need not say this is only done to the foulest of people." She pushed a jar toward me and tapped the top. "Dead spiders. To plague another with foul luck, you put one beneath their pillow and have them sleep upon it." She thrust another jar across the table. "This is snake skin. It is very lucky, as are most snakes. We value them."

I rerolled the wings and nodded as she motioned at other jars, explaining what the contents of each did. To make a man love you, you put a sprig of rowan in his sock. Donkey hairs worn in a satchel around the neck brought good luck. To drown someone, you poured water over their discarded fingernail clippings. To plague someone with hallucinations, you threaded a sprig of dwayberry with the victim's hair. To see through another's eyes, you bled upon a hawk's feather and carried it with you.

"There are other things, blessings as well as curses," Gran said, motioning at the drawers behind her. "Dolls you can make to inflict pain, ways to ward against the elements or control them. I hope you are ready to walk this road, Bethan. Once you begin the journey, it is difficult to go back."

She collected her totems and tottered back to the cabinet. I was overwhelmed and confused. I'd come home expecting her to censure me for being rash and using my limited knowledge of her practices against Silas, but here she was giving me a lesson in real, actual magic—something I'd yearned for as long as I could remember.

"I'm glad for this, Gran. Truly. Thank you. But why now? Six hours ago you said I wasn't ready."

"Because I have ill prepared you for some things, and in doing so have done you a disservice. No child of mine will . . ." She drew a deep breath and stared into the open drawer before her. "I have the tools to help you with people like Silas. He will not shame you if I can help it."

She looked at me with her brown eye, but her expression was guarded. In a person less severe than my grandmother, I'd have gone so far as to call it fear.

CHAPTER FOUR

Gran pulled dried herb bundles from the ceiling to assemble the next day's poultices. I kept hoping she'd elaborate on why she'd changed her stance on my training, but she was lost to her own thoughts, not reacting at all when I jingled my profits so she could hear how much money I'd made at market.

Deflated, I dumped the coins into her jar. The prank curse was aggravating, and Silas's boldness was a problem, but neither thing warranted the grim look on her face. "What's bothering you, Gran?"

"Stop pestering me, child. I said I will teach you magic. That should be enough for now," she snapped.

I washed my hands and began sorting our gatherings into neat piles. Lavender. Willow bark. Our diminishing supply of fennel. Gran sat to my right, empty pouches splayed before her, working in silence. I watched her thin, knobby fingers stuffing garbage herbs into charm bags and tying them off. It was foolish to push her, but the tight knit of her brows had me worried.

Nothing flustered her. Ever.

I took a deep breath. "I heard you say Silas wasn't in my stars," I said. "Does that mean you know who is?"

She jerked her face to the side to peer at me, her lips pursed in a grimace. "You are a tedious, annoying girl who asks too many questions."

"I know."

She snorted and went back to the herbs. I figured that was the end of it—her jaw was set, her nostrils flared like an angry bull—but then she dropped her peppermint leaves abruptly and spread her fingers on the tabletop, blinking at me through a veil of stringy hair.

"A blood moon hangs low in the sky. I see Silas Roberts in the shadow of a giant. A serpent slithers into moist earth. A crow falls and the wind screams fury. There is fear. There are tears. Something is lost that can never be found. You are there, but I do not know how or why. You are not alone, but I am not with you."

She closed her eyes, her long lashes resting against her weathered cheeks. "Do you see now why I held my peace? It is a terrible, useless vision until I know more."

Despite the warmth in the vardo, the hairs on my arms and on the back of my neck stood on end. My heart beat like a drum in my ears.

Fury. Fear. Tears.

I said nothing because I didn't want to know any more. Gran offered nothing because she had nothing else to give. I reached for the herb bags, my palms sweaty as I pulled open the tops and meted out the fennel.

Blood moons were witch moons—a time of dark, potent energy that made the spirits restless. Crows were death eaters. Something was lost. She'd foreseen bleak portents that somehow revolved around me.

Fury. Fear. Tears . . .

Stop thinking about it.

The work was an excellent distraction. Too much of any one component could be as bad as not taking medicine at all, so precision was key. Fennel was best served as a tea—the hot water diluting it enough to make it palatable. I fell into a wordless rhythm of measuring and assembling, tying the bags off with yarn and laying them out in the basket for the next day's market. Together, Gran and I completed a full eighty satchels—almost twice what we'd sold that day—but with Martyn's help, I was confident I'd be able to sell them all before supper tomorrow.

Gran's vision did nibble at my thoughts, though. Every time I thought I'd shoved it away, it came back again, more insistent than before.

What did it all mean? How much of it did Gran understand?

The peepers screeched dusk's arrival. Gran motioned at the hooks in the ceiling to let me know we were done. I sped through cleanup, hanging the sprigs that needed to be dried and storing the rest in wooden boxes stacked neatly in the corner. I wiped the table and swept the floor until our little home was once again spotless.

Dinner would be served at the main fire, probably some roasted game or a vat of spicy stew and fresh bread. I worked at my cuticles with a hard-bristled brush so I could handle food without fear of contamination.

"I'll see if anyone sells lemons at market tomorrow. The farmer beside me would know, I think. His family lives next to Cotter's Field." I reached for the lavender oil in hopes of masking the funk. A delicate sniff proved it helped cover the stinkgrass, but there were still unpleasant traces.

"Ahh, yes. The yellow-haired gadjo with the dirty fingers."

"No! He's diddicoy. His grandmother is a Wood. And the soil is charcoal. He draws," I said, then regretted it. It was not my job to defend Martyn, and Gran might think I'd formed an indecent attachment. I unrolled the sleeves of my blouse, which had dried over the course of our work, and reached for a shawl to cover my shoulders. "He helped me sell when I had a bad position in the square today."

Gran cast me a gleaming white grin before waddling to the corner to wash her hands. There were three basins on opposite sides of the vardo—one reserved for dishes, one for utensils specifically, and the last for our hands. More basins were stacked beneath the table as well—some reserved for personal hygiene, some for separating and washing our laundry. Gran dunked her hands in the hand-washing bowl, as I had a minute ago. She looked smug as she toweled off, and it took me a moment to figure out why: at no point since I'd come home had I mentioned Martyn, yet she'd plucked a yellow-haired man from my memory, her sight granting her access to my innermost secrets.

"Gran! Stop that."

"Do not try to keep things from me and I will not feel the

need. Now hand me my cane. I am going to the fire with you tonight."

"You are?" Gran almost never went to the fire, unless her presence was requested by the chieftain for official clan business. She said she liked to dine in the vardo because *"I prefer my own company to idle chatter."* I suspected it had more to do with the challenges of the uneven terrain, but she was proud, and it would have bothered her to admit she struggled.

"Perhaps seeing Silas will clarify my vision. Get my cane from the bucket, Bethan."

I gave her the twisted piece of oak handle first. It was about three feet tall and sanded smooth, a ball-shaped gnarl serving as her grip. Her fingers curled over the top and she made her way to the door. I offered her my arm and helped her down the steps, then ducked back in to collect our dishes and cutlery. The china was possibly the finest thing we owned, and I maintained it meticulously, as was our custom.

We teetered toward camp, careful to avoid the tallest grasses. The fireside bustling had already started—I could hear music and chatter, children shrieking and laughing. The air smelled of rich, spicy things, of savory meats and breads. I guided Gran to the western side of the fire, where the elders gathered for their meals, but she shook her head and pointed to the other side.

"No. Over there. I do not wish to sit with Wen's brood. Mikel is gassy like a too-stuffed pig and Niku never stops talking."

I snickered and helped her to an unoccupied bench. Wooden tables circled the fire so people could comfortably socialize. Only the northern section was left open as a designated spot for things like dancing, ceremonies, and clan meetings. Gran settled onto her bench, her cane resting across her lap. People looked at her curiously, most bowing their heads in respect to the drabarni, but she ignored them. "I love them, but they are tedious. Now go get us something to eat before we starve." She waved at the food tables with a sweep of her hand.

I darted off, my stomach rumbling its agreement. It was a big spread with grilled meat, stews, and breads, and I stepped around the menfolk, never crossing in front of one for fear of insult. I'd just loaded Gran's bowl and was reaching for a roll when a hard, angry poke jabbed me in my side. I spun around to find myself face to chest with Tomašis Buckland. Tomašis was a tall, skeletal oaf who'd been in Silas's shadow since childhood. He had sandy hair, muddy eyes, and a nose that was both too wide and too long.

His upper lip curled to reveal a line of crooked teeth tinged gray at the gums. "You'll regret this morning, Half-Face," he snarled, striking me again with his elbow as he reached past me. "We don't forget."

I held my chin high. "My grandmother talked to the chieftain. It's over."

"Maybe for you, but Silas's face has burned since this morning. He says he's in so much pain he can't see."

"Then he lies. I didn't curse him with burning spit."

A couple of people came to get food alongside us, and Tomašis dropped his voice, edging in close to whisper near my ear. I swatted him away like an annoying bug, but he was unperturbed. "We're watching you, witchling. We know your type."

"My type? And what type is that?"

"You know."

I didn't, but I didn't care enough to ask for explanations, either. His threats were beneath me. I circled to the other side of the table, but he stayed in pursuit, bullying his way into my personal space at every opportunity. When I reached for a piece of meat, he'd snag it and put it on his plate first. When I leaned to get bread, he stomped on my foot with his boot, my toes crunching beneath his weight.

I cringed and motioned across the fire, to where Gran sat. "Stop or I'll—" I didn't finish the sentence. Unfortunately, sometime during my exchange with Tomašis, Gran had moved. I glanced at the elders to see if she'd changed her mind about sitting with Mikel and Niku, but she wasn't there either.

A half-crippled woman shouldn't be able to disappear without a trace quite that fast. And yet . . .

Tomašis grinned and pressed his leg against my skirt, breaking all rules of propriety and humiliating me in public, since Silas wasn't around to do it himself. I wondered if that's where Gran had gone—to find Silas in the growing swarm of people so she could spark her sight. It was a shame that her absence left me vulnerable. Tomašis whacked the bowl in my left hand with his elbow, sending it sprawling. Gravy spilled over the rim to splatter my shawl, gloppy smears dripping down to splash onto the table below.

"Tomašis! Enough!"

A weaselly grin oozed across his mouth. "I'm so clumsy today, Bethan."

"Stop. Please." I removed the shawl and reached for a towel to attend to my stains. He took the opportunity to pinch my hip, his hand lingering far too long for comfort. My anger was fast and fierce—hateful words nearly split my tongue in half, but before a single one escaped my lips, Gran's voice cut across the gathering.

"What manner of mischief are you up to, Tomašis Buckland?" She pointed a spindly, crooked finger in his direction, and everyone around us froze in the face of her clear fury.

"Nothing, drabarni," he said, his voice cracking as if he'd hit manhood for a second time.

"Fondling an unwilling woman is nothing, then?"

Gran started to walk toward him.

"No! I'm sorry. So sorry."

"You are not sorry for acting out toward my Bethan. You are sorry you were caught," Gran snarled. Tomašis looked like he'd erupt into tears at any second, and as she neared him, he scampered backward, fumbling over one of the dinner tables and falling into the grass.

She advanced with slow, deliberate steps until her talon-like fingernail connected with his forehead. She knelt over him, pressing down, and Tomašis squealed like an ungreased door hinge, his hands tearing at the grass on either side of his body.

It wasn't until Tomašis's mother separated herself from the wives and hurried to his side that Gran paused, her fingernail flicking against Tomašis's pale skin.

"Florica." Gran sounded pleasant, like she greeted an old friend.

Florica's hands twisted in her skirt in obvious agitation, her gaze swinging from drabarni to son and back. "What has he done now?"

"Your boy is too free with his person. He must learn a lesson." Her wrinkly hand grabbed half a dozen brown strands at Tomašis's temple and plucked them out by the root, ignoring his pained yelp. She held the plucked hairs in front of her ghost eye, twisting them between her thumb and forefinger. "Do you know what a witch can do with a young man's hair, Tomašis Buckland? Do you know what kind of magic she can conjure?" Gran formed a fist around the hairs and blew into it before casting them into the fire by her side. It surged with the offering, rising high for a flash before resuming its steady, cheerful crackle.

"What is his punishment? What magic is this?" Florica asked.

"He will dream the dark dreams for a week. The next time he chooses to be so ill-mannered, he will not know such *mercy* from me." Gran spat on the ground, her finger swirling in a strange motion before Tomašis's face. It was a curse, a real one, done with all of the dark aplomb, to bring him nightmares. I could sense its presence, the thick energy in the air reminding me of the heavy moments just before a thunderstorm.

"Of course, drabarni. Of course. Your mercy is appreciated."

Florica hauled a sniffling Tomašis back to their tent. I was satisfied by the way she tugged on his ear and pinched his arm, telling him how he'd been raised better and ought to be ashamed of himself. He whined and squirmed; she struck him on the back of the head and hissed recriminations.

We stayed a bit longer so people could pay their respects to Gran, but we saw neither hide nor hair of Silas. Unfortunately, Tomašis's harassment had soured my mood. When the dancing began, Gran said she had better things to do than watch a bunch of young people twirling in circles, and I was happy to help her home.

After scrubbing our dishes, piling our clothes for washing, and helping Gran prepare for bed, I layered shifts against the autumnal cool and pulled my own soft, thin mattress onto the floor. I thought of the day's events, and Gran's strange premonition, and I hoped my magic training would begin soon. Gran wouldn't always be there to protect me. I had to learn to take care of myself, especially if Silas and his friends had me in their sights.

Sleep didn't come easy, but when it did, it came hard. And thanks to the woven web of colorful yarns Gran had hung from the ceiling above our heads—a variation on something she'd read about from the mystics to the west—my own dark dreams were held at bay.

CHAPTER FIVE

I woke to a rooster's crow and a still-gray sky. Gran stirred in her bed beside me. She'd be demanding food soon, and I needed to eat so I could leave for market. I washed, dressed in a white blouse and a blue skirt, and collected our dishes. The women would just be setting up breakfast, but at least there'd be bread, honey, and tea ready, and that's all Gran and I ever needed.

I walked to the great fire, the tall grass sighing as I pressed through. A cluster of matrons was already hard at work cooking. Among the women was Tomašis's mother, who chattered away while cracking eggs in a bowl, but when I crested the clearing, she went quiet and jerked her gaze away. I wondered if she'd been gossiping about me, somehow blaming me for her son's misbehavior. I nodded my respects and collected our bread, keeping to myself so I wouldn't draw ire.

The skies were turning blue when I returned home, the

muddied shades of dawn fading. Gran had fallen back to sleep after I'd left, her snores rivaling those of a hibernating bear, so I left her breakfast on the table and took the poultice basket from the shelf. I ate and dashed for the door, almost forgetting the black scarf folded on the bureau.

I tied it around my waist with a weary sigh, hurrying to Anwen's Crossing so I wouldn't have to rush my setup. Before venturing through the main gate into town, I wound the soft cloth over my head, over my mouth, and around my neck, arranging my hair so it didn't get tacked down. I was early enough that I could have claimed a table across from the well, but Martyn's offer made returning to the spot between the farm stand and the baker the smarter choice. The blond diddicoy's attention might not have been completely proper, but it had certainly sold a lot of medicine bags.

I approached the table, but seeing a paper tacked to one of the fence posts, I paused in my approach, worried someone had beat me to the space. It took a moment to realize the sign was *for* me. In the middle of the page, drawn as if lifted from my reflection, was a charcoal picture of me with my scarf. Someone— and I knew exactly who—had drawn my portrait and put it up as if to stake my claim.

I abandoned my basket on the tabletop and reached for the drawing. He'd captured the heavy lids of my eyes and the curve of my cheeks. He'd even re-created the way my birthmark darkened my face by my temple before sweeping down to my jaw, and the spray of freckles on my nose. For him to do it from memory was uncanny, and I swallowed hard at the realization that he must have been studying me all throughout the previous day to get it so detailed. There were words I couldn't read above and below, but they didn't matter—I was too transfixed by my own image to care what had actually been written.

"Do you like it?"

I lowered the page to peer at Martyn, who smiled at me from the farm stand. I didn't know what to say—I was flattered by his attention even if I shouldn't have been. He knew it, too, and his smile ratcheted up a notch.

"I take that as a yes. You want to know what's funny?" I returned the poster to the pole, trying to collect my thoughts. He took my silence as a sign that he should keep talking. "I can draw you, but I don't even know your name. That's why the title is so generic. I hope it's okay?"

I peered at the arched row of letters at the top of the picture, drawn in an elaborate, swirling style, and shrugged. I had no idea what it said, but I didn't want to confess that to him. It did make me think I should ask Gran for reading lessons, but that was probably too much right now—there were only so many hours in a day. Later, though, after my magic training . . .

"Bethan," I said, ignoring the matter of the title. I began displaying my herb bags and charms, my chest tight, like I was short of breath. My eyes stung like I might cry, too, but it wasn't sadness. Oh, no, it was far worse. I was *touched* by his kindness, which threatened the necessary distance propriety dictated I maintain.

Martyn leaned over the half door that locked him inside his stand, tucking a cigarillo between his lips and lighting it with a match. He watched as I arranged my bags into artful rows, the gray clouds of his smoke souring the air. Our men sometimes smoked pipes at night by the fire, but the cigarillo was not as sweet and therefore not as pleasant. "Bethan. Pretty name for a pretty one. I think I'll call you Bet." He peered at me through his thick lashes. "If you're all right with that."

I'd never had a nickname beyond Annoying Girl and, sometimes, Stupid Child, but they didn't really count—Gran was always irritable when she used them, so they were more criticism than terms of endearment. "Is Bethan too complicated of a name for you to say? Too long to hold your attention, diddicoy?"

I'd meant it as a jab, but he smirked and pulled out a knife from beneath his counter, using it to dig out dirt from beneath his fingernails. "Hardly, Miss Bet. I simply like the idea of having a name for you that I came up with."

"Oh? And why is that?"

"Because you're interesting. And pretty." It was such an audacious flirt, so very direct, I had to stop arranging my bags out of fear that I'd mess them up. He must have noticed how flustered I was because he chuckled from his stand. "Awful, aren't I?"

"That's one word," I croaked, forcing myself to focus on my satchels. I nudged them into straighter lines, my fingers toying with the red yarn on the bottommost bags. "You should know I can't encourage this flirtation."

"You don't have to encourage anything. All I ask is if I say something stupid, tell me so I can stop being an arsehole."

My smile was not intentional, which made it all the more frustrating. "Fine. Well, yes, you may call me Bet. If you insist."

"I do insist, and I insist you tell me if you like the title. I've been worrying about it since last night."

I winced, looking back at the poster with my likeness and the artful wording. I didn't like to confess my ignorance, but there was no way around it when he'd asked me outright, and outright lying to other Roma—diddicoy included—was frowned upon. "What does it say?"

If he was surprised I couldn't read, he didn't indicate it, instead letting himself out of his stand so he could point at the words as he read them aloud. "'The Wandering Girl's Wonders,'" he said before moving his finger to the words at the bottom. "'Herbal Remedies and Mystic Charms.' I didn't want to use the g-word. No offense meant, saying . . . you know." He ran a hand over the back of his neck before returning to his stand, his cheeks flushed. "I'm sorry. I probably shouldn't mention it in a roundabout way either."

He was so earnest, I didn't want to smile, afraid he'd interpret it as mockery. "That's . . . Thank you. No one's ever drawn me before. You're very talented. And *gypsy* is fine among Roma. You are one, yes?"

"It's in my blood—not my brain, though." He plucked another apple from his stock, rolling it across the counter and then tossing it high, almost to the cloth roof of his stand, before catching it again. His cigarillo was almost burnt down, a pillar of ash dangling from the end and threatening to plummet. "Drawing's my hobby. I can't be farming all the time, you know." He looked like he had more to say, but then a tall, broad man walked into the stand from the other side, a crate of lettuce balanced on one shoulder, potatoes on the other. Martyn threw the cigarillo to the ground before stomping it out, the ghost of his smoke drifting on the air.

The newcomer was a giant of a man, his arms so thick with muscle, I doubted I could put both of my hands around one and have my fingers touch. The similarities between him and

Martyn were undeniable—they had the same wheat-colored hair, the same bump on the bridges of their noses, the same cleft in their chins. The older man wore a red shirt to Martyn's blue, though, and deep lines crinkled the tanned skin around his eyes and the corners of his mouth.

When he dropped his crops behind the counter, dust rose up to fill the stand.

"Da, this is Bet. Bet, this is my da, Hal."

Martyn's father not-so-gently thwacked Martyn on the back of his big skull. Martyn flinched, but he tossed me a wink all the same. "Mr. Woodard would be more appropriate, I think. Good morning, Bet," his father said. He offered me a cursory nod before making his way behind the farm stand, assessing the various piles of goods in the back. Martyn watched him a minute or so before turning my way and dropping his voice to a whisper.

"I'll be busy today with him here, but maybe we can have lunch together?"

I liked Martyn and the picture he'd drawn of me, but the point remained that he was not of my people and I couldn't in good conscience let him pursue me with any amount of seriousness. "I'm not certain it's a good idea, but thank you."

"Please? I'll beg. I'm good at it." I sputtered for an answer, but was saved by a pair of women strolling over to shop the displays. I pointed at them as if their presence could ward him off, but he groaned my name, stretching out the vowel until it bordered on unseemly.

"Stop that!"

"Please have lunch with me?"

"I really shouldn't."

"That's what makes it more fun." He leaned so far over the half door of his stand, I was fairly certain his feet no longer touched the ground on the other side. "I'm trying to grovel politely, but if I'm bothering you, you can tell me to piss off."

"No I can't, that's impolite!"

"It'll be our secret. Bet the medicine girl is impolite. Another secret? She's having lunch with a diddicoy named Martyn today. Don't tell anyone."

He made such a clown of himself that I had no choice but to laugh. I didn't get to do that a lot at home—not with Gran and her perpetual seriousness, not with the others in my camp who treated me differently because I was the drabarni's apprentice. Martyn was a freedom from that gravity. He was a way to allow myself frivolity that I would never otherwise get.

Which is why, in the end, I relented.

"Fine. If it will shut you up, we'll have lunch."

"I knew you couldn't resist." He flashed me those blinding white teeth before lobbing an apple my way, narrowly avoiding walloping me in the side of the face with it. The problem was less his throwing and more my lack of reflexes. I snagged it at the last second, lifting it up to stroke the smooth, polished skin against my scarf. We shared a look, he spared a smile, and then he was gone, ducking behind his stand to help his father prepare their goods for the onslaught.

CHAPTER SIX

With his father looming, Martyn couldn't volunteer free produce to help bolster my sales, but he talked up my goods so
well, I'd sold half my stock by midday. Customers from the
previous day stopped by to repurchase, too. One woman even
claimed she'd suffered headaches for years and the only thing
that helped was Gran's willowbark tea. She bought all of my
green-tied bags that Friday, shoving her coins into my hand
with pleas for me to return with more tea the following Monday. Markets closed on Sundays for church and community
functions, and people's needs were met by the stores midtown.

I'd just assisted an elderly couple with a good-luck charm
for their granddaughter when Martyn approached my table, a
canvas bag clasped in one of his pawlike hands, a blanket in the
other. "Shall we, wandering girl?" I looked out at the square. It

was bustling. A dozen people less than twenty feet away were actively browsing tables. Martyn followed my gaze and tutted, shaking the bag of food beneath my nose so I couldn't ignore it. "You can't work if you die from hunger."

My stomach grumbled its agreement. I stood, fretful Gran wouldn't approve of what I was about to do, but I had to eat, and Martyn had been helpful.

He tucked his lunch bag beneath his arm so he could help me gather my remaining bags and put them into the basket. "You could leave the lot with my father, if you'd like. He'd make sure no one snatched it."

It was considerate, but I didn't dare; if Gran discovered I'd abandoned our goods to a gadjo's care, even for a short while, there'd be fire and brimstone and so much stinkweed picking, I'd want to cast myself into the river. "Thank you, but I'll take them with me. No offense, I hope." I glanced over at the water barrel inside his stand. "Do you mind if I wash quickly? Before we eat."

"No, not at all." Martyn stood to the side and let me dunk my hands. With no proper towel, I wiped them off on my scarf before following him to the baker's stand on the other side of my table so he could buy crispy bread. Despite its paper wrapping, I could smell it—oven fresh with a hint of garlic—and I followed its promise of deliciousness as much as the man holding it, outside the gates.

The field beyond the market was well worn, like it'd seen scores of picnickers, horses, and wagons before us. It was empty now, though, save for a doe and her fawn grazing to our north. Martyn chose a spot not too far from town, spreading the blanket so we'd have a place to sit. I watched the food to make sure it never touched the ground, especially the bread. Fallen bread was always burned in the great fire back at home. To not do so invited bad fortune.

"I hope you like Caerphilly cheese," he said, opening his canvas bag. "My mother makes it fresh." I didn't know the name, but cheese was cheese. I took the bread from him and broke off a piece from the end, keeping it for myself and giving him the softer middle portion of the loaf—the better portion, as was polite. He did the same, breaking off a piece of a pale cheese with a paler rind with his fingers and offering it to me. I laid the remaining loaf of bread across my lap and accepted, murmuring my thanks.

I eyed the bread and cheese a moment, considering wedging it up under the wrap of my scarf and eating that way, but that seemed needlessly complicated. It was only Martyn and me outside the gates, so I took the scarf off my face but let it cover my hair for modesty's sake. It felt good to be free, cooler by degrees, and I tilted my face up to the sky, enjoying the sun that precluded the nighttime chill.

"Is it good?" he asked.

"Very." And it was. The cheese was on the milder side, and salty—but tasty, too. We had our own cheeses in the caravan, some similar to the Caerphilly, but nothing that quite matched the flavor.

"Good. I prefer cheddar, but it's harder to get. Sometimes we can buy it at market, but I haven't seen many of the English traders out this way lately."

"They're in the far south mostly," I said. "At least, that is what the chieftain says, usually when he talks about horse trading. Many English stay between Abertawe and Caerdydd before returning to Gloucester. They complain about Welsh weather being too harsh, like it's much better over there."

I nibbled on my cheese and bread, my gaze drifting to the deer. They were alert, their ears pricked, watching us to see if we were a threat, and it struck me that it was similar to how I reacted to the gadjos—always ready to flee, never quite comfortable in their presence. I was the hunted, and they were the hunters. How odd that I was at ease with Martyn, who was far more them than us. He was warm, funny, and considerate, and though it all could have been a ruse, my gut instinct told me otherwise.

"Sometimes we know things and it has nothing to do with our minds," Gran had said to me numerous times before. "It is bigger, something spiritual. It is a sight in its own right. It is not like mine, not as developed, but it should never be ignored."

Allowing myself to sit with Martyn was me paying attention.

He tore into his bread, his tongue flicking out to catch the crumbs on his lower lip. "How far do you travel during the year?"

"Not as far as you might think. Just here in the fall to work the harvest, and out to Caerfyrddin in the spring for the trading. We make camp for winter in the valleys, and spend our summers on the coast."

"Not north, then?"

I shook my head. "We have family in the north, but we are separate. They have their circuit as we have ours. We both breed horses. It would be poor showing to intrude upon another caravan's business."

"That makes sense."

I smiled. "Most things do, if you only stop to ask questions."

Amicable silence stretched between us as we finished our meal. Martyn packed away his cheese and I offered him the remaining portion of bread, but he refused it. "Take it home to your gran. I lost mine last year to fever. I miss her. She was good to me and my brothers and sisters."

"I'm sorry for your loss. I will pray for her," I said.

"You pray?" His brows lifted in surprise, and I had to stop myself from rolling my eyes. I *had* said he should ask questions. What I hadn't realized was that he'd assume I was unlike him in every way and ask *stupid* questions.

"Of course. We are Christians, like you, and do many things like you. We dance and sing and marry and have children and pray to God. We simply do it our way. We are always—" I'd never tried to explain my culture to a diddicoy who'd never been taught about his own blood before, but that was mostly because I'd never wanted to spend any time with someone outside of my caravan before. It took a minute to formulate a proper explanation. "We always seek balance. There is good, there is bad. There is pure, there is impure. All things must balance for a person to live a good life."

Martyn reached into his pocket to pull out his cigarillo box, sliding one between his teeth and striking a match against his boot heel. "What determines what is good or bad? Or pure or impure? Dirt?"

"Not exactly. A dirty body is not ideal, but a dirty body can also be washed in the river. If you wallowed in filth, it would make you unclean soon enough, though. It is . . . Perhaps I should say it is a spiritual uncleanliness? Your practices determine the filth upon your soul." I looked to see if he followed.

He didn't appear confused, his expression even while he leaned back on his hands to smoke, so I continued. "To answer your earlier question, tradition dictates what is clean and what is not. These are rules passed down through the generations."

"So how would I know if I'm unclean or not?"

I tore my attention from his profile and down to the hunk of bread in my lap, my fingers toying with the crinkly paper wrap. I didn't want to hurt his feelings, but I was likely going to, and that made me squirm. "All who live the gadjos way are *mochadi*. You don't practice our ways to maintain your balance."

I braced myself, expecting him to be angry with me, but he smiled inside his cloud of smoke. Mochadi didn't mean as much to him as it did to me—which was truly the difference between Roma and outsiders, and why the separation of our people was encouraged. The outsiders blissfully wallowed in their filth.

But is he filthy?

Yes, of course.

I frowned down at the bread.

Martyn nudged my foot with his, forcing me to jerk away from him. "Guess that's that. Glad you're still sitting here, Miss Bet . . . what's your last name? You have those, right?"

"Wh— Of course we do. Mine is Jones, like my gran. Bethan Jones. A Welsh name, like yours. I told you we were not so different."

"I have cousins who are Joneses. Are you my cousin?" He leaned in to eyeball me, so close I got a coil of smoke up my nostril and had to rear back for fear of sneezing in his face. "Oh, oh. Sorry. My mistake."

"It's fine." I shook my head to clear the stench, waving a

hand about to push the smoke away. "But no, we aren't cousins. Our name was not originally Jones, I'm sure, but we took it to avoid trouble. Blending in keeps us safer in places where we are not welcome."

"Huh." He stubbed out the cigarillo and put it, half-smoked, back into his box. "You know, I could teach you how to read. It might help you blend in. I taught my sister."

My gut jumped to an emphatic no, followed by the chieftain's well-practiced *"Everything important we keep in our heads and hearts,"* but then I remembered that not a few hours ago, I'd been thinking about asking Gran for lessons. Why was it all right from her but not from Martyn? The answer, of course, was the impropriety of it all.

"You don't have to do that. I'm . . . I'll be fine. I believe you about the sign."

"I know I don't have to do it. I want to. You're smart. You'll get it quick."

He wasn't going to let it go. I may have only known him a little while, but he'd been nothing but persistent since our meeting—getting me to go beyond town limits with him was proof enough of that. It had been all right to that point, but too much of it and he'd eventually annoy me. "I'm busy," I offered, not wanting to hurt his feelings. "I come to market, I make the bags, I have lessons with my grandmother in the evening. Thank you for offering, though. You are kind."

Martyn looked thoughtful. "But if we sell your goods faster, you'd have time in the afternoon before you go back to make the bags. My brother's around in the early afternoon, and business tapers off enough that I'd feel comfortable leaving him in the stand alone."

"But the market's so loud. . . ."

"So I go to Cotter's Field with you, or if that's not allowed, we could go to the fields at the edge of my farm. It's on the way, so you'd be home with time to spare." He grinned at me. "Any other ways you'd like to try to escape?"

I had run out of comfortable excuses, and it soured my disposition. I tugged up my scarf over my face and tucked it beneath my hair. "I can't, Martyn. That's all. You said if you did anything to make me uncomfortable, I should tell you to stop. Please stop."

"I shouldn't push." He leaned forward to catch my eye, a smile on his mouth. I knew if I looked at him, I'd notice the nice balance of his features and the rich hue of his eyes, so I concentrated on the grass beside me, my fingers toying with the tall blades. "I am pushing, of course. But I'd like to spend more time with you. You don't want to because I'm not . . . I'm unclean?" He craned his head to sniff his shirt and made a face. "No wonder. I'm ripe like a sty. Been hauling all day."

I frowned. I didn't owe him any explanation, but he certainly thought he deserved one all the same. "You're ridiculous, diddicoy. Yes, that's part of it. Gran wouldn't allow it, even if I'd like to learn. It would be inappropriate."

"Aha! So you *do* want to learn."

"Is that all you heard of what I said?" I demanded.

"Not at all, but does it hurt to ask her about it? You'd sell your goods, have a lesson, and be home with daylight to spare. There won't be anything improper—just learning."

"She'll say no," I insisted.

"And once she does, I'll never bring it up again." He smiled and stood, offering a hand to pull me up. I accepted before thinking better of it, the big fingers against mine so warm that I jerked away. He was not for me, he was off limits, and I'd remember that for his sake as much as mine.

He said nothing of my recoil, instead gathering the blanket from the field and folding it into neat squares. I walked by his side back to town, quiet and contemplative. I'd enjoyed myself despite his questions, despite our differences. Reading lessons with Gran would be strict and unyielding, and there'd be few smiles. But Martyn had been interested in what I had to say. He was funny. He was generous and warm and friendly. I wasn't sure he had a hard bone in his body.

Gran very likely wouldn't allow me to meet with him, even for something as proper as education, but I would ask. I was about to commit to as much when I spied Silas standing outside the market's gate. Three of his gang attended him, the boys side by side, their arms crossed, their legs braced apart. The absent party was Tomašis, who either suffered punishment at home with his mother or was too afraid of Gran's curses to trouble me further.

I wanted it to be an unhappy coincidence, but Silas's look was too keen. He stomped my way, his boots kicking up clouds of dust. My teeth ground together as he neared. I clutched my basket and bread to my chest and forced myself to meet his gaze so he would know my defiance.

Martyn paused at my side, his brows lifting. His attention swept from Silas to me, and seeing my displeasure, he tensed.

Silas spat on the ground. "What are you doing with him? This isn't proper." He eyed Martyn up and down, his frown so sour it could curdle milk. I took a step away from Martyn's side, putting enough space there that another person could have easily slid between us. It was not enough for Silas. "No! Come here." He pointed beside him like I'd heel simply because he called. To be addressed in such a way was embarrassing, especially in public. An old woman near the gate to the market watched us through slitted eyes; another woman near her whispered to her daughter and pointed.

I motioned at the gadjos observing us, and past them, at the milling crowds ever so ready to take Roma to task for any number of invented sins. "Keep quiet," I barked, my voice a furious whisper. "There's trouble enough for us without your help. If you wish to speak to me, do so in camp, with Gran or your father to witness."

Silas said nothing as he stalked toward me, his hand darting out, fingers manacling my wrist. He jerked me toward him. My body collided with his chest, one of his hands sweeping to my lower back and holding me like we were dancing.

"Hey," Martyn said, his tone uncertain.

"It's all right." I pushed away from Silas, but he held strong, glaring at Martyn over my shoulder.

"Go, gadjo, and don't think to look at my girl again."

"He's diddicoy, and let me go. Have you learned nothing these past few days? Ask Tomašis about his dreams!" I slapped at Silas's shoulder, but that only made his grip tighten, his fingers digging painfully into my side.

"How much Romani blood?" Brishen demanded. "A thimble's worth?"

"Less. Look how *yellow* he is up top," Cam replied.

"Shut up. You blather like women," Silas spat. His eyes never left me as he delivered the reprimand, though they did narrow when he said to me, "My father said your curses have no power. Your grandmother frightens children, and I am no child." He shook me again like a ragdoll, hard enough that my teeth rattled and the bread slipped from my hand to hit the ground.

"Now look what you made me do! You stupid boy." Such brave words, and yet I was so anxious, my heart pounded in my ears. I wrenched from his grasp to gather the bread so I could properly dispose of it later, but the moment I stood straight, he grabbed me again.

"You all right, Bet?" Martyn asked from behind. I couldn't see his face, pressed as I was to Silas, but the tone was upset.

"I will be once he leaves me alone," I said.

"You heard her, friend. She's not interested in your attention."

Silas let loose with a string of expletives in Kååle that Martyn wouldn't understand before whirling me about and throwing me at his friends like a sack of potatoes. Brishen, a squat brick of a boy with a too-round face and an enormous nose, caught me and pulled me to his body, his hands pinning my arms to my sides so I couldn't catch him with a flailing elbow.

I glanced back at the gates to see what the spectators were doing, worried they'd gone for the constable, but they remained, looking disgusted *and* hungry for the promise of violence.

"Or what, diddicoy? Or did you lie about being one of ours?" A cold smirk oozed across Silas's mouth. He streaked his fingers through his hair as he circled Martyn, looking him over from head to toe. Martyn was taller than him by half a foot, wider by as much, but that didn't intimidate Silas. Why would it when he had three of his cronies at his back? "What are you? A blacksmith? A carpenter's son? Or let me guess, a farmer? It doesn't matter. You're unfit for our girls—especially my girl."

"Never yours. Ever, Silas." I shook my head and looked at Martyn, my eyes stinging with shame. We were so proud, so proper. So many of us were good, honest people, and yet here was the outlier, "proving" what outsiders whispered among themselves whenever they spoke of us. That we were ne'er-do-wells and troublemakers. That we couldn't be trusted. "Ignore him and go back to town, Martyn. He's goading you. Please."

"I'm afraid I can't do that." Martyn spun with Silas, never again giving him his back. "I can't leave you with him, not like this."

"She's not upset. She's spirited, as all our girls are. She's too much filly for a rider such as you." Silas snickered, and Mander, Cam, and Brishen echoed him in foul chorus. Brishen was distracted, so I kicked at him, my boot striking the side of his knee and buckling his leg. I tore free of his clutches, but then Cam swooped in to loop his arm around my shoulders, his movements smooth like a dancer. I struggled, but Cam had me tight while Mander snagged the side of my blouse, letting me know he'd take over guard duty if I somehow escaped my newest shackles.

Silas smirked at Martyn with another oily grin. "Some fillies kick. Perhaps I'll hobble her when we get home."

I didn't so much see Martyn throw the first punch as I heard it crunch into Silas's face. There was a wet snap and Silas staggered, blood exploding from his nose to dribble down his lips and chin. His eyes rolled back and his whole body tilted, his heels the fulcrum to his seesaw. I thought he'd fall, and secretly hoped for it, but he righted himself at the last second, growled, and charged Martyn, striking him in the middle and sending him sprawling in the grass on his back.

"Stop!" I shouted at them. "People are watching!" But neither boy paid me any heed, the two of them wrestling like cats. Footsteps approached from behind, and I tried to see who was coming so we could run if need be, but Cam's grip kept me anchored, his shoulders too broad to see around.

"ENOUGH." The command was so loud, it echoed across the hills and startled the birds in a nearby tree. They swooped up at the sky in a choreographed dance.

Martyn rolled off Silas with a muttered oath, his hand slapping at the dirt on his trousers as he regained his feet. Mander and Brishen slinked away like kicked dogs while Silas, their leader, stayed prone on the ground, his breath coming fast, blood staining his nostrils and drying to crusts on his cheeks.

"Da," Martyn murmured.

I heard the crunch of grit beneath boots as Mr. Woodard approached. Cam loosed me and I collapsed onto my knees in the field, the bread once again tumbling from my grasp. I silently apologized to it for my poor treatment as Mr. Woodard overtook us, his shadow huge and long. I glanced from his stoic face over to Martyn's resigned one, and then down to Silas, who glowered at me despite his injury, his features blackened by Mr. Woodard's looming shadow.

"I see Silas Roberts in the shadow of a giant," Gran had said when she'd spoken of her vision.

In that field outside Anwen's Crossing, I did, too.

CHAPTER SEVEN

Mr. Woodard offered Silas a hand up, but Silas smacked it away and scrambled toward Cam. His cronies hauled him to his feet, the four huddling together, half-crouched and hackles up like rabid wolves.

"I don't need help from the likes of you," Silas snarled. "Come to us, Bethan. We're your people, or have you forgotten?"

It was meant to shame me, but all I could muster was a tired shake of my head. I looked toward town, the knowledge that I had work left to do weighing on me. I'd have preferred to go home, to burn the bread and seek Gran's council about so many things, but I had forty bags left to sell.

"You would choose the gadjos over your own?" His hands raked through his sleek black hair, flattening it to his scalp. "Betrayer."

"Can't you see she wants to be left alone? Go home," Martyn said.

Silas stepped toward Martyn, his lip curling. "As for you, you're nothing. You're dead."

Martyn stood taller, like he'd gladly go at Silas a second time, but Mr. Woodard slapped a hand across his son's chest, holding him back. "Violence begets more violence," the older man said, but his eyes remained on Silas. "I apologize on behalf of my boy, but threats do nobody any good. We'll go back to work; you go on your way."

"You don't tell me what to do, pig farmer." Silas spat on the ground to punctuate his insult, and Mander, Cam, and Brishen were quick to do the same. Silas extended a hand my way, once again trying to coax me into standing with him, but I ignored his dirty, blood-crusted fingers. Not five minutes ago he'd said he would hobble me like a mare.

I walked away then, from him and the boys and Martyn and Mr. Woodard, to return to my table in town. I was too ashamed to look at the Woodards and too angry to look at my own people. I wanted to escape it all—to concentrate on my work so I could get home to Gran.

"I will not leave you here," Silas called after me. "Not unchaperoned. It's indecent." I walked through the gates, pretending I didn't see the curious looks of the bystanders who'd assembled during the boys' fight, pretending I couldn't hear Silas shouting, "Bethan! Stop!" as I pressed through the crowds, the throngs of market people closing around me to cloak me from his view.

Martyn jogged to catch up with me. We walked side by side, never saying a word, not when he ducked into his stand to work, not when I displayed my remaining goods on my table. Mr. Woodard joined him a short time later, but didn't spare me a glance.

Hours passed. Customers came and went; many referred to me by the young man whose grass-stained clothes sported the evidence of his scuffle. Sometimes, when the crowds thinned, I caught Martyn looking my way, and sometimes, when our eyes met, he dared to wink at me.

I manufactured smiles for him despite the heaviness in my chest. It seemed like the right thing to do when he'd fought for my honor.

Later, when the shoppers came in singles instead of droves and my table had only six bags left, I shot a nervous glance at Mr. Woodard as he sorted his remaining produce before calling out to Martyn.

"Thank you," I managed. "Silas is spoiled and terrible. We're not all like him. He's shameful."

Martyn leaned over the half door of his counter, his arms folded, a piece of straw migrating from one side of his mouth to the other. "That's obvious. You're lovely. Is he courting you?"

"No. I think he would if he could, though. He's the chieftain's son—our leader's son. He doesn't believe rules apply to him." I gathered my leftover bags, laying them in the basket next to the bread. "I hope you don't get in trouble with your father. You were defending me."

He shrugged. "If anything, he'll whack me for throwing the first punch, but I can live with that. That boy was an arsehole."

"I'm sorry."

"For what? You didn't make him an arsehole . . . or is that one of your witch abilities, like the warts on your gran?" His grin was all teeth, and I shook my head. I glanced Mr. Woodard's way, at his broad back flexing as he stacked and restacked his boxes of crops. I didn't want Martyn getting thrashed for Silas's awfulness, and if a kind word from me would tip the scales, I had to try to talk to him.

Before I could say a thing, though, Mr. Woodard stopped laboring and looked my way, his expression hard, his eyes pinched tight so the crow's-feet crinkled at the edges. I braced for disdain, but instead, he said, "Martyn, I want you to walk her home. I don't like how those boys looked at her. Stick to the main roads and make haste." He rubbed his hand over his mouth. "Your parents should be told those boys are looking for trouble, Bet."

I cast my eyes down and nodded. "My grandmother knows, sir. Thank you. Martyn doesn't have to walk me home. I'll be fine."

Mr. Woodard shook his head. "I'm not so sure either of you would have been fine if I hadn't come along. Four versus one, Martyn? Terrible odds." He reached for his son's chin, tilting his head to examine him for injury. "I didn't raise a stupid son, but you wouldn't know it. Have your mother look at that when you get home."

Martyn jerked from his grasp and waved him off. "I'm fine, Da. He didn't touch me. They were being arseholes."

"Arseholes or not, you can't do anything if you get kicked to death." He shook his head and reached behind him, producing a big bag of pears in a burlap sack. "Those are for her," he said, motioning at me. "Home early, both of you. Keep the wind to your backs."

Martyn let himself out of the stand, the pears nestled into the crook of his arm.

"You heard the man. Shall we?"

I gathered my basket, reaching for Martyn's sign on the post to take home to show Gran, but he gently tugged on the end of my scarf to pull me away. "Leave it. At least I can be sure you'll come back if that's there."

"And if it rains and ruins it?" I asked.

"Then I have another reason to draw you."

Considering how much I liked the first portrait, I wouldn't object to a second, and my hand slid from the paper. "Fine. I need a lemon or a lime if there are any."

"Wait here." Martyn darted off into the marketplace. I tried to follow his tawny head, but it was no use, even with the dwindling crowds. He ducked down an alley and disappeared from my sight, only to reappear a minute later with a pair of lemons in hand that had seen better days—it was late for such a fruit. They were likely some of the last in the Crossing.

He dropped them into the sack with the pears. I pulled a penny from my coin purse, but he waved me off. "My treat."

"But . . ."

"No buts. On me." He motioned me ahead of him. I worked my way through the market, past pushy vendors thrusting end-of-day trinkets beneath my nose, some promising bargains, others outright pleading for business. Martyn stepped in front of me, using his superior size to carve a path. I almost lost him in the chaos twice, so when he offered me his hand so we could stay together, I took it without thinking, my fingers wrapping around his. He gave me a reassuring squeeze and ducked around the well, barging onward with me at his heels.

The moment we were past the front gate, I took a deep breath. He squeezed his fingers around mine, reminding me that we were tethered, and I gently disengaged, thankful that he didn't try to recapture my hand. I was grateful he'd defended me, and I wouldn't deny I found him pleasing, but that changed little about our circumstances.

"You look lost in thought," Martyn said as we rounded the first wheat field. "Like you're trying to figure out why the sun shines or the sky is blue."

"There's a tale about that," I started to say, but my story got tangled around my tongue as I spotted a crow perched on the fence post ahead of us. Its black head tilted back and forth, its eyes shining like onyx beads. It was so calm, so curious. We were only a few feet away and it did not move. Martyn stretched his hand toward it, his finger lifting like he'd allow the thing to perch if it so desired.

"If it pecks you, it'll hurt," I cautioned. "Or it could be sick. Crows aren't known for friendliness."

That caught his attention, and he jerked his hand away. "True. I've never seen one so willing to get close before, is all."

Neither had I, and it bothered me, especially in the wake of Gran's vision. If Silas had been in the shadow of a giant, and this was the crow, that was two of her portents manifesting in a few hours. My fear and tears were only a matter of time. I shivered and stepped back, peering at the wheat field beside us. The ominous scarecrow loomed at the bend ahead.

"When's the full moon?" I asked, more to myself than to Martyn.

"Tomorrow night. It's the blood moon. Da says that's what they call the first full moon after the equinox. Why do you ask?"

I didn't want to tell him about the vision, afraid he'd think it a silly superstition from a sillier girl, so I shook my head and walked toward the caravan, my steps brisk. I wanted my grand-mother's company more than anything in the world. I wanted to tell her what had happened and what I'd seen. I wanted her to know about the blood moon. But first I had to get past the scarecrow.

"That thing is hideous."

"Who's hideous? Thomson?" Martyn's grin stretched so wide that the corners of his mouth nearly touched his ears. He shoved the pear sack at me so he could hop over the fence, walk-ing up to the scarecrow and smacking its patched slacks with obvious affection. "You'll hurt his feelings. Thomson's a good sort. I made him."

"Why would you do a thing like that? He's terrifying."

"He's not inviting the crows to tea, is he?" He put his hands around the scarecrow's waist and hoisted it, repositioning the bag of nightmares on the big rusty hooks of its pole. Thom-son's head lolled to the side, stitched eyes fixed on the ground. "That's better."

"Better by what standard? And does this mean this is all Woodard land, then?" I motioned at the wheat fields surround-ing me. We were close enough to Cotter's Field that I could see our horses grazing in the easternmost pasture. Martyn had mentioned that his land backed up to where we were staying, but I hadn't realized it was *that* close.

"Indeed. This is ours, and the barley farther down the way. The vegetables are from the gardens behind the farmhouse yon-der, past the hills." Martyn climbed back over the fence to join me on the road, careful when he reclaimed the bag of pears from my grasp.

"I can carry that, you know. It's not far now," I said.

"I know you can, but I like doing nice things for you." He smiled at me. "I'm hoping my chivalry will convince your grandmother to let you take those reading lessons."

I doubted it would matter a whit, but I held my peace. We walked along, his trousers swishing with his steps, my skirt rustling with mine. It was a companionable silence, and so peaceful that when he erupted with a startled bark, I gasped, my grip tightening on the basket handle. I jerked my head toward him, my stomach sinking when I saw the panic on his face.

"Martyn?" I cupped his elbow, squeezing it, and he shook his head back and forth, his tongue sliding over his upper lip, his shoulders tense.

"And I gave you all that sass about Thomson, too, but, well—" He pointed to the side of the road. There, stretched into a zigzag of gold across its black scales, was a smallish snake, only two or so feet long.

"A serpent slithers into the moist earth."

I frowned.

"It's stupid. I'm big, it's small, but I was bitten as a boy. Adders don't kill, but they hurt like the devil. My leg swelled up for three days." Martyn glanced behind him, at a fence post similar to the one where the crow had roosted before. "Seems all of nature is out today, and acting ornery."

The snake wasn't ornery so much as lazy, the cold weather driving it closer to its winter hibernation, but I didn't say so. Martyn was afraid, and fear skewed perception.

I tugged off my scarf and wadded it into the basket before walking on. It wasn't long before I could hear the caravan children hollering from the fields. Dogs barked. Someone played a pipe whistle. The sun sank toward the treetops, and soon it would be dusk, the peepers singing their last before the cold winds came.

I paused to smile at Martyn, gently pulling the pears from his grasp. "I should go. I'll ask Gran about the reading lessons tonight, but after what happened with Silas, I'm not sure it's a good idea."

"He doesn't scare me. Your gran does a bit, just from what you said, but if she says no, that's the end of it. Doesn't mean I can't enjoy your company at market."

I nodded and looked down at his dusty boots. "Thank you, again. For earlier with Silas. For the pears."

"You're welcome, Bet." Before I could pull away, he lifted his hand to my face, his calloused fingers gliding over my cheek with the birthmark. The touch was tingly and warm, like holding his hand had been, and I pulled away from him, fleeing the diddicoy boy from Anwen's Crossing who made me feel too much.

CHAPTER EIGHT

Two steps into the vardo and Gran sent me off to collect dinner. I was swollen with the need to tell her about the day, but she'd hear none of it until our bowls were full. Even then, with both of us seated at the table and spoons poised, she insisted I wait.

"Too much time with your mouth open, evil thoughts will sneak in." It was an old decree of hers. Talking while eating invited trouble, so most of our meals slanted quiet. I struggled with it that day, squirming, shifting in my seat, toying with the stew with my spoon more than putting it into my mouth.

"Sit still. You are not a child. We will talk of your day shortly."

"Yes, Gran." I gobbled it down to get it over with, quiet as I took my bowl to the basin and rinsed it. Gran whacked her dish on my hip a short time later, letting me know that she was finished, too. I took both bowls to the river for washing. When

I returned some minutes later, Gran had her yarn and knitting needles on the table and was busy making loops.

"Tell me," she said as soon as the door was closed. "If I have a bad stomach later, it is because you rushed me through my meal."

"I'm sorry." I slid into the chair across from her, my eyes lowering as I tried to figure out where to start my story. I'd been so eager to expel words, I'd never considered the best delivery. "I've made a friend at market. I mentioned him yesterday."

"The yellow-haired man."

"Yes, Martyn. He defended me from Silas today." She arched a brow at that, and the words flowed thereafter, from the sign Martyn drew of me to our lunch date, Silas's arrival, and the fight in the field. She never said a word, not when I told her about Silas in the giant's shadow, not when I told her about the too-brazen crow and the adder. I'd thought those matters were direly important, but her silence suggested otherwise.

"The scarecrow's name is Thomson," I said in closing, because hearing my own voice was better than hearing nothing at all. "Martyn made him."

Gran pushed the knitting aside and stood, heading to the corner of the vardo with her witching goods. She searched the top drawer, choosing jar after jar and peering at the contents before banishing them back with their brethren. Eventually, she found what she was looking for—a jar of feathers. She set it on the table and added a spool of thread and needle to the pile before she sat back down across from me, sectioning off two feet from the spool and threading it through the needle.

"You will wear this through the blood moon," she said, her long fingernail fishing around inside the jar to capture a feather.

She pulled it out and wrapped a thread around the shaft. "Over your clothes like a necklace."

"What is it?" I accepted it, and was about to tie it off behind my neck, but she stopped me with a squeeze to my wrist.

"Not yet. It is a hawk's-eye charm, and we have to enchant it before you can wear it." She returned to her chest of supplies to retrieve a silver knife with an etched wooden handle from the drawer. She slid it across the table at me, hilt first.

I slapped my hand down on it to stop it from skittering off the side.

"The single most important thing to know about magic is that there is always a price. Making the impossible possible is difficult, as it should be, so I must weigh results against what I am willing to pay. It is never a gratuitous thing. This makes some people—people like Silas—disbelievers. They see my unwillingness to perform on command as a sign that the magic is untrue. Let them drown in their ignorance. When it is time for them to know my wrath, they will know it—and there will be no mistaking it."

She moved behind me and rested her hands on my shoulders, digging her fingernails in like cats' claws. "With the right tools, we can accomplish anything, but anything is also expensive. Do you understand?"

"I think so." I picked up the knife and turned it over, weighing the heavy, cold metal against my palm. The silver blade gleamed like new, but the wear on the carved grip suggested it was very, very old. "So what's the currency?"

"Many things, but the most common is the sanguine coin." She leaned over my shoulder to stroke my wrist, her nails tracing along the spidery blue veins beneath my skin. "Your blood on one side of the eye, mine on the other. It will let me watch you."

"But touching blood is generally forbidden." Her clutch on my shoulder tightened, and I winced, tripping over myself to explain. "I am not arguing, Gran, but I am confused. How is this allowed for something that's not healing?"

"I am drabarni. You will be drabarni. When our people cut themselves, we stitch them. When the babies come, we pull them from their mothers' wombs. Blood is a necessity of our trade. It is why we keep our vardo separate."

"Oh."

She hadn't quite answered my question.

"Mmmm. Now, the things you saw today—your crow and adder—I do not know if they relate to my vision or not, but we must be vigilant until the blood moon is past. The charm will allow me to see you from afar, and to help you if you need it. You are an annoying girl who does not know when to shut her mouth, but you are my annoying girl, and I will care for you to the best of my ability."

She jerked the sleeve of my blouse up to my elbow, revealing my left forearm. She tapped the thickest part of my palm, below my thumb where my birthmark went from solid wine to a smattering of wine-colored freckles. "Cut here. It does not need to be big, just enough to saturate the thread. To fuel magic, your own essence is always preferable to someone else's, but sometimes we cannot give our rituals what they require without doing irreparable harm to ourselves, and so we harvest from other resources."

I had questions I didn't dare to voice. A small enchantment cost small blood—that I understood. It stood to reason, then, that bigger enchantments cost bigger blood. Gran had claimed some impressive feats of magic in the years before I was born, which suggested impressive amounts of blood had been spilled.

Was it Romani blood? Or gadjo blood?

And who would volunteer for such a thing?

I must have mulled a little too long for Gran's taste, because she tore the knife from my grip. A heartbeat later, there was fire in my hand. She'd sliced me from thumb to lifeline, the flesh opening and seeping crimson into the grooves of my palm, a coil winding around my wrist. I yelped, as much in surprise as in pain, my eyes wetting as I hunched over, instinctively cradling my injury to my stomach to protect it from hurt.

"Gran!"

"I am sorry. It is unpleasant, but if you wish to do magic, you will know much worse in your lifetime. This is the ugly part of our craft." She peeled my hand away from my midsection, and when I refused to unclench my fist, she jabbed my shoulder with the butt of the knife. "I am not going to kill you. I am getting your blood on this thread. Would you waste your sacrifice? Was it for nothing?"

"I . . . No." I relinquished my throbbing hand to her untender mercies. Gran wasted little time dipping both the hawk's feather and the thread into my pooling blood, and when the cut's flow dwindled, she squeezed the wound to reopen it, like I'd become her personal inkwell. I swallowed my whimper, afraid she'd decide I was too craven to follow in her footsteps after all.

"We join your lifeblood to mine. Like this." She stabbed herself in the fleshiest part of her middle finger, unflinching as the skin split and a dome of blood rose, only to drizzle over the

79

hills and valleys of her liver-spotted hand. She was ambivalent to the pain, like years of ritual bleeding had hardened her to the discomfort. "Paint the other half, Bethan, to complete the charm," she said, offering herself to me.

It took me longer to saturate my side than it had taken her to do hers, but I wanted to be thorough. Rushing could ruin it, and I didn't want a first-time failure looming over my head forever.

When the thread was damp and rust-colored, I handed her the charm for inspection, hoping she'd find no fault with my work. She twisted it this way and that, eventually nodding with approval. "Blow on it to dry it," she instructed, and I did, thinking how simple it all seemed. Was a drabarni working with blood no different from a baker working with flour? Was the blood a commonplace tool used to glue more important components together?

"Lift your chin," Gran said.

She fit me with the foul necklace, tying the thread off behind my neck with two tight knots. I cringed when the feather brushed the soft skin of my throat. If she noticed, she said nothing, instead patting the charm and making her way to the basin in the corner. She worked at the blood staining her hand with lye and a scrub brush. "You must keep it on through the blood moon. There are no exceptions."

I fingered the heavy thread. Two days was a long time to wear a bloody bird feather, especially when I was expected at market and I'd already had problems with the locals. "May I tuck it beneath my scarf?"

"No. It will block my view. Wear a dark blouse so it is

harder to see," she said, toweling off her hands. "The yellow-haired diddicoy will not let anyone bother you much, yes?"

"I suppose." I got up to approach the mirror on the wall. It was smaller than my head, oval-shaped, and framed by oxidized copper. It was extravagant, something finely made and valuable, and I doubted anyone else in the caravan owned such a prize. The surface was smooth and clear save for the bottom, where a cluster of lumps distorted the glass. I stooped so I could peer into it, to see how awful the necklace looked around my neck. It wasn't as obvious as I'd feared, though I did pull my hair over my shoulders to hide the thread. "Do we need magic words to make it work?"

"Yes, but that is for tomorrow. Magic is time sensitive—its effects diminish quickly. Three days before it goes cold and needs to be recast. Curses can go longer, but curses and spells are not the same." She stepped aside from the basin and motioned me over. I practically dove for it, wanting to scrub myself to the bone thanks to the tacky film soiling my fingers. Each dunk of my hands in water resulted in a pink pool, and when I was done, I opened the window to throw the water out. I'd wash the basin in the river in the morning, as I did every morning, and collect fresh water for Gran's personal uses.

Gran shuffled around behind me, pulling on her sleeping clothes. She let the sun determine when and how long we slept, and with autumn's chill came early nights.

"Gran, there's one more thing. It's probably stupid to ask." She eyed me from her bed, her fingers adroitly weaving her gray hair into a plait. "Martyn, the young man from market—"

"The yellow-haired man," she interjected, tilting her face

to peer at me with her brown eye. "You do not have to keep identifying him. I know who he is."

"Yes, him. He's offered to teach me to read. Lessons. They'd be before supper, during the day so it'd be proper, and only after market time. I'm only asking because I gave my word to him that I would, but I know it's not really—"

"Ask me after the blood moon."

That was not the answer I'd expected. I thought she'd worry about the diddicoy's influence, or that I longed for the company of someone outside our caravan. She'd forbid it for my own good. The logical, sensible part of me said that would be the right thing for her to do, to sever the tie before it tightened. The other part—the part that whispered fanciful promises and tingled when Martyn flirted with me—secretly delighted that she'd left the door open.

Heat flooded my cheeks. "Thank you."

"Do not thank me yet, girl. It is not a yes." Shivering, she pulled her blankets up to her chin. I took that as a sign to pull out the winter furs. I knelt before one of the storage trunks, sweeping the sundries aside to burrow for the blankets below. Gran had packed them away with lavender sachets, so they weren't overly musty, but I'd hang them out the next day, weather allowing, for good measure.

I laid one over her and tucked it tight around her feet. They were often cold, something she attributed to age and poor circulation, so I leaned over her to rub them. As I stood there, fingers pinching and kneading over her socks, she reached for me and gently squeezed my wrist.

"Sit," she said, motioning me to her side. It wasn't a big bed, but with enough wriggling I was able to perch beside her legs. Her thumb swept over the back of my hand, as close to a loving gesture as she'd ever come. Gran wasn't the type to pull people to her bosom and smother them with affection. She expressed her love in other ways—small touches, hard-earned smiles, and pats on the back. For her to be warm like this was a rare treat, and one I'd appreciate while I had her grace.

"Your parents. Your father. He was not one of us. Did you know that?"

"Yes."

She nodded and her eyes closed, her tongue flicking at the corner of her mouth. "He loved your mother very much and was willing to give up his own people to be with her. She loved him, too, and would have followed him to the ends of the world if he had asked. By clan tradition, she should have been outcast for her choice, but she was a well-loved drabarni and the people needed her healing skills too much to send her away. They did not welcome him, though, despite his efforts to learn our customs. Men like Silas are rare, but not rare enough, and they made your father's life difficult. He stayed for your mother. Loyal, true, never complaining, though he often came home with bruises he refused to explain. The fights were never fair, but he survived.

"Your mother felt terrible about it. She often told him he should go, leave her and find another, but he said he could bear it as long as he had her. Her one regret . . ." Gran paused to look at me, peering for a long time. She wore a strange expression, her customary hardness replaced by something I didn't recognize and couldn't name. Uncertainty, perhaps. It was in the creases of her brow, in the slight gape of her mouth and the wideness of her eyes. Seeing it made my heart heavy, and I stroked her gnarled, frail fingers despite the ache in my palm.

"I know—the chieftain told me," she added, almost as an afterthought, "that your mother's one regret was putting a good man through this life. She died proud of you, proud of what she and he had made, but she regretted what this life had done to the man she loved.

"And your father, for all that he was good, could not raise you. Without your mother to soften the blows, without her station as drabarni to ward off the less emboldened, he would die, and so he left the thing he wanted most in this world: you. The last piece of her he could claim. *This* is how you came to me as you are. Not because a gadjo was scared of your markings. The choices we make in life stay with us, Bethan. There are few opportunities for second chances."

I'd fallen into a listener's trance as she talked, letting her story lull me, but I was shaken fully awake when she suddenly dug her fingernails into the tender meat of my hand. "Tell me you understand what I am trying to say! I am old. I do not have words to waste anymore. The things I have left to teach you— there is so much. Let us hope for both our sakes that you learn quickly."

I swallowed past the lump in my throat and nodded. Not only was she reminding me of her mortality, but she'd drawn parallels between my mother's life and my own. In her descriptions of my father's pain, she made me see Martyn's beaten face. I'd have been stupid not to see the danger, for him and for me. A smart person learned from their mistakes, but a smarter person learned from other people's mistakes, or so Gran liked to say.

"Say it, Bethan," she barked, giving my hand another hard squeeze. "Say what I want to hear."

"I understand, Gran. I wish I didn't, but I understand."

She gave me a long look—a heavy look—and I knew without asking that she was searching my eyes for far more than just my agreement. Whatever she saw must have satisfied her. She released me and settled back into her blankets. Her eyes fluttered closed and she let out a chest-rattling sigh.

"Good. You are not as silly as I thought. Sleep, and sleep well. Tomorrow will be a long day for both of us. Far longer than any before it, but we will prevail. One way or another, we will prevail."

CHΛPTER NINE

I twisted and turned beneath my blankets for hours, sleep as distant as the stars. Gran's proclamation for the coming day had sounded so ominous—as ominous as when she'd given the initial portent—that my mind raced with terrible possibilities. When she nudged me before dawn, I was exhausted, my eyelids leaden with sleep, my bones weary.

"Up for food. Up for enchantment. Up for market," she said. I burrowed deeper into my warm nest, but she ground the tip of her cane into my shoulder, the pressure increasing the longer I dallied.

She would not be denied.

By the time I'd put away my bedding, washed downstream, dressed, and collected our breakfasts, Gran was already seated at the table with her tarot cards in one hand and a silver coin in the other. The coin was old and foreign, the stamp on the top side too worn to reveal its origins. She flipped a card and scowled, only to flip another, then another. Twelve in all were displayed on the table, many of them swords, some wands, with the Devil, the Tower, and Judgment sprinkled throughout for flavor.

"Worthless," she griped, pushing the cards away and motioning me to my chair.

"You saw nothing?"

I put her food before her. She stabbed into it and lifted her spoon only to turn it over, a lumpy, mealy spoonful plopping back into the mix with a wet smack. "No. I had hoped to spark more vision with the cards, but it is the same. The shadow, the crow, the snake."

"I can stay home if that will help."

She took her first bite, cringing. The better breakfast would be at sunrise, with spicy sausages and eggs and coffee, but she'd likely skip it on account of her lameness. "My experience tells me we are better embracing what we know. You *can* change fate once it is cast, but Destiny does not appreciate thwarting. She can be cruel. Whatever it is that comes for you, you make it through. I have seen that, but I cannot say the same if we alter the course of your stars."

We ate in quiet until our bellies were full. I did the washing up, and then Gran was motioning me to her side.

"Come."

I hovered by her elbow. Her fingers reached up to dance along the hawk's eye charm, her lips murmuring words I couldn't understand. I wished she'd speak more clearly, but she was too lost in her private thoughts. The silver coin flitted back and forth between her fingers, glinting in the early-morning light.

I didn't expect her to toss it at me. It bounced off my chest to roll across the table, and I slapped it to stop it from plummeting to the floor, scooping it into my palm.

"Many magic users have a focus—a trinket, a charm, something—that they keep with them always. It is a tool to channel the will, and the longer you use it and keep it, the more powerful it becomes." She snatched the coin back from me. "I chose this because I carry it always. It is always near when I need it. What you choose is up to you. It does not have to be costly, just something you keep close and value."

She looked at me expectantly, but I didn't own much of anything myself—I didn't wear much jewelry beyond my earrings, and the things I held dear were largely immaterial. What should have been a simple decision felt disproportionately complex, and I cast my eyes around, desperate for something to put forth.

I must have looked lost, because Gran pushed herself from the table to shuffle to the corner, rifling through her things until she found the black cat figurine with the chipped paint. "Take this. It is my old focus, a toy from my childhood, and it served me well. If you want to replace it with something more personal later on, that is fine. Sometimes our foci change as our priorities change."

It was a personal gift, a caring one, and I smiled as she slid it onto the table before me. "Thank you, Gran. I am touched."

"Good. Now pick it up." I did, and she laced her gnarled fingers with mine, the cat token between one set of joined palms, her coin between the other. "I want you to think of the eye of the hawk and how it can see prey from miles above. I want you to will that sight into the charm. Banish all other thoughts and distractions until I speak. When I say the words, repeat after me. Do you understand?"

"Yes."

" '*Yes*' what?"

"Yes, Gran. I understand."

"Good." She closed her eyes but I did not, too curious not to witness my first real magic. There was no sound beyond Gran's deep, even breathing. I followed suit, embracing a deep, trance-like stillness where nothing existed but the hawk. I pictured it soaring on the wind with wings spread, its body gliding above treetops. I imagined its eyes scouring the ground, able to see any and all things as it searched for its next meal. I imagined the feathers in jars, ripe and ready for magic, and the blood drizzled on the one Gran had chosen to bind us.

I don't know how much time passed—a minute, two, ten—but when Gran finally spoke, it felt intrusive, like she'd shattered a sacred quiet. "For one day and for one night, grant to me your hunter's sight. The blood is tithe, the task is true."

The spell sounded strange. Perhaps it was because the first sentence rhymed and the second did not, or perhaps it was because doing magic evoked images of mighty sorceresses conjuring with dramatic monologues, beseeching everything from the ancestors to the elements to God himself.

I repeated Gran's words, willing the hawk to grant Gran its sight, and then . . . magic happened. A thick, pulsing heat blossomed between our joined hands. The warmth intensified, surging to a scalding heat, but I refused to pull away, gritting my teeth, groaning as the power leaked from the sides of our hands, shining over our bodies, glimmering across the wall. I tingled from fingertips to elbows, the energy inside me rushing the blood through my veins and quickening my pulse. My fatigue was gone. I could have danced for hours or run around the vardo until my legs gave out. It was too much, too fast, but it was ecstatic, and I never wanted it to stop.

"It is done," Gran said.

Her words were a hammer crashing down, the spell bursting apart on the anvil upon impact. The inferno fizzled to a tepid throb, the light no longer painting us ethereal. The lightning left my body, my pounding heart the only evidence that anything had happened at all. I pulled my hand away from Gran's to touch the charm, but it felt the same as it had before—sticky and crusty.

I frowned. "But can you see through my eyes?"

"The mirror and my sewing. Bring them to me."

I slipped both before her as she settled into her chair. She pawed through her sewing basket, pulling a wooden needle from her pincushion and stabbing the tip of her finger with it, squeezing her flesh when the crimson dollop didn't ripen how she wanted.

"Push the mirror closer," she barked at me.

As soon as the copper frame touched her chest, she tipped the finger so she could splash blood across the mirror's smooth surface. A ripple passed over the glass, like she'd disturbed a very small, very still pond. I stood transfixed as a hazy fog formed in the middle, swirling like a storm cloud before dissipating and revealing a faint, but clear, image. The mirror's reflection showed the interior of the vardo, from the perspective of the charm.

"It works. It really works," I whispered.

"It does. This is your work, Bethan. I would have aided had

you needed it, but your will alone was enough. You have an affinity. It is good." She looked so proud of me, like I'd finally earned the apprentice's mantle she'd thrust upon me all those years ago.

It felt good to please her, to be accomplished on my first try. My eyes stung, emotion threatening to overwhelm me, but I sniffed it away and stood taller, my spine made of iron. Perhaps I should have been afraid, but I wholeheartedly trusted Gran. She'd kept me safe for seventeen summers. I expected no less despite the omens.

"Do not bask too long, silly girl. Bind your face and get to market. Sell what you can, but do not tarry. The blood moon is upon us, and the nearer I am to you, the better I will feel. I do not trust this night."

I collected the herb bags and headed for the door. As I was about to step out into the cold, she called for me to wait before draping her own old, knitted shawl over my shoulders. It wasn't much to look at—the yarns were sky blue, the edges trimmed in silver—but it was thick and comfortable and would keep me warm against the cold.

"I—" Gran peered at me, her brown eye coursing over my face, worry crinkling her brow. "You are strong. You are mine so you are strong. Remember this."

"Yes, of course. I understand."

I didn't, not truly, but neither did she. The vision hadn't been kind. She squeezed my shoulder and told me to go.

I ran to town, my fast pace keeping me warm. When I walked through the front gates of the market, it was a ghost of the town I'd come to know. The empty tabletops shimmered with morning dew, and the shelves sported the shimmering labors of a few industrious spiders. I could have grabbed any position in the square I wanted, but I went back to the table next to Martyn's stand. My drawing curled at the edges, thanks to two days' exposure to the elements, and I took it down and smoothed it out, bending the corners into shape. I'd just tacked it back into place when Martyn appeared, a crate of apples perched on his shoulder.

"Good morning."

I smiled at him, moving around behind my table to display my herb bags. "And to yourself."

"How are you? You look nice. Warm."

"Thank you." My hand strayed to the hawk's eye, my instinct to tuck it beneath the collar of my shirt so he wouldn't behold something so ugly, but I wouldn't be stupid. Gran and I had made it to protect me from the blood moon, and that was more important than looking pretty. "I'm well. And you?"

"Good! I have something for you."

"Enough presents, Martyn. It's too much."

Gran might see . . .

But he didn't know that, and so he smiled, abandoning his crate on the counter to stand by my side, close enough that our elbows touched. He pulled a scroll from his pocket and offered it to me by tapping it against the tip of my nose. I snorted and tore it from his grasp. "I won't be able to visit much today," he said. "Market's closed tomorrow for the Sabbath, and people tend to stock up. I wanted you to have this, though."

I unrolled the thick, cream-colored paper, smiling at the new portrait. It was black chalk, but there were touches of color here and there, too—a peach flush along the cheek, a dash of red on the lips—and he'd captured the sepia of my eyes almost perfectly. I was looking far away, my scarf pulled down, like he'd caught me in the middle of a daydream. I was glad to see he hadn't shied away from drawing my birthmark, using a wine color to trace out the curve over my eye and down along my jaw. He even showed the splash of wine freckles on the column of my throat.

There were words above and below the picture again, which suggested he expected me to hang it beside my table. I wanted to, but I didn't dare. There was a reason I wore a scarf to market every day. Advertising how different I looked from everyone else wouldn't do me any favors.

"Thank you, but I can't. Hang it, I mean. I can bring it home, though." He looked disappointed, and I rushed to explain. "I love it, but you know I've had trouble. I cover myself to avoid it."

I was afraid of what he might say, afraid he'd take the picture back because I refused to hang it, but then he turned his body toward mine, leaning forward and leaning slow. His face was scant inches away from mine, his hands braced on my shoulders when he said, "I won't let that happen again."

"It will, though. The birthmark draws more attention, and the gadjos already treat my people as lesser. You can't change every mind." I brushed my fingers over his, the touch clandestine and exciting, and also completely unacceptable. I stepped back, forcing distance between us again. Gran had told me about my mother's folly with my father, and of dark omens on the blood moon. I would not be foolish and disregard her counsel. Not for any man.

My eyes skipped to the drawing in my fist. "Thank you for this, though. I will keep it close. You do beautiful work."

Martyn looked like he had more to say, but then Mr. Wood-ard appeared, pushing a wheeled cart with squash rattling around inside. He nodded and greeted me with a casual, "Bet," before motioning Martyn back into the stand. Martyn dared to skim his fingers over the scarf at my cheek before joining his father.

Watching them set up for the day, it occurred to me that Gran had witnessed our exchange through the hawk's eye. My face flushed beneath the scarf. I hadn't done anything wrong, but if she wondered about my feelings for "the yellow-haired man," she would wonder no more. There was an intimacy to the exchange that couldn't be denied.

I hadn't pursued it, but I also hadn't discouraged it.

I slid the drawing into my basket and sat down behind my table. I watched the square come to life around me. The baker arrived, and then the linen merchant stacked her bolts in pleasing, colorful heaps at the end of her table. In no time at all, the empty shelves and vacant tables transformed into a fully stocked bazaar ready for commerce.

I didn't think I'd see much in the way of customers for a while, but as soon as the shopkeepers turned their signs from Closed to Open and the street vendors settled into their seats, people swarmed. It pleased me to get a buyer almost right away and without Martyn's help—Gran's reputation for quality curatives was spreading. I waited on the man at my table, and then the woman after him, and the man after her, and the steady stream of business didn't seem to be ebbing. By lunchtime, my voice cracked and my feet hurt. I didn't have much time for a break, but I managed a biscuit from the baker and a glass of water. I would have visited Martyn, too, but Mr. Woodard sent him back and forth to the farm to restock their inventory. He was too busy.

Midafternoon became late afternoon, the sun sulking its way toward the west and its inevitable decline. I had a dozen bags left and an elderly couple shuffling my way, but I waved them off and packed my goods, promising a Monday return. I wouldn't risk my safety for pennies. I glanced to my right. The Woodards were still inundated with customers, though their bins had been ravaged and picked over. I wanted to wave good-bye to Martyn, but I wasn't going to displace paying customers for the privilege, so I headed toward the gate on my own. My scarf was wound tight around my nose, and this time I kept my eyes fixed on the ground so no overeager vendors would jump into my path.

I was almost outside when the hot hand clamped down on my wrist and nearly tore me off my feet.

CHAPTER TEN

I would have fallen on my face had it not been for the sea of bodies surrounding me. I slammed into an elderly man instead, my herb bags tumbling from my basket to litter the road by my feet.

"I'm sorry! I'm—" The hand tugged again, harder, cutting my words short. There were so many people, so many passing faces, that I didn't immediately recognize my captor—but when he jerked me back a third time, crashing my body against his, I knew.

Brishen was Silas's shortest friend, a squat, wide man-boy with too many freckles and a nose that resembled a pig's snout. His rubbery fish lips stretched into an unkind smile. He moved his hand higher on my arm, toward the elbow, pulling me back in the direction I'd come from. I tried prying his fingers off me, but his grip was ironclad. People glared at me as though bumbling into them were my choice, no one seeing my struggle or caring. They were so intent on getting their shopping done before the Sabbath that they could only spare a moment's annoyance for a floundering Romani girl.

"Brishen, please. Gran watches," I hissed, but that just made him pull all the harder, wrenching my arm at an unnatural angle. He paid no mind to my pained yelps, forcing his way through the market. I staggered behind him out of necessity, trying not to further injure my arm.

I knew from my days in town that the crowds thinned near the back gates, especially late in the day. If he pulled me through an open space, I could kick out at him—maybe distract him long enough to clamor for my freedom—but as we passed the well, another set of hands wrapped around my free arm, and Cam fell into step beside me.

"Cam, no. Please. I want to go home." I repeated his name, hoping to get through to him, but all he did was peer at me like he couldn't fathom my upset. Gran always said not to trust wolves, as wolves didn't understand anything but other wolves. Looking into Cam's pale eyes, noting his impassive expression, and feeling his fingers dig into the flesh beneath my shawl, I saw her words rang true. Cam had all the warmth of a northern blizzard.

The crowds were densest near the front gates, where the market touched the town square. I searched for Silas in the swarming shoppers, but the faces blended with the chaos. I knew he was there, though; he was the plan maker, the one at the root of my problems. Sure enough, I spotted him lingering near Martyn's stand, behind the biggest cluster of people, where he wouldn't easily be spotted. I looked for Mander and Tomašis. If three of the boys were present, the other two couldn't be far, but I didn't see them. Perhaps they were searching for me in the market still, or waiting outside. They weren't smart enough to stay away. Tomašis maybe, because of the nightmare curse, but I didn't count on it.

Silas beckoned the boys close, his hands grabbing for me before I was even within arm's reach. Brishen and Cam flung me at him like I was a ball to be tossed from player to player. Silas held me as close as he could without our bodies fusing, his face pressing into the side of my neck so I could feel his breath. For the first time, I was glad for the scarf wound around my head—it kept me from feeling his lips against my skin.

"Silas, no. Stop," I rasped, wriggling in his clutches. "Why me?"

He nuzzled at my hairline, so close I could feel the smile stretching his mouth. "Because you're fiery and beautiful. Because I like that you run. Because you are drabarni and I'm the chieftain's son and together we'd be royalty. So many reasons, Bethan."

"Except I don't want it! Gran talked to your father. She knows what you're doing. She sees all now. Whatever stupid thing you plan to do, don't do it."

"Shut your mouth." The words were at odds with the smile on his face. He looked so pleased with himself, so very sure, that I knew something insidious was afoot. I wasn't given long to worry about it.

He put two fingers in his mouth to whistle and then dragged me behind him. He shoved past customers, snarling and spitting when people wouldn't get out of his way. One man shoved back and shouted in anger, but Brishen stepped in front, leaving Silas a clear path. I dug my heels into the ground to try to slow

Silas down. There were no people to block him. My heels got no grip in the yielding earth. I kicked at the back of his knee to offset his balance. He stumbled forward, losing his grip on me, and I yanked my arm free. I turned to run, but the crowd was too thick for me to get far, and Cam was right there to close in, his arm looping around my waist and hauling me back.

Silas picked himself up from the ground and brushed off his knees, his curses colorful. I swung my head around, trying to get my bearings. We were almost back at my table. I spotted the back gate ten yards away, which meant Martyn's stand was close. The crowd parted enough that I could see him behind his counter, empty vegetable crates stacked behind him, a sack of potatoes in his hands. Martyn spied me at about the same time and, seeing me wriggling like a worm on Cam's hook, his face turned red. He threw the potatoes aside and vaulted the counter.

"Don't. There are too many." I'd have said more, but Silas lunged at me. His fist struck my face so hard, my head rocked back on my neck. My vision splintered into white shards. The pain was extraordinary, and I slumped in Cam's arms, forcing him to hold my weight. The world spun around me, a blur of shattered rainbows. There was no noise except for an odd buzzing between my ears, like I had bees in my skull instead of a brain.

Spittle struck my scarf, droplets spraying my forehead and eyes as Silas screamed in my face, but I couldn't understand him over the buzz. I couldn't seem to speak yet, either. My tongue felt like a fat lump of meat in my mouth. When my head had finally cleared enough to make out Silas's words, of course they were filled with venom.

"You will never put a hand or foot on me again. My father is chieftain. You will *respect me.*"

People had started to notice the spectacle, and bodies closed around us in a ring, with me, Cam, Silas, and Brishen at the center. The gadjos yelled angry things at Silas, but most were racial epithets and didn't spare me, either. One man told Silas to "collect his gypsy whore and go home." I wanted to call that man to task for disgracing my honor, but I felt too dazed, too terrified to find my anger.

While the rest of the crowd jeered, it was Martyn who thrust through the circle and jumped on Silas's back, one of his arms wrapping around his throat. Silas bucked like a horse, trying to shake him off, but Martyn was far heavier, and his grip was too strong. Brishen rushed at him, punching Martyn's head, and Martyn huddled close to Silas's back to avoid getting struck in the face. I could hear the hard *whoomp*s as Brishen's knuckles smashed against skin and bone in rapid succession.

I screamed, thrashing away from Cam. He let me go, but only so he could jump into the fray. Still off balance from Silas's punch, I tumbled to the ground. I realized I'd lost my basket and Martyn's pretty picture somewhere as I struggled to my feet. Cam tried to peel Martyn off Silas's back, his feet kicking out at the backs of Martyn's legs, but Martyn clung despite the abuse. He was in pain, and I could tell by the sweat on his brow that he couldn't keep it up much longer, but he fought valiantly, three against one and holding his own. Silas let out an angry shriek, collapsing onto the ground and dragging Martyn with him. Cam grabbed one of Martyn's feet and wrenched back, and Martyn cried out.

"Stop! Stop it, all of you!" I shouted, rushing in. I shoved at Brishen's shoulder and stomped on Silas's fingers when his hand encircled my ankle. Silas screamed, and I wanted to give him another kick, but I was afraid of striking Martyn. Instead, I rushed at Brishen, who was still pummeling Martyn's face. My first swipe was a miss as Brishen turned his head, but then my sharp nails found their target and left a long gouge along his cheek, opening the meat and drawing blood. He hollered and spun around, smacking at the cuts as if he could swat the pain away.

"Motherless bitch," he swore, swinging one of his beefy arms at me. I managed to duck, my head swimming with the motion. I stumbled into some of the people behind us. One stranger's hands pulled me in as if to protect me, while another's thrust me away as if to send me back at Brishen.

"Bet. BET!" I heard my name, at first thinking it was Martyn calling me, but when I raised my head I saw it was Mr. Woodard who'd pushed his way through. His weathered face looked strained, the grooves next to his eyes and mouth more pronounced than I'd ever seen them. I looked at him, he looked at me, and he motioned toward the gates behind us. "Run home. Go. Get somewhere safe."

I hesitated, not wanting to leave Martyn to Silas's cruelties, but then Mr. Woodard hoisted Cam like a bale of hay and threw him off his son. Mr. Woodard was a big man—a huge man by our people's standards. The boys were half his weight and size, and it was clear he wasn't going to allow any more nonsense. I took my opening to leave, surprised that people stepped aside to let me pass.

I knew I couldn't run—I wasn't yet steady enough on my feet for that. But I managed to get outside and onto the road.

The skies had turned a murky charcoal with approaching dusk, but there was no moon yet.

Perhaps that meant I'd get home safe after all.

I walked far slower than I wanted to. It wasn't so much from the pain in my head—though that was far from pleasant—as it was from the dizziness. Too many steps too fast and the world spun like a child's top. I walked alongside the fence, the wood touching my hip, my hands gripping the topmost rail for support. Gran must've known what had happened to me, but I'd broken free, so there was no need for her to come. When I got home, she'd know what to do. She'd never let such blatant disrespect go unpunished.

By the time I turned the corner of Cotter's Field, the sun was gone and a cold wind crooned its nighttime song. It shook the wheat to either side of me, some of the taller blades snapping beneath the onslaught. I pulled Gran's shawl tight around my shoulders and walked on. Soon Thomson's dark, saggy outline loomed against the sky, his burlap head cocked as he stared at the ground.

Another burst of wind whipped the leaves and dirt at my feet into a frenzy. I put up my hand to shield my eyes from the debris. It was hard to see, but I could smell the caravan fire's smoke wafting on the air. I was close. I hiked up my skirt to run for it when I heard someone call my name from the field behind me. It sounded like Martyn, so I paused and listened. If it was Silas, not only would I run away, I'd scream loud enough to wake the dead in their graves.

"Bet? Bet, wait. Are you all right?"

I walked toward Martyn's voice. The crops swayed as a form pushed through, and then he was there, a head above the wheat, working his way to Thomson. It was dark, but there was enough light for me to see the cuts and bruises on his face and his torn shirt. Mr. Woodard had gotten him free of Silas, but not before Silas had taken his pound of flesh.

"I'm so, so sorry," I whispered. I walked to him, and thus straight into the fence, and I looked down stupidly at the slats. I was addled, my mind slow thanks to the punch, and it took me far too long to remember that I had to climb over if I wanted to get to him. I did so carefully, less for propriety's sake and more because I didn't want my nausea to return with the jostling.

Martyn neared and reached for my hand. I let him have it, and then he pulled me toward him into a hug so fierce, I thought he might crush my bones. I didn't mind, though. There was a comfort to him that was different from Gran's comfort. Hers was the strength of stone—cold and aloof but ever present and steady. His was a hot cup of tea on a cold night, warming you from the inside out.

"My father sent them scurrying and said if he saw them in the Crossing again, he'd have them put in lockup. It's safe there now, Bet. You won't have to stay away. Please don't. We'll make it work."

I didn't want to think about the future. I wanted to cleave to the illusion of safety in his arms in this moment. Like all illusions, though, it had to end sooner or later.

For us it shattered when a sack came swinging out of the field to bash Martyn in the back of the head.

CHAPTER ELEVEN

I should have known it was a trap when they dragged me to Martyn's stand. Of course he'd rush to defend me. Of course he'd follow me from Anwen's Crossing to see me home safe. Of course Mander and Tomašis would be waiting for him with a burlap sack and ill intent.

It was Mander who struck the blow. It hit the base of Martyn's skull with a sickening, wet thud. Martyn cried out and stumbled into me, slouching, and I tried to hold him up, but he was heavy and I was not. He fell to his knees before me as Tomašis stepped forward and punched him in the side of the head, in the soft spot above his ear. He raised the sack of stones, thrashing Martyn's side with it over and over, raining strikes against Martyn's ribs and back. Martyn slumped into my middle, as limp as a dishrag. Something was wrong. Something was *terribly* wrong, and though I couldn't claim Gran's healing knowledge, I knew enough to say they'd done great harm to Martyn Woodard.

I pulled him to me, pressing him into my chest to huddle over him so I could protect him from the blows. "Stop! STOP!" I screamed, but it did no good. Mander's heavy bag swung at my shoulder once, twice, thrice. There were sharp things inside— pebbles and pieces of glass and metal—and they bit into tender flesh with every blow. My back felt like it was being flayed open, and rivers of tears streamed down my cheeks. Warmth seeped along my sides like hot kettle water, and I knew without looking that what I felt was blood.

Breathing heavily, Mander dropped the bag at last. His crazed expression reminded me of a horse facing fire. Dark splotches sullied his cheeks, his throat, and his white shirt. It was everywhere, from his hands to his trousers and the toes of his boots, yet not a single drop spilled from his veins.

I crumpled, my body still shielding Martyn's as Tomašis ripped the scarf from my head and the thread from my neck. The hawk's eye fell to the ground, and I stretched for it, but Tomašis stomped his boot down, crushing two of my fingers and Gran's charm in one go.

"We're too close to camp. Move them," Mander said. The wheat near Thomson was chest high, but farther in, it grew taller—at least six or seven feet. Tomašis pulled me up by my hair, off Martyn and away from the fence, and I thrashed in his grip, digging my fingernails into his wrist. He responded with a series of hard, fast slaps to my cheeks.

"Silas won't want broken goods," Mander cautioned. Hearing his name, I screamed as loud as I could, hoping my voice would carry on the wind, but Tomašis clapped a hand over my mouth to quiet me, still dragging me away through the crops. Mander hauled Martyn's limp body behind us, Martyn's head lolling forward.

We stopped in the middle of the dark wheat field. Tomašis held me against him while Mander dropped Martyn's battered body in a heap. Martyn's chest was rising and falling, so I knew he was still alive, but the labored rattle spoke to severe injury, and I could see the ugly stains soaking the thin fabric of his shirt. Daylight was gone, and with it all colors. There was no red to see, only dark splotches. Yet I could smell the blood— like the inside of an abattoir.

I wailed against Tomašis's hand, so he wadded up a corner of Gran's shawl and stuffed it into my mouth. He fed it to me until I choked, and I bit down on his fingers, relishing in his startled cry. The rebellion cost me. He thrust me to the ground, his knee on my spine as he ground my face into the dirt. I kicked, furious and terrified as he wrenched my arms behind my back, tearing the scarf from my throat to wind around my wrists. He pulled it so tight I couldn't feel my fingers.

I closed my eyes and groaned into my gag. I wanted Gran. I wanted her to save us with magic and fury, but they'd taken away her hawk feather. She'd likely seen the trouble, but she hadn't seen where they'd dragged us, and with wheat and barley everywhere, it would be hard to discern one field from the next. I had to believe she'd come, though. I had to believe the nightmare would end. She'd told me I'd make it through the night of the blood moon.

But in how many pieces?

"What now? Just wait?" Mander tilted his face up, his hand wiping Martyn's blood off his chin.

Tomašis climbed off me, his booted foot pressed to my neck to keep me still. I shrieked my displeasure, but he pretended he didn't hear. "Silas said he'd meet us."

Mander glanced down the field, scanning for Silas's approach. "You see that scarecrow back there? It was looking at us. Unnatural."

"It's a scarecrow. Nothing to worry about."

"Didn't say I was worried. Said it's just not right-looking." Mander stopped talking long enough to pull something from his pocket. My eyes were so heavy with tears that I couldn't make out what it was, but then my nose filled with the familiar, too-sweet smell of tobacco. He stuffed his cheek full of leaf before sliding the tin container back into his pocket.

Minutes. Longer minutes. Tomašis was quiet, but Mander was restless. He paced, he sighed, he nudged Martyn with his toe until Martyn groaned. "Got an idea," he said eventually.

"Oh?"

"While we wait for Silas. Follow me."

"We're better off hiding here."

"Trust me." Mander hefted Martyn under the arms to drag him back. Tomašis hauled me along by my boots, my stomach raking over uneven terrain, small rocks and broken wheat stalks scraping my neck and chest. We stopped not long after, Tomašis dropping my legs to help Mander with something.

Run, I thought. *You should run.*

But I was gagged and bound and too dizzy to push myself up to my knees. My front ached. My back screamed from the beating. My face was bruised from Silas's punch and my scalp tingled from all the hair pulling. I was well and truly bested. I breathed into the dirt, wishing I could make myself invisible.

A *whoomph* sounded beside me, and I turned my head to see that Thomson had been thrown from his hooks. I'd never liked the scarecrow, but the hay spilling from his sides and the burlap head separated from his overalls felt irreverent somehow.

Mander lifted Martyn as best he could, grunting under the considerable weight.

"Help me. He's a fat one," he said to Tomašis.

There wasn't an ounce of fat on Martyn Woodard. He was big and solid and strong from his farm work, but I couldn't say so. Couldn't talk, couldn't move. All I could do was watch helplessly as they raised Martyn toward Thomson's menacing, rusty hooks. They propped him up in Thomson's stead, two hooks under his arms, two under his thighs. The ones in his legs dug into his pants and cut into his flesh, but the boys didn't care.

This was their revenge, the revenge Silas would have told them to exact.

Martyn sagged on his perch. He wasn't dead, but there was little doubt he teetered ever closer to that dark precipice. He let out a plaintive moan before his head flopped to the side, as still as Thomson had been in the same position minutes ago. I watched his chest and counted the breaths and the seconds in between. Each time, the count seemed to dwindle.

He was dying.

They've murdered someone for the crime of being kind to me.

I screamed into my gag, shaking my head back and forth as fresh terror took hold. While Mander and Tomašis were still preoccupied, I rolled my body into the wheat. I was unable to find my feet or walk, but I was so desperate to get to my grandmother, to get help for Martyn, that I'd inch along like a worm if I had to.

Then six black boots blocked my path. Silas, Cam, and Brishen stood side by side, all of them winded and flushed from running. I glanced up. Silas peered down at me, then up at Martyn on the hooks, and a delighted smile stretched across his lips. I could tell he relished this moment, stepping over me to examine Mander's grim work. I yelled into my gag again, and Cam kicked my flank in warning.

"He's not dead," Silas announced, his disappointment evident. "He lingers like a bad smell." Silas punched Martyn's bloodied middle with all his might, but Martyn made no sound of protest. He gave no indication of feeling even as his body jolted on the hooks. If some piece of Martyn was in there still, he had faded to a place where pain could no longer find him.

It was, perhaps, the only mercy he'd seen that night.

I closed my eyes and prayed, not to God or the spirits, but to Gran. She'd come. I knew she'd come, even if she had to check every field in Wales to find me. She moved slowly, but she moved surely, and if she rallied others to her side, they'd be there soon. The camp was only ten minutes away. The hawk's eye had, at the very least, told her I'd been taken on my way back from town. She could narrow down my whereabouts, especially if she'd caught sight of Thomson's post.

Gran. Help. Please.

As if in response, a biting wind shredded through the field, tearing through my clothes. Goose pimples appeared on my arms and legs. I tucked my knees into my middle, trying to ignore my body's aches as I willed Gran to avenge me in the field.

Faster, faster.

"What do you want to do with him?" Tomašis asked, shouting to be heard over the banshee-like gusts of wind.

"Leave him for the crows. They'll take his eyes and pull the meat from his bones. A proper pig funeral." Silas crouched before me, a blood-crusted hand sliding beneath my chin to tilt my face. His nose was still swollen from Martyn's punch. A small scrape marred his chin. He pulled the shawl from my mouth, pinching my cheeks so hard my lips puckered like a fish's. "What to do with you? Whoring yourself out to a farmer. Were you so eager for a man?"

He thrust me away and motioned to his friends. Brishen and Cam lifted me, their arms looping around mine as they pulled me to my feet. They turned me to face Martyn, and I jerked my gaze away. A hand plunged into my hair and made a fist, forcing my head back.

Silas prowled around me like a starving lion. "Do you see? *This* is what happens to those who cross me." He stopped behind me, his hand stroking over my hip to toy with the ends of my disheveled braid. I struggled, desperate to escape his touch, but Brishen's and Cam's grips were true.

The wind howled even louder, making the wheat crop shimmy in a frantic dance. That was when I heard it—*her*—a harsh, gravelly voice screeching its despair.

"I come, I come," the wind promised.

I saw Silas had heard it, too. His brows shot upward. "Who's there?" he demanded.

"I will find you. I am in the fields!"

The voice was distinct enough that the boys whipped their heads around in search of its owner. There was another blast, and another, but the display wasn't for me. It was for them—a warning. A curse. A promise.

Mander spun as if he expected to find my grandmother standing behind us in the field. Tomašis looked like he might be ill. The blood moon shone down upon his face, revealing a scared, bewildered boy who realized too late that the monster was coming and he had nowhere to hide.

"Have you heard that voice before, Tomašis?" I taunted him. "Did you dream the dark dreams with that sound in your ears?" I had no business being so brave, but words were all I had.

"Shut your lying mouth," Silas snarled behind me.

"She comes for you, too, Silas. She comes and you know what she brings."

Silas grunted, and the hand that had been toying with my hair yanked, and the end of the braid came undone, a stray curl pulled so hard that it tore from my head. The blood came hard and quick, dribbling over my scalp and trickling along my hairline and cheek. I throbbed. I ached. I suffered in almost every way, but I gritted my teeth against the pain, stronger knowing that Gran was there—if not in body, then in spirit.

"Silas, we should go," Tomašis insisted, nearly jumping from his skin as the wind writhed around him, the wheat an endless, hissing witness. "We don't want to cross the old woman. We should go."

"I will not be put off by parlor tricks or superstition," Silas spat. "I am the chieftain's son. I am not a fool!"

My eyes met Tomašis's, and despite the pain in my face, I

forced my brightest smile as tendrils of my loosed braid started to whirl around my face in the wind. "She's coming for you, Tomašis. For all of you."

Tomašis ran as if Hell itself had been unleashed. He shoved his way past his friends and jumped the fence railing, abandoning us all to the threat of the drabarni. Silas shouted his name and demanded he return, but Tomašis was either too far to hear or too afraid to heed.

"Do you think you're clever? Scaring him?" Silas stalked around to shove the shawl back into my mouth, grabbing my cheeks and shaking my head back and forth until my vision spiraled. "Look at me, Bethan. Look at me!"

I refused, casting my eyes to the blood moon above. It was full and golden and hung low in a blanket of never-ending stars. How could it be so beautiful when what happened beneath it was so ugly?

"You will mind, girl. You *will* mind. Hold her up."

Cam and Brishen stood me up tall, but their expressions were strained now, their eyes panicked. They were no longer so sure of Silas and his plan, but they'd come too far to leave at the last bell toll.

By contrast, Mander leaned against Martyn's pole like he had no cares, periodically spitting out wads of tobacco. His arms were folded across his lean chest, one of his legs crossed over the other. He grinned at me, the smile distorted around the lump in his cheek. I looked down, not wanting to meet his gaze.

Silas rustled with the fabric of my skirt, but it wasn't until his hands pulled my skirt up around my waist that I understood what he was about. I screamed into my gag, my legs buckling, but the boys held me firm, one of them thrusting a knee between my thighs.

The wind promised wrath. Its wail stood in for my own voice, its gusts for my rage. My hair billowed past my face. The wheat stalks around us snapped in half like they'd been stomped to the ground by a marauding titan.

It was not supposed to happen—it could not happen— except it would, and it did. Beneath the blood moon, Silas Roberts stood in the shadow of a giant. The crow had fallen in the guise of a felled scarecrow, and despite my struggling, despite my screams and protests, a pale serpent slithered into warm, deep earth.

CHAPTER TWELVE

My heart was cold like stone.

I stood motionless as Silas pulled himself from me, my skirt falling down to my ankles. The wind blew so hard I should have floated away like a feather, but I did not stir. I kept my eyes fixed upon Martyn's broken body, but I did not see. I did not weep for what was lost because I did not feel.

Silas walked around from behind me, adjusting his trousers. His face was blotched from exertion, beads of sweat dotting his brow. I didn't scream when he removed my gag. I didn't flinch when he trailed his fingers over my cheek and down over the scratches on my chest to press his palm against my gut. His eyes narrowed thoughtfully. "We'd have strong children, I think."

The wind blasted again, so hard the four boys staggered. Brishen and Cam had to let me go to keep their balance, and both crouched low against the gale. Silas rocked back on his heels and Mander clung to Martyn's pole to anchor himself. Somehow, perhaps by Gran's magic or my own resolve, I held strong, my spine straight as if it, too, had gone to stone. I could hear Gran everywhere, whirling and snarling around me, her voice filling the vast darkness.

Before, her approach comforted me. Now I couldn't even muster relief. I was dead inside.

"We should go before there's trouble," Cam said, looking unsettled for the first time that night. As his eyes scoured the wheat field, his palms swept down the front of his trousers to wipe away sweat that shouldn't have been there on a chilly autumn night.

Silas waved the boys to the fence. "Go. I'll follow."

After they'd gone, Silas stepped close to me and placed his hands on my shoulders, his thumbs brushing along the sides of my neck. I didn't look at him, so he cupped my chin and tilted my face up to catch my eye.

"There are two choices, Bethan. You walk to the caravan by my side, or I leave you with the diddicoy and you wait for him to die. Don't be stupid."

I didn't answer, but held my ground. Frustrated, he pinched my cheek, digging his nails in, and when that didn't spur a reaction, he shoved me to the ground. I landed hard on my hip. There was pain, but I didn't cry out. I recognized the trauma, I knew my body suffered, but I didn't feel connected to it; it was foreign. By defiling me, he'd removed me from my own hurt.

It was not me that had been beaten and compromised. It was *she,* and in that moment, *she* was not me. I just lived in her skin.

Silas loomed over me still. "Dumb sow. Rot with the farmer

if that's what you want. You deserve each other." He spat, and the gob landed on my cheek and dribbled down my neck. Then he stomped away from me and pressed through the wheat, vaulting the fence to join Brishen, Mander, and Cam.

I listened for a long time, hearing the rustle of their bodies through the wheat, the pounding of their boots when they hit the dirt road, and finally, silence.

I rolled onto my back to peer at Martyn on his hooks. He was too still, though every few seconds I thought I saw his shirt flutter. It wasn't the wind's doing—that had disappeared with the boys—so maybe there was something left of him after all.

I wanted to hope, but stone didn't know how to hope.

A distinct drag-shuffle gait drew my attention from the pole. Gran approached from the belly of the wheat. She carried no lantern or torch, but I could tell she was close when her voice rang out like a bell. "This way. This way!"

"Coming, Drina. I cannot see."

The chieftain.

"Move faster. She's near. Bethan!"

I wanted to cry out, to tell her to come to the scarecrow's perch, but the words tangled around my tongue. I breathed deep and closed my eyes, willing my body to respond to my commands. It was not mine in those moments, but hers—the other's—and *she* was intent on finding the deep, quiet place where there was no hurt.

The crop rustled near my feet. I rolled my head to it, expecting to see Gran hunched over her walking stick, but the chieftain found me first, his horrified gaze swinging from Martyn on the pole to me on the ground, my hands tied behind my back.

"He couldn't. He didn't—" He covered his mouth, his

words cooperating no more than mine had. What he didn't see, and what I plainly saw from where I lay upon that cold ground, was the inevitability of it all. He'd made excuse upon excuse for his boy. He'd dismissed Silas's misdeeds as rambunctious. A tousle of the hair instead of a sharp word. The chieftain hadn't held me down while his son violated me, but he was complicit in my attack in his fashion.

Clearing his throat, he called out into the field, "This way! I've found her."

I heard more wheat snapping as Gran trundled our way. She appeared beside the chieftain, standing at his elbow. Her back was hunched over, and her hair, free of its bun, slithered over her shoulders.

Gran peered down at me where I lay on the knitted shawl she'd given me. Her gaze traveled from one end of me to the other, assessing the hurt. Her head swung up to the young man on the hooks. She lifted her cane and poked Martyn, but got no response.

"Help me down," she growled at the chieftain.

He offered Gran his arm so she could lower herself to my side. Her joints popped as she settled beside me. Seeing Silas's spit, she lifted her hand to my face but paused short of contact, like she was afraid I'd burst apart with the touch, a dandelion given over to seed.

"May I? I do not want to . . . After what happened, I do not . . ." She drew in a ragged breath. We were so close that I could see the redness around her nostrils and the dew at the corners of her eyes. Had Gran cried for me? In all our years together, I'd never seen her shed a tear, and yet it was all over her face. I could hear it in the wetness of her breaths.

I rejected the touch and rolled over to expose my wrists instead, showing her the binding so she could loosen it. The scarf pulled away and blood rushed to my fingers, which throbbed as if I'd dunked them in boiling water. I climbed to my knees, waiting for the world to stop its relentless spiral, before cleansing my own cheek.

Gran's hand glided over my hair, a gentle petting that was her affectionate gesture of choice during a rare soft moment, but it reminded me too much of Silas fondling it before he tugged a hunk out. I wanted her to stop. I *needed* her to stop. I swatted her away with a hiss.

"Of course. I am sorry." She motioned for the chieftain to help her stand. He lifted her, cradling her against his chest like a baby before righting her, his hands supporting her elbows until she steadied.

He reached his hand out to me as well, but I didn't take it. I said nothing, shoving myself to my feet and bracing against the vertigo. I extended my arms to either side of my body for balance, until the whirling slowed and eventually stopped. I wadded my skirt to wipe the seed from my legs, not caring that the chieftain could see my bare skin. I had no idea if he turned his face away so I wouldn't dishonor him, or so he wouldn't dishonor me.

Unclean. I was unclean. How could one ever be clean again after such a thing?

"It was not fruitful," Gran said, watching me scrub. "I would have seen it. There is no child."

I had to tell Gran what happened, but the words eluded me. I gestured at the pole, and she hobbled over to Martyn, reaching her hand up into his trouser leg to grab his ankle.

She tilted her head back, closing her eyes. "There is no time, Bethan. He is too close to gone."

I twitched. It wasn't much, but it was enough to tell me I could still feel something through the dullness. I tried talking again, and failed, breathing in through my nose and out through my mouth. It took a whole precious minute of Martyn's dwindling time for me to manage a gurgled, "Save him."

"I know no medicine that can make the insides stop bleeding. The best we can do is—"

"SAVE HIM!" My voice echoed through the fields, shattering the stillness of the clear, cold night. Gran peered at me, her lips pinched with displeasure, but she did not chide me for my rudeness, instead tilting her head back to regard Martyn's pulpy face.

"There is a way, but you have to understand what you commit yourself to. Magic has a cost. A high cost. I told you this before. You will have to do things you never—"

"I'll give anything," I said.

"'Anything,' she says. No, this is not your price to pay. You will reap what is sown, but our hands will be ever stained red." Gran jabbed a finger into the chieftain's chest, startling him. "That boy of yours is a poison, and poison must be purged. Bethan wants to save this young man—it will be your son who pays the price to fuel her magic."

The chieftain looked ill. He staggered away from us, his hands raised in supplication, his head shaking back and forth, making his woolen cap tumble to the ground. "No. He's a boy. Just a boy. He can learn. He can—" His voice broke on a scream. Gran had lifted her hand in his direction and was swiveling her fingers like she twisted a door handle, though she grasped only air. The veins bulged in the chieftain's throat and his eyes went bloodshot.

"Drina, no. I beg you," he pleaded.

His face ripped open along the scar traversing his cheek, the age-old hurt flayed wide as if she'd dug her fingers into his flesh and peeled back the skin. Blood welled in the wound, and he slapped his palm over it to stifle the flow. Gran advanced on him, pointing a taloned finger perilously close to his eye.

"Do not forget who you pledged yourself to, Wen Roberts. Who *owns* you. I brought you here to behold your son's evil deeds. Is your own ruin so easily forgotten? Do you think I would allow history to repeat? I told you to warn him off. I told you to correct him. *You failed.* As his chieftain and his father, you failed, and my Bethan and her diddicoy suffered for it."

Days ago, when I'd eavesdropped on their private conversation, it'd been clear that my grandmother and the chieftain shared a past. What awfulness had occurred that Gran could claim to "own" the chieftain and he'd not refute it?

"I know, Drina. I know." The chieftain's head hung low, his shoulders slumped. "I cannot help but love my son."

"That is your burden, not ours. Fate punishes us for our transgressions eventually. Perhaps your hens are home to roost at last." Gran dropped her hand from his face and turned to Martyn, her fingers manacling his ankle. She scowled. "Death takes us feet first, and he is slipping. Can you climb to him, Bethan? To his mouth? I know you are in pain."

"I'm fine." I wasn't, but I approached the pole regardless, putting my hands on the big rusty nails embedded where Thomson's feet used to be. I pressed my weight down to see if they'd shake loose, but they were sturdy in the wood. "What do you want me to do?"

"Take his last breath. Suck it down and hold it inside of you. Death will not stake its claim while you have it."

She'd said she didn't allow cats near her because they'd steal an old woman's last breath, and yet it seemed I was to be the cat to Martyn. I had so many questions, but there was no time for any of them. I had to trust and I had to climb.

As I scaled the pole, I winced in pain, the aches and injuries no longer out of mind. But it did not stop me, and soon I was nose to nose with Martyn. I looked at the cuts and bruises on his chin and cheeks, at the swelling in his eye and the knot forming on his temple, and I felt another twinge. The wall that separated me from She Who Inhabited My Skin was shifting. But I didn't want to feel. Feeling *hurt*.

I shut my eyes, swallowing my emotion. Stone was safe.

I looped my arm behind Martyn's body, my gorge rising when I made contact. Closeness with anyone—even Martyn—was nauseating. And yet I had to endure for his sake. I tipped his chin up and forced his head back. We looked like lovers, but there was nothing romantic about our first kiss. I cupped his bloody cheek. I smeared my lips to his. With a hard jerk on his jaw, I opened his mouth and breathed him in, his cold death settling into the pit of my belly.

CHAPTER THIRTEEN

Breaths, as a rule, are warm, airy things, but Martyn's death rattle was frigid and thick, like icy porridge slithering down my throat. It tasted like raw meat and pennies.

"You can feel it?" Gran asked, her hand sliding from Martyn's leg. "It is a distinct sensation. Like—"

"I'm frozen on the inside."

In more ways than one. I cannot feel.

"Yes, precisely. Now climb down. We need to store the breath before its magic fades."

Question after question popped into my mind as I eased my way down. *What will happen if the magic doesn't work? Did we deny Martyn a true death? Will he linger between the living world and the spirit world, never finding peace without that last breath?* I trusted Gran, but it was easy to fall prey to worry. Martyn being lost forever could very well shatter whatever fragile strength I still claimed.

The chieftain unhitched Martyn from his perch, his hand pressed to Martyn's stomach to hold him steady while he worked the hooks from his legs. Free, Martyn slumped forward, his big body too heavy for the chieftain to catch. He landed face first in a heap on the ground, appearing dull and boneless, more like a pile of meat than human. The chieftain murmured an apology—to Martyn, to me, to Gran, perhaps to all—before looping his arm under Martyn's shoulders and dragging him.

The walk to the caravan took a while. Gran's gait was labored thanks to her overtaxed joints, and the chieftain struggled to haul Martyn. Halfway there, Gran reached for me, her fingers gently brushing the back of my wrist. I pulled away, concentrating on the tingling sensation in my toes instead of my trauma.

"I could not see you. I saw fields of wheat before they took your charm, but that is all. It happened so fast, there was no time for magic to save you beyond the wind. I hope you can forgive my poor preparation."

"It's not your fault." I'd never blamed her and I never would. She'd foretold a terrible thing and she'd told me why it was better I suffer it than not. She'd made me a charm; she'd sent the wind to dissuade the boys. She'd come to collect me herself. She'd done all she could.

Gran was not to blame that I'd endured Hell.

Silas was to blame. He and his horrible friends.

After a few more steps, I glanced at Martyn, and my thoughts skipped to the Woodards. Mr. Woodard would be unrelenting in the search for his missing son, especially after the fights with Silas. If he reported it to the constable, there would be trouble. People might do to us what Silas had done to one of them.

"Mr. Woodard saw Silas provoking Martyn," I said. "He'll make assumptions if Martyn doesn't come home."

The chieftain grimaced. "I've considered this. It would not be the first time one of our girls ran off. If the drabarni allows it, I will visit the Woodard patriarch and tell him I believe you two escaped together after the fight. You'll have to avoid town, Bethan, but that should not be difficult. It will give you a few days to do what you must."

"And what about the field? It's a mess."

He thought for a moment. "I'll send the men to wash it away before dawn. There will be no trace. The crops are damaged— the scarecrow, too—but a gadjo will not assume magic, just bad weather."

"You have excused Silas's wickedness in the past," Gran observed. The chieftain did not deny it.

On we walked. When we were close enough to camp that I could smell the spice of dinner on the air, Gran stumbled into my side. I flinched. Any touch was still too raw to bear, but I bit past my instinct to jerk away and offered her an arm.

"I ought to be holding you up after what happened," she said, despair and regret in her voice. *That is true,* I thought.

From the outskirts of camp, I could hear the lively music from the fire; my people were blissfully unaware of the tragedy that had played out a field's length away. My thoughts strayed: Would Silas be among them? Would the other boys? Were they celebrating what they had done? Or did they hide like rats in the bowels of a ship?

I do not wish to know.

The chieftain struggled with Martyn's weight, but he followed Gran and me all the way back to our vardo. Gran lit the candles on the table and by her bed before collapsing into her chair. The chieftain stood in the doorway with Martyn in his arms, looking uncertain. All I wanted was for him to leave and the night to end.

I pulled my mattress from the corner and laid it out. "Put him there," I said. I'd sleep on the bare floor—the soreness of hard wood on my back didn't matter. The chieftain eased Martyn onto my bed, taking a moment to adjust his limbs so he looked less like he was dead and more like he was sleeping.

It was a lackluster illusion. I wanted my mental picture of Martyn Woodard to be a sunny, smiling flirt smoking a cigarillo, not the pulpy, battered mess on my bed. I covered Martyn's body and face in a patchwork afghan, tucking it around him until it looked like a death shroud.

"I should go. I need to get the men to the field, and talk to Silas. To see if he'll apologize."

As if that could ever—would ever—be enough. I gave the chieftain a sharp look. It must have unnerved him, because he left without another word. I was glad for it.

I wanted nothing more than to be done with this day, but there was much still to do. I grabbed the basin to scrub Silas's taint from my body. I'd bathe in the river as soon as I could, but a cursory wash would have to do until the morning. I took the bowl, lye, and a rag outside, squatting in the grass and rubbing myself raw. Silas had bled me with his rough attentions, and when one basin of water turned pink, I emptied it out on the ground and poured another from the pitcher. No matter how much soap I used or how many cloths I took to my legs, I still felt dirty. By the time I was through, there was a fresh ache from my savage scrubbing.

Frigid, I quickly changed into unsullied wools. They did little to warm me. Martyn's breath was a lump of ice in my middle that made it impossible to get warm. Gran's blue shawl had been left in the field, so I grabbed another from the peg on the wall and wrapped it around my shoulders.

I wadded up my clothes and thrust them into a burlap sack. I could see bits of Thomson's hay on the blouse, and Silas's taint staining the inside of the skirt, and I swore then that those garments would never touch my skin again.

I thought Gran would be asleep upon my return, but she was awake and still propped in the chair. She motioned me close and attended my wounds, dabbing at my scalp with a cloth and rubbing salve onto the cuts on my shoulder. When she finished, I sank into the chair across from her. She said nothing, and I watched as her fingers coursed over the tabletop in meditative circles. She did that sometimes when she was looking for unknown truths with her sight—it helped lull her to the still place where visions were born. In that moment, I hated it, and I hated that she could do it. I didn't want to shoulder the burden of her psychic vagaries.

"Stop it," I said. "Please, stop."

"If you insist." She turned her face to the window to peer at the blood moon hanging low in the sky. It painted her face with shadows, the hollows beneath her eyes and cheeks so pronounced, she looked skeletal.

"We are losing time," she said, turning back to me. "I know you are tired, and soon you will rest. For now, though, we must store the diddicoy's death rattle. Are you ready?"

"Yes," I said, my voice flat.

She reached for me across the table, her warm fingers tangling with my frigid ones. " '*Yes*' what?"

I jerked away and huddled inside my shawl, my teeth chattering with cold. "Yes, Gran. I'm ready."

"We need the mirror," she said.

I took it from the wall and slid it before her, but she pushed it my way with a shake of her head. "The breath is inside of you, Bethan, not me. You must deliver it. Blow on the glass. Force it out and do not stop until all the cold is gone."

I braced my hands on the table and leaned down, my breath clouding the surface. I inhaled and then blew air out in a steady stream, but the sludge remained inert.

"From your gut. Go deep," Gran said. I clenched my abdominal muscles and strained, my eyes bulging, my cheeks ballooning. Martyn's breath lurched from my stomach, lodging in my chest and rising with every heave until it polluted the back of my throat. It was sticky in texture, a rancid wad, and I ejected it onto the mirror in much the same way I'd seen the boys eject their sputum in the mornings. A breath shouldn't look like riverbank mud, yet that's what I spewed—runny sludge.

I glanced Gran's way, awaiting instruction, but she waved at the mirror and I turned back just as the muck absorbed into the surface, the glass whirling with strange, dark fog. A shadowy image of Martyn Woodard's face took shape within, but unlike the corpse in my bed, mirror Martyn was whole. There was no blood. There were no bruises, cuts, or broken bones.

I wanted to feel hopeful that we could save him, but feelings remained beyond my grasp. I eyed the mirror like I'd eye a stick on the ground—with detachment.

Gran picked up the mirror and nodded, tapping on the image of Martyn's mouth. "It is good. It is a strong picture. Three days."

"'Three days' what?"

"That is how long his breath will last. After that, it will disappear and he is gone."

I waited for further instruction.

"We have things to discuss. You have questions. Explanations and answers are forthcoming. But that can wait until morning. For now, you must rest and restore your strength."

I nodded, standing to help her into her bed.

"You don't have to sleep on the floor," Gran said. "Take my bed. You are hurt."

"No. My body is young, even if it is injured."

And I cannot feel. A hard floor is nothing to me.

Gran fussed about it, but I helped settle her into her bed before creating a nest next to the table with the extra blankets.

"At least take my fur," Gran said, pulling it from her legs.

"No. You need it."

She frowned. "Are you certain?"

I extinguished the lantern to end the conversation. Gran drifted off shortly thereafter, but I stayed awake long after, staring at the darkness, my knees gathered to my chest. The floor was hard and cold no matter how many blankets I piled beneath me, and my mind kept replaying what had happened in the field. I would thrust the thoughts away and try to focus on the work ahead of me instead, but my thoughts always returned to the hands on my hips.

The hands on my hips.

The. Hands. On. My. Hips.

CHAPTER FOURTEEN

My sleep was restless and full of nightmares—the tangled yarns hanging from the ceiling did nothing to save me that night. I woke before Gran and the sun, my eyes fixed on the wall until the first slivers of daylight penetrated the slats of the vardo. I rose and hurried to the river, dreading the cold water but needing it, too.

I waded out to my waist, the current washing away some soil, but not all my filth went bone deep. I worried someone would discover me exposed, so I finished quickly, unable to ignore the bruises riddling my body. My wrists were raw and red from the bindings. Yellow and purple marks marred my upper arms. My fingers and toes were black-and-blue from where Tomašis had stomped on them, and my shoulder ached every time I moved.

My face was sore, too, from Silas's punch, and when I got

back to the vardo, I went to where the mirror normally hung, but the space was empty. We'd moved it into the bureau drawer, and I pulled it from its silk nest to peer at it. I was met not with my own reflection but Martyn's sleeping face. Somehow, in the delirium of insufficient sleep, I'd forgotten about that.

I studied it awhile, frowning when I realized it had faded since the last time I looked at it—the edges were shadowy and the image shimmered, as if I were looking at a pond stirred by the wind instead of a solid glass surface.

I must've lost time while gazing at the mirror, because Gran's voice startled me. "Good morning. How are you feeling?"

"I'm fine." I wasn't fine, though. I was anything but. I was a hollow shell, but I would go through the motions of being Bethan so I wouldn't have to face the myriad of awful feelings swirling beneath the surface.

"We must go to the fire to tell our people what wickedness has occurred," she said.

I inhaled sharply. I hadn't thought about having to face the clan. Or worse, my attackers—what would I do seeing them? How would I feel? Would I crumble? "I won't speak of it. It's forbidden," I whispered. Any woman would have struggled after an attack such as mine, but for Roma, it was more complex. Purity was valued. Private matters were kept private. Women did not speak of carnality for fear of being labeled mochadi. "I am a woman with no husband. They may shame me—think me impure."

"The rules are complicated when it comes to personal matters, but I promise you, the shame belongs to Silas and his boys. Not you. Never you. You are *righteous*. We could cast the five of them out for their crimes. We could disavow them from our people forever if you prefer, but someone needs to bleed to save your young man. If you wish to do the magic, we must lay down our terms."

"Someone needs to bleed to save your young man."

Five someones, perhaps?

Is there any choice?

I had no reply. I just wanted it to be over with.

Gran lifted a hand to stroke my hair, but she must have remembered my recoil in the field, because she placed it back on my arm. The gesture made me realize that my hair had to be covered. Silas had stripped my girlhood away from me, and I was a woman. No matter the reason, I couldn't escape the laws of propriety.

I pulled out my brush, streaking it through my hair hard enough that my scalp tingled before gathering the rest into a bun at my nape. I tried not to think much about it, the task unpleasant but unavoidable, but when I fashioned the scarf around my head, tying it for the first time, Gran let out a pained groan.

"Oh, Bethan. I am sorry. I am so sorry." The granite shell protecting my heart cracked. With one selfish act, Silas had forever changed my identity—my life would *never* be the same. Among my people, I'd be pitied. Some might shun me for wickedness beyond my control. Touch was hard to take from Gran, so what would it be like from people less close to me? Especially men? I couldn't stand the thought of it. I was to be drabarni with an aversion to doctoring half my people?

It was a deep wound, an *emotional* wound, and I stared straight ahead, tears stinging my eyes. My knees wobbled and nausea roiled in my stomach despite a lack of food. I had to sit to keep from collapsing to the floor. Gran left her bed to stand behind me, her hands going to my shoulders and squeezing. I flinched at the contact, but reminding myself it was Gran and she meant me no harm, I calmed.

Life is unfair.

"I am loath to say it, but it is good for the caravan to see the fresh bruises, so they are reminded of why the boys are ours." She fussed with the wayward strands of hair at the corners of my vision, tucking them behind my ears. I pushed away from her, heading outside without another word.

We walked to the clearing together. Gran shuffled by my side, a quiet, steady presence, who held me up as much as I held her. As my panic rose, my heart fluttered and my tongue felt dry. I reached for my newfound emptiness, for *she* who looked through my eyes but did not see. For the one who walked among lively songs and laughter but did not hear. *She* was my curse and my sanctuary. I would let her wear my face and yet remain far away, more ghost than girl.

Gran pressed on, surer on her feet than she'd been the night before on the road. I stayed with her up until the lip of the great fire's clearing, my legs stopping abruptly. My fingers tightened around Gran's. She offered a small squeeze in return, leaning in close to my ear.

"It is much to ask, I know," she whispered, "but I need you to be strong for me again."

We approached the great fire, where most of our people were having their breakfast. The chattering voices tapered to quiet, and I felt my face flush. Word had already traveled, though that wasn't surprising. News in a caravan changed hands as quickly as money. All eyes fixed on us as Gran approached the northern benches, and then—with my help—stepped onto one so she stood taller than all the others. I stayed before her on the ground so she could use my shoulder for support if needed.

"Last night, a great wrong was done to me and mine." Her voice had thrice its normal volume, sounding as big and furious as it'd been when it tangled with the wind. "A great wrong was done to a diddicoy, inviting the wrath of outsiders."

She paused to let her words penetrate, her brown eye scanning the sea of faces. Each one looked my way, some hands clasped over hearts, others clinging to their loved ones. I looked to see if I could find any of the boys in the throng, but they were nowhere. Their relatives were, though, and would carry Gran's words.

"I am your drabarni, and yet that did not stop five"—she paused to splay her fingers, wiggling each of them so all bore witness—"five from harming my charge. Do you forget who I am? Do you forget what I can do?"

Gran's arms stretched up to the sky. The flames of the fire rose, surging to the heavens with a furious roar. I stood steady, unflinching, but those on the other side skittered back, afraid. Wind whipped her hair, and her clothes snapped around her slight body. She'd always been thin and bony, but in that moment, I would have sworn she was giant.

Gran tilted her head back, her eyes closing as she screamed, "RETRIBUTION COMES THIS DAWN. Present, confess, know my benevolence. Deny your sin, the cost is threefold. No one harms my charge. *No one.*" She cast a finger over the sea of our people. "You all bear witness, you hear my demands. Now go. Send me the five today or send them to a dark fate. This is my decree. GO!"

There was a frenzy of movement, families finding each

other in the crowd, whispering. Some people looked Gran's way. Others were too afraid. They dispersed back to their tents and vardos. Gran peered at me from the bench. She reached down, brushing her knuckles over my cheek.

"I hope you are ready. This is an unpleasant journey."

I hoped I was, too, but there was no way to know until she told me what bringing Martyn back would entail.

It was a silent procession home. We climbed the steps, and Gran paused to look behind her, in case anyone was coming to confess. I worried in some ways that they would. If they begged for forgiveness, must I grant leniency?

"I will tell you all you need to know soon," Gran said, stealing my thoughts. "They will pay for their deeds, *that I vow.*"

CHAPTER FIFTEEN

Gran went to her bureau drawer and pulled out a thick piece of parchment and a quill with a notched tip. Sitting at the table, she began to write. I watched her hand scrawl down the page, the ends of her shawl brushing over the letters and smudging the ink at the edges.

She brought the paper to me, her finger hovering over the words as she read them aloud. "Fingers for touch, an eye for sight, a nose to smell the air. Teeth for taste, an ear for sound. Some blood, some skin, some hair."

I accepted the paper from her when she offered it. "That sounds like a spell."

"It is an ingredients list. Far easier to remember when it rhymes." She arched a sparse gray brow at me. "The words of a spell are only important if they help you focus your will. The

Irish witches say nothing when they bless or curse. It is all hand motions. Magic is in the heart, not on the tongue."

"I understand, Gran." The blocks, circles, and swirls before me were all so very meaningless. What I remembered was Gran's last lesson, when she'd explained that magic had a cost proportionate to the end result. The ingredients list was a list of gruesome tithes.

"I'll have to harvest these?" I asked. "To bring him back?"

She nodded. "One part for each sense, to wake them from sleep. The hair, skin, and blood will come from the yellow-haired man himself. Not a lot—just enough to tie him to his own ritual."

"And if taking my due kills the boys?"

She eyed me slyly. "Would you care?"

I pondered the question. Before, I would have said that I couldn't kill, no matter the circumstance. It was a sin. It would tarnish my soul beyond reach. I would be banished for such a wicked deed. But the stranger that lived in me now said the ends justified the means. Death was not the goal, but if it happened in the course of restoring Martyn's stolen life, so be it.

I was no longer afraid. Fear existed beyond the stranger's scope.

"I won't try for it, but if it comes, I'll persevere." I laid out the list on the table, my fingers smoothing the curled corners.

If Gran was shocked by my acceptance, she didn't indicate as much; instead, she reclaimed her list and notated in the margins. She'd run out of space and was about to flip the paper to the other side to continue writing, when a knock sounded on the door.

My spine straightened, an animalistic urge to flee surging

inside of me. Gran sensed my distress, sensed that I'd become prey before predator, and offered me her hand. I clung to it, my desire to not be touched feuding with my desire to anchor myself to her.

Gran swept her thumb across my knuckles. "Their fates are yours. You can harvest them for what you need and banish them as *mochadi*. You can harvest them and allow them to stay. You can bind them to you to serve. You can kill them all if it pleases you. Whatever you choose, I support you."

I nodded but said nothing, the options swirling in my head. Another knock sounded, and the voices outside hushed. Gran patted my hand and shuffled to the door, swinging it open to see who dared approach in the wake of the fireside proclamation.

Standing on the steps, tearstained and wrapped in a heavy brown sweater she'd belted at the waist over a long skirt, was Florica Buckland. "He's an idiot," she said in greeting, her voice breaking. "He's an idiot who listened to stupid boys and it made him a stupid boy, but he's big enough to admit he's wrong. Have mercy on him. On me. He's my only son."

Tomašis. I expected to want to lash out at him, to lust for blood, but all I could do was marvel at how unchanged he was. He was afraid, yes, but he was unfettered. He carried few weights, despite proving his cowardice twice—first when Gran plucked his hairs at the fire and again when she sent her winds to the field.

"Come. You are not to speak unless spoken to. Either of you." Gran pulled her chair around to my side of the table so there'd be space for all inside the cramped quarters. I slid the enchanted mirror from the table and into my lap. I wanted Florica and Tomašis to see only the corpse lying on my bed beneath its death shroud. Martyn's former liveliness in the mirror was not a comfort either were owed.

I couldn't bring myself to look at Tomašis. He hadn't delivered the blows that felled Martyn, but he'd held me strong while another did. He'd allowed the murder to happen—he'd *relished* it happening—and when his courage abandoned him, he'd run back to camp, not once opening his mouth. Had he, the men may have come. Had he, I may not have been assaulted.

He'd more than earned my ire.

Florica knew it, too. She glanced between us, her tall son hiding behind her like she'd wall him off from the wicked witches ready to pass judgment on his head.

"I'm s-sorry," Tomašis stammered. "So sorry. I shouldn't have . . . I should have . . ."

Tomašis's pained screech drew my gaze. He was doubled over, panting, his hands holding his stomach like his insides had burst. His fingers bunched up the white fabric of his shirt.

"Do. Not. Speak. Unless. Spoken. To," Gran snarled. She whipped her head around to glower at Florica, her eyes narrowed to slits, her lips pursed into a thin line. Florica retreated, stepping away until her backside struck the wall. "You have raised a stupid boy, Florica."

"Yes, very stupid. Like his father."

"I am not so sure it comes from the father."

"Perhaps not, drabarni." Florica sighed and dropped her head until her chin touched her chest. "I am sorry for his crimes."

"Do not be sorry for things you have not done. It is his job to be sorry." Gran rose from her seat and circled the table to stand beside Tomašis, who was sobbing. She grabbed a fistful of his hair in her hand like she had at the great fire and jerked. Tomašis howled as the strands came free. He dropped to the floor with a mewl, wrapping his arms around his mother's legs, his face pressed into her hip. She didn't offer him comfort, but she did let us see her desperation to save his life. Tears dribbled down her cheeks and dripped onto her thick-cabled sweater.

Florica started to speak, but remembered she wasn't allowed and clamped her mouth shut. Gran twisted Tomašis's hairs and nodded at her. "Speak."

"Drabarni. He'd do anything to make amends. He wasn't there when Silas dishonored her, and I know he should have told someone about what happened in the field, but he was afraid. He says the chieftain's son is not always kind to his friends."

"He held me," I said quietly, my hands gripping the sides of the mirror. "Tomašis held me as Mander beat a man to death and struck me with a bag of rocks. Silas wasn't even there yet. It was his choice."

Gran shoved Tomašis's hairs under his nose and he wailed again. "What I find most offensive about you, worm, is that you've already experienced my power. You dream the dark dreams still, and yet you risked it anyway. Of the five, you were aware, and yet . . ."

She turned her attention my way. "What do you want to do with him? Ask it and it is yours." Looking at Tomašis's sniveling, huddled form, part of me wanted to take my due and kill or banish him, but Florica's presence lent me pause. She'd committed no crime, and yet if I doomed Tomašis to bloody sacrifice, she'd forever mourn.

"Tomašis must be punished," I said carefully. "But he did come, and that holds weight. I don't think Florica should lose a son when she's done nothing wrong."

Gran snorted. "Hardly nothing. She thrust a loathsome monster from her loins. However, I may have an idea that will satisfy your honor and yet spare Florica her tears." Gran shuffled to the door and thrust it open, letting a gust of cold wind rip through. She pointed down the rickety steps. "Take your idiot outside, Florica. I make no promises, but perhaps he will yet be spared."

Florica kicked Tomašis off her leg and walked outside, head high, her son slinking after her like a whipped dog. People whispered outside, at least a dozen strong, my clansmen gathered to witness Tomašis's sentencing. I glared out at the faces.

Gran closed and latched the door before hobbling back to her chair. "Ignore them. Their fear binds them from acting out against us. That is the way it should be—the way it should have been for the boys, too, the fools."

Gran captured one of my hands and began to stroke my fingers. She tilted her head to the side, and a bevy of difficult emotions flitted across her face before settling on resignation. "You have gleaned by now that the chieftain is bound to my service, yes?"

When I nodded, a wan, joyless smile stretched across her lips. "I have not explained before because it is painful for me to discuss, but it is time." She turned in her seat so she could pull out a drawer, and rifling through the contents and digging deep, far beneath the folded cloths and miscellanea, she found a framed portrait. She wiped a thick layer of dust from the glass and thrust it at me. It was no bigger than a dinner plate, and the face painted on it was crude at best, but I could make out a man with strong features and dark hair. His eyes were green, his nose was long, and a thick, dark mustache hid his upper lip.

"Your father. His name was Joseph and he was a cobbler by trade, as his father was before him. He was from Pontypridd. I told you how he fell in love with your mother and how poorly our people treated him. What you do not know is that it was the chieftain himself who caused Joseph the most pain. Wen was young and stupid and he tormented that poor man despite your mother's pleas."

The chieftain was such a gentle man that I had a hard time believing it, but Gran—seeing my doubt—waved me off. "Good men sometimes do bad things. It is the degree of bad that dictates if his goodness remains intact. In Wen's case, he was redeemed on the eventual." She took a deep breath, peering at the portrait for a long moment and licking her lips. "Your mother was young—a new drabarni. She threatened Joseph's tormentors, but to no avail. She was carrying you at the time and could not tax her body with great magic. She could not lash out at those who hurt her husband.

"Then, one day, it went too far. Joseph was walking back from town with supplies for your mother when he encountered Wen and his friends on the road. There was another beating and Joseph had to run. Wen chased him all the way to the river and Joseph slipped into the water. He could not swim and was dragged downstream."

Gran squeezed my hand, the strain on her face making her look older than time itself. "Wen was wise enough to run to your mother for help. Heavy with child, she searched for Joseph on the banks, finding him clinging to a rock at the river's bend some ways away. He was full of water and fading. Your mother, she . . . she did what she had to do."

"What was that?" I asked, quietly, gently. Curiously. Gran's crumb of information was more than she'd said in years about my mother.

"I was getting there," she snapped, then flinched, realizing how she sounded and to whom. "I am sorry. This is difficult for me and I should not have barked. But, what was I—oh, yes. Your mother made a great sacrifice that day to save the man she loved. She had to be careful what she conjured with you in her belly, but she succeeded in the end. Joseph would live after a long period of rest—you were born before he woke, three weeks after his drowning. Imagine everyone's surprise when you bore her magic upon your skin. She had not harmed you with her spellcraft, but it had marked you dark on one side and light on the other."

Gran's fingertips traced along my wrist, over the wine-colored freckles. "You were a robust baby. You brought great joy, but there was sadness, too. Joseph would wake soon, and that was good, but your mother's sacrifice had changed her. She was not who she was before she revived him. She did not want him to look upon her and be repulsed, or worse, feel guilt for what she had done to save him. She was not confident her clans-men would not continue to torture him, either, and so she had to make a decision, perhaps the hardest of her life.

"She spared the chieftain's son—Wen—for two reasons. The first was that Wen admitted his part in Joseph's near drowning and pledged himself to her service for the rest of his life. The second . . ."

She hesitated, lifting her eyes to me, tears welling in the

corners and leaking into the deep crevices of her cheeks. "The second reason was that the chieftain vowed to tell both Joseph and the clan that Eira the drabarni had died during childbirth and that her last wishes were for Joseph to leave and let their daughter be raised by her people. To save Joseph's life, Eira had given thirty years of her own to fuel the magic. She had gone from maiden to crone in the span of a day. She looked nothing like the woman she had been, and so she became someone new. Eira became Drina, and Wen bound himself to me."

CHAPTER SIXTEEN

The stranger in the portrait was no longer such a stranger. I was present there, in the arch of his brows, his half-smile, and his dimpled chin. My resemblance to him explained why I'd never suspected my relation to Gran—there were few similarities between us, and those that existed were masked by age. Perhaps I had her nose, and perhaps our shapes were similar, but with her stooped-over posture, it was difficult to say.

I hugged the picture to my chest and dropped my head, regret cracking my icy armor. I'd never know the man. Gran would never see the lost decades. Had she not been carrying me when Joseph drowned, she could have used blood to fuel the spell—hers or someone else's—but to keep me safe, she'd had to give up half a lifetime.

No wonder she was always aloof. She resented me for what I cost her.

"No. No, no, no." Gran reached for my arm and clung to the sleeve of my blouse. "Never, not once, did I harbor ill will toward you. I loved you. Love you. I am not warm often, but it is because our road is fraught with hardship. I want strength for you. To harden you in ways I was not hardened. All parents want better for their child than they themselves had. Perhaps I did you a disservice, but my intentions were pure. You are my world, Bethan. You are the living proof of my great love."

Her great love. Joseph. My father.

I looked down at his foreign-yet-familiar face.

"It changes nothing," I said. "It doesn't matter." Such lies were not becoming of the Romani. Everything was changed, all of it mattered, but the blood moon had brought too much strain for one night. My energies were limited, and what I had in my reserves had to go to Martyn's ritual. I slid the portrait across the table and reclaimed the enchanted mirror, tapping the sleeping facade in the glass. "You said you had an idea for Tomašis."

"Yes, of course." She pulled her hand from my arm and sat up in her chair. Her spine had gone to steel. My dismissal had hurt her, that was evident, but there would be time later to soothe her, when the pressing business was done. "If you wish to spare him, to allow him to live on among his people, I would recommend binding him to you. He will not volunteer as Wen had, as he is a lesser man than Wen, but you can force it. Such relationships can be helpful. As for punishment?" She paused, frowning. "The eye. He crushed our hawk's eye, and it hampered me in finding you. There is, too, that of all of them, he knew my strength and disregarded it. If he is too blind to see what is right before his face, sight is wasted upon him."

I considered it, watching Gran twirl Tomašis's hairs between her fingers. "That's just, you think? It isn't too severe?"

"No. I am angrier with him than the rest, Silas aside, because he already suffered my curse. He disrespected me by disrespecting you a second time despite my warnings. As for taking it from him"—she paused thoughtfully—"eyes are sensitive things. Removing one is a revolting chore, and one you must be cautious with, lest you kill the person you take it from. I will do it for you tonight, but you will have to learn. You never know when the time will come that you will need to take another. For magic. For medicine."

"I . . . All right." I wasn't overeager, but if I was willing to levy the sentence, I had to be willing to play executioner, too. Gran was merciful to take responsibility for Tomašis's tithe, but there were four boys who hadn't come yet, and she wouldn't be the one chasing them around. I'd bloody my hands soon enough.

Gran motioned at the open bureau drawer behind me. "Put the mirror and the portrait away. I will summon Tomašis. The hour grows late." I wedged the frames side by side into the drawer, a piece of perfumed silk stretched over the tops to keep them hidden from prying eyes. Gran stretched her cane to the door latch and pushed on it until the door swung wide. Our gathered audience gasped, murmuring quietly among themselves.

"Bring the boy, Florica. The rest of you leave. I am sorely tempted to sic the shadows on you for eavesdropping." That killed the talk. People clamored to get away, the dry field grass snapping and hissing as they fled back to their tents and vardos. "Idiots," she murmured beneath her breath.

Florica stumbled up the steps, her face bloated with tears. Tomašis didn't look much better, slouching beside her, his hand entwined with his mother's, his face pressed into the side of her neck.

"You are fortunate, Tomašis Buckland. My granddaughter is feeling magnanimous. You are not banished, and you will live—" Florica erupted with a happy shout, and Tomašis hugged his mother with relief. Annoyed that she'd been interrupted, Gran jabbed her cane into Tomašis's side, hard enough that he squirmed away. "I am not finished, boy. You are not banished, and you will live, but under two conditions. The first is that we bind you to Bethan. You will serve or you will suffer, it is that simple. Perhaps, if you are a dutiful and loyal toad, she will release you one day."

I didn't relish the idea of having any kind of tether to such an odious boy, but I could see the practicality of it, too. A boy bound into my service, required to do as I willed, meant he could no longer endanger me. There was safety in that, in a place where I did not feel very safe anymore.

"The second condition is that we take your eye," I said before Gran could get to it. I wanted to be the one to deliver that blow. Perhaps I was hoping to sate a desire for vengeance I hadn't really acknowledged yet, but when Tomašis crumpled, I felt nothing.

"My eye?" He looked pleadingly at his mother. "Help me, Mama."

Florica covered her mouth with her hand and looked away. She was red-eyed and red-cheeked, her brows knit together in an unbroken dark line of hair. "You helped m-murder a man, Tomašis. You wronged the drabarni's granddaughter. It is a mercy that you will see the sunrise." She dabbed her face with her sleeve, slapping her son's hands away when he clawed for her arm. "Be grateful for your life and the knowledge that you aren't banished."

"B-but my eye, Mama. MY EYE!"

"That's the tithe, son. Have a seat and we will get started." Gran stood and shoved her chair toward him. Tomašis shrieked and scampered into the corner, his face awash with terror. "Wait outside, Florica," Gran said. "You have my word he will be returned to you quickly."

Florica pressed her hand to her mouth to muffle her sniveling as she walked out of the vardo. Tomašis darted after her to escape, but Gran lifted her hand and gestured and the door slammed in his face, the latch locking and trapping him inside. He screamed for his mother but all she could do was sob, the walls far too thin to keep out the sound.

Gran snagged Tomašis's ear and dragged him toward the chair. She looked frail, but she had unfathomable strength when necessary, and she efficiently steered a boy a full foot taller than her into a seat with little effort. "Tie him. I doubt he will be still," she said to me, pointing at a stack of scarves folded neatly on the shelf beside her bed. I grabbed them all, thinking they wouldn't be strong enough to hold him, but then I remembered how secure my bindings were in the field after Tomašis tied me, my arms pinned behind my back, allowing Silas to . . .

No.

No, I will not think about that.

I chose a red scarf and circled Tomašis. He sat very still before me. I thought he was paralyzed with fear until I saw his eyes beginning to droop. Then his head dipped forward, his chin touching his chest.

"Sleep," Gran whispered. She'd bespelled him, using his hairs as a focus. She flicked his ear to check his responsiveness, and getting nothing, she opened the window to cast the hairs to the wind.

"You are merciful." I wove the ends of the scarf through the rungs of the chair and around his wrists in figure eights, concentrating on the task to mask my irritation.

"Am I?"

"I was awake during my attack." I wrapped a second scarf around his neck, letting it bite into his skin more than was necessary. "Martyn was awake when they beat him senseless."

"I plan to wake him for the last of it. Tie his legs and arms as well."

I did as she said, then strapped him across the forehead and chin so his head couldn't loll. Gran returned to the corner and pulled out the ritual knife we'd used to make the hawk's eye charm. She pressed it to Tomašis's cheek, the flat silver against his skin.

"Always make a visible mark, so they cannot hide from their wrongs." She stepped aside, offering me the knife handle first. "It is densest here." Gran carved a path over Tomašis's cheek with her fingernail, showing me where to cut. "Remember to go deep. You want it to last as long as your bond."

I did not hesitate. I slashed at him, the edge flaying him open from the side of his nose and diagonally across his cheek, to just above his ear. The skin ripped open, the blood criss-crossing in rivers down his cheek and dripping from his jawline onto his crisp white shirt.

Gran leaned in, squinting her brown eye to assess my work. "Good. Perfect. Now we must bind the two of you together. Do you have the cat fetish I gave you?"

I retrieved the bag I'd stuffed my soiled clothing into and rummaged through the pocket of my skirt. Touching the soiled garment made me shudder, and once I'd found the charm, I thrust it away like it bore disease. If that wasn't a plague, nothing was.

Gran guided me back to stand between Tomašis's splayed knees. "Here. We will need a drop of your blood to seal the bond. Do you want to do it or shall I?"

I opened my hand for her, the knife flat across my palm. My consternation when we'd made the hawk's eye charm seemed silly in the wake of worse hurts, and when she took the blade and jabbed me in the center of my palm, I didn't flinch. She scraped a crimson bubble from my palm, letting it rest upon the silver before pressing it to the open wound on Tomašis's face. Not having to touch him myself was a blessing.

"Will him into your thrall," she said. "Claim him. Own his soul, Bethan."

I pinched my eyes shut, my free hand squeezing the cat figurine until it dug grooves into my palm. I pictured Tomašis indentured to me as the chieftain was indentured to Gran. I wanted it; I demanded it; I would not be denied. Tomašis was mine. The magic simply had to acquiesce to that reality.

And it did, answering far faster than it had with the hawk charm. Heat scalded my bleeding palm, startling me enough that I nearly dropped the cat, but I gritted my teeth and held on. When I opened my eyes, I saw a golden glow spilling out between my fingers. It flared bright, like a star, the burn worsening for a heartbeat before the effect burst apart. Magic sprinkled from my hands in a wash of golden dust that dissipated upon contact with the floor.

I hadn't touched Tomašis, and yet when I looked up at him, my magic had closed his wound to a fresh pink scar and scorched off most of the blood. His mark wasn't as blatant as the chieftain's, but it bisected one side of his face, impossible for him or anyone else to ignore.

"Focus on the scar. You can feel it—him—through it. His blood is now yours." I'd witnessed Gran manipulating the chieftain with magic, reopening his old wound, and I wanted to see if I could do the same. I gave the cat fetish another squeeze, envisioning myself ripping open the meat of Tomašis's face, my fingers pulling the flesh apart. Sure enough, the scar beside his nose burst, and the neat seam unraveled like stitches before my eyes.

I could do it. I could hurt him at will, and knowing that the power had shifted, I actually managed to relax a little in his presence. It was the first hint of peace since the field, and I was grateful for it.

"Good. Now for the rest of it." Gran tapped his shoulder twice to wake him. Tomašis's eyes popped open. He hollered, the muscles in his neck and forearms cording with strain as he pushed against the scarves, his face turning red. He'd gone from restful to very much aware in no time at all.

"Welcome back, toad. You now bear Bethan's mark. If you betray her, she can reach into your chest and squeeze your heart until it explodes. She is your mistress, and you would be wise to remember that." Gran limped to the front of the chair and grabbed a scarf from the stack, wadding it into a ball. Tomašis looked from it to Gran and snapped his jaws shut, desperate and scared. Gran simply pinched his nostrils closed, shook her head, and waited. "Silly boy. This is a kindness to your mother. This will muffle your screams."

He succumbed quickly, greedy for air like a pig at a trough. His maw opened and Gran stuffed the scarf inside, deep enough that he gagged and couldn't spit it out.

Like he'd done to me.

She let go of his nostrils and tutted. "Bring me an empty jar, Bethan. And you can put the knife away. This is delicate work. I will have to use my fingers, as unpleasant as that is. We'll need boiling water from the fire later, most certainly."

I did as instructed, pulling a jar from her supplies and sliding it onto the corner of the table. Tomašis looked at it and then at me, his red face darkening to purple, tears welling and then spilling down. He sobbed behind his gag, but it didn't stir me because nothing stirred me. His cruelties had stolen my ability to care.

Gran used two fingers from her left hand to widen Tomašis's eye—one finger pulling up on his brow, the other pressing down on his upper cheek. "See how I've opened him up? I go in from the corner. . . ." Her long, curved talon pressed not where the pink and white started, but the skin beside it. "Now all you do is slide in and scoop. It pops out surprisingly easily. I will have to sever the cord afterward, of course."

Gran pressed her fingernail in, and Tomašis screeched, his chair thudding against the floor as he rocked back and forth. Gran was undeterred. As she went in a second time, Tomašis's screams hit glass-shattering pitch, and though his pain did not

bother me, the gore made me jerk my gaze away. I was not beyond revulsion, after all.

For what was most likely a minute but felt like an eon, I listened to the awful, rhythmic squelching sound of Gran's work.
It reminded me of when I did our laundry at the river, when the
clothes were saturated and I had to knead them to wring them
out. Finally, after much sloshing and sucking, Gran deposited a
freshly severed eye into the jar.

I stared at its unseeing brown iris, at the stringy bits of
meat hanging from the back and the way the blood smeared the
inside of the glass. It was awful, yes, but it had to be better than
looking at the gaping hole in Tomašis's face.

Gran retrieved her healing kit from the shelf and brought
it to the table. She chose fresh linen cloths, once boiled to keep
them free of contamination, and two jars of medicinal salves
from the basket.

"This will heal quickly," she said, turning back to Tomašis.
"Ask your mother to fashion you a proper eye patch. I want you
to drink the tea I give you twice a day for a week to keep the
fever down."

It was strange to watch the torturer become the healer in
such short order, but that was the essence of Gran, wasn't it?
Good and bad, both sinner and saint. She damned and blessed
in equal measure, depending on how the wind blew. She was
drabarni. She was magical.

She was fierce and terrible and wonderful.

And she was my mother.

CHAPTER SEVENTEEN

Tomašis was the only one of the four who dared show his face that first day. I wondered whether the other boys' mothers were pleading with their sons to come to us, and whether their fathers, like the chieftain, refused to believe that their boys could commit such heinous acts. My conscience would be clear as I collected my tithes, but for the parents who hadn't heeded Gran's advice for a chance at mercy, I had to wonder, would theirs?

The next day, I rose early and grabbed our bowls to get breakfast. The grass had the first crusts of frost on it, the blades snapping beneath my boots. People milled about the fire, drinking tea and talking animatedly, likely about last night's travesties. As I approached the main table, every voice quieted, and I wondered how many people had already seen Tomašis or learned of his fate. I refused to shy away, meeting their gazes with my own cold, steady one. Some people looked down, affronted by my boldness. Others offered tight, awkward smiles, like they weren't sure how to proceed.

And then there was Brishen.

He stood across the clearing, talking to one of the elders, nodding and smiling like it was any other day. I wondered if he'd even considered coming forward or if he'd convinced himself that he hadn't directly murdered anyone so he had nothing to repent for. I slapped porridge into my bowl so hard that it splattered over the table and across the front of my blouse and skirt, but I was too angry to care much about the mess I'd made.

Brishen must have felt the weight of my stare, because he craned his head my way, peering at me through the dancing flames and smoke tendrils of the fire. I thought he'd have the good grace to look discomfited by my presence, but instead, he smirked.

"The new look suits you well, Bethan," he shouted. He lifted his hand in a mock salute and turned back to the elder, effectively dismissing me from his thoughts. The elder reached for Brishen's ear and yanked it, dragging him away from the fire and chastising him for his insolence. I wanted to chase after him right there, but I swallowed my growl and stormed back to the vardo. When I crested the home path, Gran awaited me, holding the door ajar, her eyes narrowed.

"What is wrong?"

"Brishen next," I spat, brushing past her to slide both bowls onto the table. "Brishen today."

"As you wish."

We ate in silence, but my thoughts whirled with every bite.

Brishen had undoubtedly heard about Gran's proclamation, but he simply didn't care. Could he possibly believe that the chieftain's son held so much favor? That because Silas had always been beyond reproach, his friends would be, too? Perhaps he had not seen Tomašis's face.

"Idiots. Vain, self-serving idiots." I slapped my spoon down into my porridge and shoved away the bowl. Normally Gran would chide me for wasting hard-earned food, but she reached for the parchment piece from yesterday instead, skimming it and nodding.

"The hungry roots," she said. "The hungry roots for Brishen, I think."

"What does that mean?"

"I learned about it from an old Welsh woman with fair folk blood. They place high value upon the trees. Roots dig deep—they twist and writhe beneath the soil for nourishment. If you feed them, they are yours to command. Tomašis is yours now—he will do as you say. You will need him to lure Brishen to the woods."

"And what do I do when I get him there?"

Gran pulled the knife from her bureau and slid it across the table. "Go to the southern woods, where the elms thrive. Bleed upon the ground, offering your essence to the trees and beseeching their roots. You are learning to harness your will. It is the same as the charm or the binding." She retrieved a plain apron with a big pocket on the front from a nail on the wall and placed it on the table in front of me. She took her seat again, wincing as her knee joints popped. "You will want to wear that, and you will need the knife and your focus piece, of course. What do you plan to take from him?"

The eye was already accounted for on the ingredient list, so I could choose any of the other four senses. I pictured Brishen in my head, how I'd last seen him in camp. Squat body, wide across the shoulders and chest, with a long torso and short legs. Dark hair, light-brown skin, heavy brows over a nose with a turned-up end, freckles splashed across his cheeks, and a softness around his face that made him look younger than his sixteen years. His mouth was wide, too, with rubbery fish lips that peeled back to reveal his one true beauty—two rows of straight white teeth.

Perfect teeth.

Teeth for taste.

"A tooth," I said, tapping my lip. "From the front."

Gran nodded. "You will want pliers and gloves."

Both were with our herbing tools. We used the pliers to clip reedy stems or snap stubborn branches from trees and shrubs when we gathered. They were old and the handles were rusted, but they worked. The leather of the pale-brown gloves was soft from so much wear. The fingertips were stained on both hands, and while I'd only ever seen Gran use them for our herbalism, now that I was more familiar with her magical practices, I wondered whether they had been deployed for far darker work.

Like pulling teeth, perhaps.

"Is that all I need to know? To command the roots? How do I take the tooth itself?"

"You pull it? Do not ask ridiculous questions, Bethan," Gran said, her tone clipped. Oddly, there was comfort in her snideness. She'd been soft in the face of my troubles, but what I needed was familiarity, and Gran's crotchetiness was as familiar to me as the ground beneath my feet.

I smiled a little, surprised I knew how to do that still, and stood to don the apron and gloves. The knife and pliers clunked together when they struck inside the front pocket. Gran handed me the black cat figurine, and I added it to the mix, the weight of my mystic goods pulling on the apron string around my neck.

"Do you have any other questions?" Gran asked. I had a slew, but by the set of her jaw I presumed she'd find most of them ridiculous as well, so I shook my head and turned toward the door. "We will burn what you bring back with Tomašis's eye so neither pollute the vardo. The ash is all we need for Martyn," she called out.

"Yes, Gran."

"'Yes, Gran' what?"

"Yes, Gran, I understand."

"And Bethan?"

"Yes?"

"Be careful."

"As careful as I can be."

I ducked behind a pair of vardos to get to Tomašis's tent, avoiding as many of my people as possible. The few that spied me quickly looked away, but I was too preoccupied to care. Gran's instructions weren't thorough, but they were straightforward, and if the key to magic really was learning to channel will, I could piece it together on my own.

All I needed was for Tomašis to play decoy.

I rounded the corner that led to his tent. Florica was outside beating the dust from a threadbare rug with her broom. I didn't want to startle her, so I cleared my throat to announce my presence, my hands primly folded together against my skirt. She paused and turned around, and seeing me, let the broom slip from her grasp.

"Bethan," she warbled.

"Tomašis, please. I need him."

She looked like she wanted to argue, like I was a child asking for her friend to come play, but when I cocked my head, she closed her mouth and ducked behind her tent flap. Furious whispering was followed by furious rustling, and finally Tomašis emerged, his eyehole covered by a wad of linen secured with a black scarf.

He peered at me, and I peered right back at him. His face was red, and there was sweat on his brow despite the cold. I wondered if he was feverish, perhaps, but Gran had given Florica enough herbs to keep him in good health. If he heeded her advice, he'd recover soon enough.

"Bring Brishen to the southern woods, at the riverside. Be there in twenty minutes, no later," I said.

"Why?"

"It's not up to you to ask why. Bring him to the clearing at the center of the trees and keep him there until I come."

He looked so wary, I thought he'd refuse me—I was ready for it—but before my fingers twitched, before I could utter a single word of warning, his shoulders slumped in resignation. "Fine."

"Good." He didn't reply, but that was fine—obedience was more valuable to me than politeness. As long as he produced Brishen where and when I requested, there'd be no quarrel.

I made my way to the river's edge. The area was thick with trees, the overhead canopies so dense that sunlight couldn't pierce through to touch the ground. The shadows proved a breeding ground for thick roots that rose from the earth like gnarled serpents. When the wind stirred the branches, I was reminded of Gran's shrieking gale in the wheat stalks in Thomson's field.

I rejected the association and gritted my teeth, concentrating on finding steady ground amid the root tangle. I needed to be surefooted when I gave my offering. I pulled the gloves from my apron pocket and slid them over my fingers, flexing to test the leather. The big knife came next, and I rotated my arm to find a suitable spot to cut. Gran never told me how much blood I'd need, but a deepish cut that would clot quickly was my aim. I eyed the back of my forearm, some inches above my wrist, where the fat hugged the bone.

The knife glinted as I arced it down, with brutal ease. The pain was immediate, and the shock stole my breath away. I stomped my feet and swallowed a curse, an awful, steady throb racking me from wrist to elbow. I unfurled my arm, breathing deep to keep from crying out. The wound bled true and my essence painted the roots, leaves, and rocks all around me scarlet.

As the flow slowed to a drizzle, I returned the knife to my apron pocket and pulled out the cat figurine, my blood-slick glove smearing red over its golden eyes. I closed my eyes and dug deep, going to that still place where I focused my will and birthed magic. I envisioned the roots coming to life. I envisioned them rising at my command like twisting, thrashing monsters.

The ground beneath me shifted.

I dug my heels into the packed earth to be sure it was real. It stirred again—a low rumble, a tremble some feet below. I crouched to keep my balance. So close to the earth, I could see the smallest roots worming their way up through the under-brush to reach for me, their fibrous hairs waving at the heavens. There was another shift and the midsized roots churned their way to the surface, crawling and slithering toward me like dirt-crusted snakes. I smelled damp earth and decomposing leaves, and despite the cold autumn day, I was reminded of spring.

One of the roots dared to tickle the hem of my skirt, its pointed end stroking the thick fabric. I stood and stepped back, only to have another root slide across my leg. Its cold, bumpy exterior grazed my skin near the lip of my boot. I yelped and ducked behind a thick tree trunk to get away. The roots crawled over each other, tearing up the earth in an impatient frenzy.

Gran had called them the hungry roots. Like anything starving for nourishment, they yearned for their next meal.

CHAPTER EIGHTEEN

The tangle of roots writhed, hissing as they stretched for the sky, some slapping the ground with famished fervency.

"Hush," I barked, afraid Brishen would hear the clamor when he approached. They stilled *so* absolutely, I worried they were no longer in my thrall. I pointed at a tiny tendril near the toe of my boot and willed it to move.

It waved at me. I still had control.

I slipped behind a fat trunk and waited for Tomašis to bring Brishen to the clearing. It didn't take long for their voices to carry through the trees; the boys' heads were together, their thumbs notched into their pockets.

"What's the plan, then?" Tomašis asked.

"Not sure yet. Cam wants to torch the vardo with the old woman inside it, but Silas won't go for it. He's still pushing for the match with the half-face. She'll need a husband after their rut, and the diddicoy is gone." The boys paused at the edge of the roots, boot to boot, and Tomašis glanced from the river to the trees and back to Brishen. His fingers worried at the seams of his trousers, his weight bouncing from foot to foot.

Brishen eyed him. "Something wrong? It's as if you have ants crawling on you."

"No, nothing wrong. I wanted you to see what they did to me is all. Come where there's better light." Tomašis stepped over one of the thickest roots, bringing Brishen into my enchanted patch of ground.

"Go. Take Brishen only. Leave Tomašis alone," I commanded. The roots exploded to life. They erupted in a frenzy of churning dirt, the thickest ones waving like the tentacles of a subterranean beast. Both Brishen and Tomašis screamed, trying to fumble their way out of the area. Tomašis was aided by the roots—two midsized ones nudged him to safety. But the largest roots caught Brishen around the waist and hauled him into the writhing mess. Thinner roots wound around his arms and legs, jerking him off the ground and dangling him like a helpless doll.

"Hold," I commanded. They stilled, but not before squeezing Brishen hard enough that his eyes bulged.

I stepped out from behind the tree. He was three feet off the ground and tilted forward, his stomach parallel to the ground. Seeing the hem of my skirt swishing his way, he lifted his head, and on some level, it pleased me to see his face blanch.

"Let me go."

"No."

He shouted for help, and I pulled the big knife from my apron to flash it under his eye. His scream was a piglike squeal.

It suited him—his nose, the roundness of his cheeks, and the flush of his skin. Brishen was a pig, and pigs made piggy noises.

Some feet away, Tomašis whimpered. He was in crab position, his weight supported by both feet and hands, but otherwise he looked unharmed, if not a little scared.

"Are you hurt?"

"No," he managed. "I'm fine."

Brishen thrashed inside the roots' grip. "Tomašis, get help. Get my father. Get Silas or the chieftain."

"Tomašis doesn't go get help, Brishen. He leaves people to their fates, whether they're diddicoy who are beaten to death or girls who are abused. Don't you remember?" I slapped the flat of the blade against his cheek to punctuate the point.

He reared away from me, slamming his eyes closed. "You can't have it! You can't have my eye!" he screamed.

"I don't want your eye." I crouched low, so we were nose to nose, and waited. After a long, silent moment, he dared to peek at me, promptly changing tack and trying to stare me down. I never flinched, not when he snarled, not when he spat and struck my apron with his sputum. I would not break, and in the end, he was the one to look away first.

I reached up to squeeze his cheeks with my gloved fingers, grabbing his jaw and forcing him to look Tomašis's way. "Tomašis admitted his wrongs. For it, he gets the privilege of staying among us. Not you. You'll bleed and then you'll leave. I'm banishing you forever. No family unless yours goes with you."

"The chieftain," he said, the words muffled from my hold.

"The chieftain will let me because his son has my blood on his hands."

Brishen screamed for help again, and I smacked him atop the head with the knife flat, growing irritable when he wouldn't quiet. "They can't hear you. We're too far from camp." He didn't stop, his voice shredding through the grove.

Tomašis groaned behind me, like he, too, was pained. For all I knew he was—from fever.

I waved in the direction of the caravan. "Go home and take care of your eye. Say nothing to anyone."

He didn't have to be told twice. He found his feet and ran, as fast as he'd run from the field that night. Brishen called after him, pleading for him to send help, but Tomašis never spared him a glance. He was too busy putting distance between himself and the impending horror. He was too busy saving himself once again.

"Coward!" Brishen hissed, his voice raw.

"He *is* a coward, Brishen. A terrible coward, but it might not be such a bad thing. It's what saved him, after all."

I stepped away from Brishen. Fear made him wheeze, and as he strained against the roots even harder, balling his hands into fists inside their constraints, the veins in his temples throbbed purple. The roots hadn't loosened their grip, nor would they as long as I held them in my power.

It was satisfying to see Brishen's big body so helpless, but I didn't want to look at him anymore. I found him revolting. I eyed the roots near my feet. The big ones were too big for delicate work, but the small ones were strong and thin and could hold open his swine maw for me.

"Open the mouth wide. Do not pull too far or you'll kill him."

Brishen looked confused—his gaze swung around, searching

with red-rimmed eyes for whomever I spoke to—but he understood better when the roots pulled his limbs taut to either side of his body and tilted him forward, belly down. He answered with more screams, more futile struggle. Two thinner tendrils snaked up over his chest, crawling along his neck and jaw like hairy serpents. Brishen snapped his lips together in defiance, but the roots were finely pointed and strong. They pried his lips apart, worming inside and coiling along the roof of his mouth and on his tongue.

The roots flexed, pulling, and Brishen's nostrils flared. But they did their work. His mouth was held open, so I could have my due.

I approached, fishing into the pocket of my apron for the pliers. I stopped a hair's breadth from Brishen's quivering frame, the first doubt niggling at me. Gran had taken the eye, and that had been her sin, not mine. It had been on her soul, not mine. This would be the first tithe I'd taken myself. I couldn't give it back. I couldn't undo it. All the rivers in the world might not be able to wash that stain away.

But what is left to salvage after Silas's attack?

And what of Martyn?

It was the memory of Martyn's face—not the handsome, smiling one from market, but the pulpy, bruised one from the field—that spurred me on. Without the tithe, he would not see his breath restored, and a tooth was just a tooth. It would not kill Brishen to lose one.

It would have been hypocrisy to shirk my own duty in the face of my fear.

I forced the pliers inside Brishen's open mouth and up the top row of teeth, stopping at the center right one. The tooth was white and straight and perfect, and I guided the long nose of the pliers around it, clamping down on the enamel. As I began rocking the tooth in the socket, Brishen screamed. I kept wiggling the pliers back and forth, loosening the tooth from the pink flesh of the gums one hard pull at a time. The task was far more laborious than I'd anticipated, and I ended up using the knife to cut into his gum above the tooth to get at the root. The drool rolling down his chin went from clear to red in short order—my borrowed gloves were slick with his fluids. Brishen shrieked and whimpered, his face red and his shirt smeared with his own spit, but I continued working him over.

Finally, the tooth was loose enough for me to twist. I gave it one last hard tug, and it popped from the socket. Both my hand and my pliers were so wet they flew from my grasp to land some feet away. The hungry roots crawled for them, eager to consume the piece of man, but I kicked them away and swooped in for my prize, cradling it inside my palm.

The tooth was more red than white, the top portion stringy with bits of Brishen's flesh.

It's done.

It's done. It's done. It's donedonedone. . . .

Gran would have relished this moment, Brishen's pathetic mewls and bloodied spit evidence of a victory, but for me, collecting the tithe had been an unpleasant necessity. My muscles were tense and my heart was racing, thanks to the adrenaline surging through my body. I braced for regret to slither its way into my belly, but it never came.

"You will go back to town. You will get tea from Gran to heal your tooth, and then you will gather your things and go. You will not return."

Brishen's body shifted inside the roots. It was drenched in sweat, and as he lifted his gaze my way, his eyes were full of fear and hate. It did not stir me. Nothing stirred me, not as my hand clasped around his tooth, not as I gestured at the roots.

"If you do not, I'll feed you to them. They're starving. They'll rip you apart from the inside and feast on your innards."

It didn't matter if it was true or not. All that mattered was that he believed me, and when the roots shook him because I willed them to, he looked afraid. I wiped the blood from my blade on the apron and slid it back into the pocket along with the pliers and cat figurine.

"Release him," I told the roots, and they dropped Brishen to the ground in a heap by my feet. He curled into a ball and looked up at me, his bottom lip trembling. His meaty fingers clasped the bottom of my skirt, wadding it up in his palms as he started to sob.

"Please," he begged. "Mercy."

My emotions simply weren't there—no fear, no excitement, no satisfaction. Surely no mercy. I was a void. My stranger self had certainly made the task easier. I would continue to the next boy and hope that I didn't lose my resolve.

"Gather your things and go. What mercy I had set with the blood moon." I jerked my skirt from his grasp and walked away.

CHAPTER NINETEEN

The blood on the apron told an incomplete story. I circumvented the caravan, not wanting to have to explain myself to anyone—they'd know Brishen was banished soon enough. I saw no reason to call attention to it prematurely.

For once I was glad Gran parked away from the others.

The knee-high grass hung limp beneath the seasonal frost. Soon winter would come, and with it, the snow and the feeling that I'd never be warm again. I paused on the vardo steps before going inside, pulling off the apron. I didn't want that soil in my home.

As I folded the apron, I heard approaching footsteps. I looked over my shoulder just as the chieftain turned our corner. He raised his chin and, seeing the bloody cloth in my hands, went still. His mouth opened with questions he didn't dare give voice to. Instead, he cleared his throat and motioned for me to go ahead of him, so I cast the apron over a barrel and climbed the steps.

Inside, Gran had an iron pot waiting on the table, but that pot had never seen stew. Incense, sometimes, and medicinal pastes, yes—but never food. That day, it saw a plucked eye, oil, and a smattering of herbs.

"All is well?" she asked, hovering by her cabinet with its oddities, a jar of pale blue powder in her hand. "Put your tithe there."

"It's done. The chieftain is here." I dropped the tooth into the pot, sloughing off the meaty bits still stuck to the gloves before peeling them from my fingers. They, too, needed a washing, and I brushed past the man in the doorway to bring the pitcher of water outside. I rinsed the gloves in a bucket we kept by the wheel. Water wasn't good for leather, but they'd been waxed enough that a quick pass wouldn't do much harm.

I worked quickly, the chieftain watching me all the while. He was silent, even as I laid the gloves out to dry and climbed the steps. He followed, glancing from me to Gran, waiting for her to acknowledge him. She finished fussing with her jars before bothering to turn his way.

"Yes?"

"I am sorry to intrude. I spoke with the Woodard elder. He is sending one of his sons off in search of Martyn and Bethan. I suggested they might be going to Caerdydd. He believed me, though he expressed concerns over the fight. I told him that was the reason you fled. To avoid more violence." The chieftain glanced at me, nervous, and nodded at the pot. "Who is that?"

"Brishen," I said. "I told him he was banished. His family may come to you seeking intervention."

The chieftain frowned. "I see."

"And they will get none, will they Wen?" Gran pressed.

"No, though the other elders may argue it with me."

"I will speak with them. An attack of this nature warrants expulsion at the very least. The boys are lucky to get away with their lives. They would not if it were up to the gadjos." Gran cocked her head my way. "Who is next, after Brishen?"

"Cam spoke of burning us alive inside our vardo. We need to be prepared."

"We always are." The reply was for me, but her attention was fixed on the chieftain, her fingers whirling circles over the glass surface of the jar.

"You cannot help him, Wen. He did not come last night," she said softly.

The chieftain winced, much like I winced whenever she sampled my thoughts without permission. "I tried, Drina. He insisted it was not how Bethan explained it. That they were besotted and ought to marry. I said you saw it otherwise in the glass and he . . ."

"Called me a liar?" I said, my voice flat.

"All but, yes." The chieftain's shoulders sagged. "I am reconciling myself to losing him. He is a bad, spoiled boy and a stain upon my family name. I ought to be glad he is going, but it is hard. He is still my son."

"Bad boys get what they deserve." I motioned at the black pot with the tooth inside, no longer numb, but furious. Silas's casting us as secret lovers in a play he acted out in his head was delusional madness, but was that so surprising? Who besides the mad would so readily dismiss the drabarni? A drabarni who'd learned magic craft from the British witches in her travels, at that? Gran didn't flash her power, but it was feared and respected in equal measure by our people. Silas refused to believe only because he hadn't witnessed it with his own eyes.

Or because he believed I belonged to him, he was willing to risk her wrath.

I washed my hands in the basin. There was no mess because I'd worn gloves, but the ghost of bloody deeds past compelled me to reach for the bristle brush. I sawed until my fingers puffed and reddened.

Gran and the chieftain lingered behind me, silent. Gran was busy sprinkling her strange powder over the tooth in the pot, but I felt the weight of the chieftain's gaze upon my back again. It made me uncomfortable.

"I do not wish to see this change you, Bethan. To see you become cold-hearted," he said.

I said nothing, and did not turn around to face him.

"She is my daughter. Her heart is iron," Gran said. "She is kind and good, but she is strong, too. Strong enough to do anything she wishes to do. Anything she has to do to bring back the diddicoy."

There was pride in her voice that I would have relished on any other day. Now, after the attack, I simply toweled off my hands.

The chieftain sighed as he opened our door. It squealed on its hinge as if echoing his sentiment. "I suppose, but I worry. For all of us, but especially for Bethan."

"That is what makes you a good chieftain," Gran replied. "Your caring."

"I do not feel like a good chieftain. I failed my people and my son. I am sorry for you, Bethan," the chieftain said quietly.

"If I could take your pain away, I would." He left with footsteps so heavy on the stairs, the vardo shook on its wheels.

I glared at the space he'd just occupied. *He* would take away my pain? *He* would know it? I wanted to strike him. Shake him until his teeth rattled. Until his person was reduced to meat, until his body was not his own anymore, until his heart was encased in cold glass one minute, only to fill with molten fury the next, the chieftain could *never* understand.

"Scowling makes you ugly," Gran said to me. "He means well, but he operates from ignorance. A man cannot under-stand a woman's burdens, especially ones such as these. I worry that he still wishes to save his son. His conscience makes him untrustworthy. He may warn Silas away to protect him, or per-haps even shield Silas's friends."

"Would the chieftain betray you that way? Would he refuse to honor the banishment?"

Gran reached for the matches on the overhead shelf, but she was so short that she had to use her cane to hook the box to pull it down.

"Love makes us do foolish things. I of all people know that. If he thought he could change his son's stars, he would. It is easier to believe the lie of redemption than the truth that some people are beyond it."

She slid the matches across the table to me in invitation. "We burn the flesh from the tooth and store it with its ashes. If we work swiftly, you will have time to prepare for the next boy. You said Cam, but if the chieftain shows his hand, Cam will expect you. Mander, perhaps."

I struck the match. I didn't expect wet flesh to ignite so quickly, but whatever powder Gran sprinkled over the tooth and eye made it do just that. There was a puff of acrid smoke and then an odd fizzing sound as blue flames devoured the offerings. The smell was revolting—like beef roasted hours too long—and Gran opened the shutters, letting the awful stink out and the cold air in.

Soon, all that was left in the pot were ashes and the tooth. Gran offered me a tobacco box with a sliding lid to keep the ashes safe, and I used a wooden spoon from our herbing to collect everything inside.

"What will we do about Cam's threat?" I asked. "It sounded like Silas didn't like the idea, but if Cam's desperate enough, he might ignore Silas's dissent." I closed the box and handed it to Gran, and she tucked it away with the rest of her ritual things, going so far as to hide it beneath her jars of feathers and dried chicken feet.

"Fire does not scare me. A gadjo from Scotland showed my mother—your grandmother—how to talk to flames. If Cam tries to burn us, he will live long enough to regret it and not a moment more."

She sounded so confident, I felt I could put that one worry aside. It didn't hurt that she'd controlled the fire at the center of the caravan so well the morning before—she had been an extension of the flames themselves. If Cam wanted to attack her with her chosen element, he was a fool.

I tapped the ashes remaining on the spoon into a refuse jar, then tossed the spoon into a bucket outside, adding it to a pile of river washing.

"May I see your arm, please?" Gran asked when I locked the door. I offered it to her, and she inspected the cut I'd made to feed the roots, her finger hovering over the ragged edges. "This is too much, Bethan. Not so deep next time." I wanted to point out that she hadn't given me very clear instructions about the ritual, but I got distracted watching her reach for her tray of medicines.

The squat clay pots were painted different colors to indicate the contents' purpose, and Gran chose the orange one, flipping the lid and covering the tip of her finger with a smelly substance. She rubbed it over the gash, actually worming her way inside the wound to smear in the ointment. It stung, but I didn't complain; she keeping me safe from infection.

Gran wrapped me in linen from knuckles to wrist. "No more cutting. We must come up with some other way to work Mander's offering. I just wish we had time. . . . There is so little time."

She pushed the medicine aside, reaching for her list and scratching out two lines. I wondered if those had been Tomašis and Brishen's names.

"Something more traditional for Mander. Tonight, after dinner, when the clan is gathered by the fire, you will sneak into his vardo. Look for a hairbrush, a pillow—anything with his trace upon it. The bigger the sample, the better. We can conjure something tonight or do it in the morning depending on when you return."

I didn't fancy the notion of creeping about in other people's homes, but it wasn't like Mander would offer me his hair, and plucking it from his head would cause a fuss. While no one would deny Gran and me our vengeance, they wouldn't be happy that we were harming their sons before turning them out.

"Should I send Tomašis to do it in my stead?" I asked.

"No. Not only would I not trust him because he is stupid,

but he was also the last person seen with Brishen. Silas will be suspicious. I hope Tomašis lies well, for his mother's sake if not his own. There would be something cruelly ironic about having spared his life only to have Silas end it for disloyalty."

I hoped Tomašis lied well, too, though less because I was a charitable soul and more because I'd gone through the trouble of binding him and didn't want my efforts wasted. I sat at the table, quiet, and watched Gran fold her list and tuck it away. She gathered her sewing basket from the floor and rifled through the contents. I was dismissed, apparently. Most days, I'd cherish free time, but idle time meant idle thoughts . . . and I didn't want my thoughts to drift back to the wheat field and leave me vulnerable to emotion—I wasn't ready to feel yet.

I tapped my fingers on the tabletop until Gran cast me a look that suggested I should sit still before she made me sit still. I decided to work with our herbs. Days ago, I'd complained that herbcraft bored me, but its easy monotony was exactly the distraction I needed. I pulled the canvas bags and colored yarn from the drawers and took the clustered herbs down from the hooks in the ceiling.

Gran watched me. She cocked her head as I reached for the fennel stalks above my head, but before I could bring them down, she pointed to another hook. "No. Not that. Give me the dwayberry." I did, handing her the sprig with its deadly berries and dusky-purple flowers. The cutting was drying out, the petals on the blossoms shriveled to wrinkled silk.

"This. For Mander," she said.

"Poison him with nightshade?"

"No. Well, it is a poison, yes, but we can use it to poison his mind instead of his body. If you can get his hair . . ." She trailed off, retrieving her list again, and I could tell by her crooked smile that whatever idea she'd conceived pleased her. "If you get the hair tonight, we can send him a living dream—dream magic. The enchantment creates illusions in the mind, and it takes only a single drop of our blood. If we conjure a truly potent vision, Mander will focus on it instead of you, and you can corral him. The trick is to find something frightening enough to hold his attention."

"Thomson," I blurted, without thinking twice. "He didn't like Thomson. He said as much in Martyn's field. He thought he was scary."

"Who is Thomson?"

"The scarecrow. He's terrifying. Or was terrifying, before they ripped him apart."

Gran's eyes swept over to the bag holding the clothes I'd worn during my attack. I hadn't burned them yet because I hadn't had the opportunity. She reached inside to pluck a few pieces of Thomson's straw from my blouse, twining them around the dwayberry, one of her pointed fingernails bursting a fruit so its juices ran down her skin. "This. Tonight, you get a piece of him. His essence." She paused to eyeball me, a grin prefacing her unmelodious cackles. "And tomorrow, you control his nightmare."

CHAPTER TWENTY

It didn't occur to me until after we'd eaten dinner to ask Gran what she meant by *"corral him."* She peered at me over her bowl of soup, her brows knit together as if I asked only stupid questions.

"If Mander believes he cannot move, he will not move. Control his vision, control him. You can take whatever you need while he is under your sway."

"Oh. Of course," I said, as if it was evident, though it was anything but.

I picked up our bowls and rinsed them in the dish basin. I'd take them to the fire to wash them in boiling water later, when most were asleep. After I'd gotten Mander's essence.

"Is your conscience bothering you yet?" Gran asked my back.

It was, perhaps, her way of testing my mettle for the

178

gruesome tasks to come. Or perhaps it was her odd way of seeing if I was all right in the wake of Brishen's tooth removal. I swept the washcloth over a bowl and shrugged.

"No, should it be?"

"It is not a matter of should. You are good, and good people do not do the things you have done or are about to do. But that is the nature of magic: it is transactional. Nothing is free. You take pieces of these boys' lives to pay for the yellow-haired man's life. When your doubt comes upon you—and it will—you must cling to the knowledge that those you harvest wronged you and the sacrifice is just. If you plan to be my successor, you will be in this position again one day—sooner than you would like. There is little room for half-measure or hesitation. The best you can do is take tithes only from those deserving of the pain. These boys are deserving of the pain."

"Yes, Gran." I stacked our empty bowls beneath the window, my eyes drifting to peer out into the night. Clouds played peekaboo with the moon while a silver fog rose from the ground, wispy gray tendrils tickling the vardo side. "I should go," I said, turning the washed bowls upside down so they'd drip dry. "It's a good time to sneak to Mander's vardo with the fog."

"Yes. Be careful. Get what you need and come back. And take these." She handed me the shawl from her shoulders and the ritual knife, patting its handle with a murmured, "In case." I bundled up, scarf over my hair, shawl on my back, the blade tucked close to my body. We'd been through a lot in a short time, that knife and I, and I felt better with it near.

I scrambled down our front steps and toward the back of the camp. Mander's family was parked on the opposite side of Cotter's Field, far from me and Gran, and I darted through the dark alleys between vardos and tents, my head low. The fog nipped at my heels, swishing past my knees to hover around my thighs. It was so thick I couldn't see the lower half of my skirt. I looked like a disembodied torso with a red shawl and a long black knife clutched in my hand.

I kept a row of goods wagons between me and the fire. There was no music that night; people spoke in hushed tones, their conversations grave. I had to assume that either Brishen's absence had been noticed or the chieftain had simply come out and announced his banishment. Part of me was tempted to eavesdrop for details, but the fear of being caught kept me back. I didn't want anyone thinking I took pride in my actions. It was an ugly necessity and nothing more.

I hurried on. Nearing Mander's vardo, I heard a different set of voices. Recognizing Silas, Mander, and Cam, my mind flashed back to the night in the field, to the abuses heaped one on top of another. I retreated, a primitive instinct to flee overriding what my mind wanted me to do, but I forced my feet to stop.

I must stay. I must stay.

I took a deep breath.

The boys were alone. Their parents had likely gone with the rest of the adults to the fire. It was clear from their lowered voices and urgent whispers that they were up to something. As much as it sickened me to get close to them, I had to find out what. I ducked behind Mander's vardo and crouched, the fog sweeping over my head keeping me hidden.

"Gone. Niku said he saw him heading toward the woods with Tomašis, but he never came back," Cam said. "I went all the way to the river to look for him, but there's no trace. Do you think he was banished? Or did the old witch kill him?"

Mander spit a wet mouthful of what I assumed was tobacco to the ground. "Tomašis's mother wouldn't let him out from behind her skirts earlier. She said he was too sick to see anyone. His eye, she said. If he's so sick, why was he out with Brishen? Something's not right."

"That's why we should burn them," Cam insisted. "I know you've claimed Bethan, Silas, but this is too much."

Silas hissed like a rabid raccoon, and that small sound was enough to make my hand clamp down on the knife hilt. I could picture his sneer in my head—the curled lip, the pinched brows, the narrowed black eyes. All I wanted to do was run around the corner and plunge my knife into his heart, to terrify him the way he'd terrified me and Martyn, but that would resolve nothing. I had to remain calm and quiet despite my trembling body.

"You're such a woman sometimes, Cam. Brishen is strong. The drabarni looks like a wind would knock her over. And we have yet to witness her magic, remember."

"*We* haven't, but *others* have. You're going to get us killed, Silas. Banished or killed, and I'm not sure which is worse. You may not believe the old woman has power, but my mother says she saw the hag freeze a lake solid once to punish a fisherman for cheating us. My mother—" Cam's voice was cut off with a shout.

The vardo rocked before me, the furniture and trinkets inside hissing and thudding as they skidded around. Something heavy had been slammed into the vardo's side. Judging by all the grunting and squabbling that followed, I had to assume it was Cam's body.

"Don't feed me your superstitious nonsense, or I will pound you into the earth," Silas barked.

"Do not think being the chieftain's spit makes you immortal!" Cam yelled. "We have to strike first. How you can't see that with Brishen missing is—"

The violence escalated. I backed away from the vardo in case it went sprawling onto its side with the rocking. I could hear Mander trying to calm his friends, telling them to stop turning on each other, but he was ignored.

"You dare lay your hands on me?" Silas shouted. "The chieftain's son? You dare?"

"Yes, I dare. We followed you to that field, we did what you asked us to do, and you repay our loyalty by refusing to see the threat before your nose? You may as well hand us to the drabarni trussed up like roasted pigs on platters. Not all of us can hide behind our fathers, Silas. I warned you about touching that girl before we got to the field. I told you it was foolish, that it wouldn't get you what you want, but you didn't listen. Now you're making us pay for your stupidity."

There were so many things I wanted to ask Cam. Why did he let Silas touch me if he knew it was wrong? Why hadn't he told him to stop? Why had he stared at me with his cold wolf eyes and pretended none of it mattered? He had a baby sister— would he have allowed something like that to happen to her?

I wrapped my arms around my knees and buried my face in my skirt, my teeth clenched on my tongue so I wouldn't scream.

"If you were so afraid of the drabarni, why didn't you go

see her when Tomašis did?" Silas taunted. "She gave you the chance. Why not give her an eye, too?"

"Because you told us not to, you son of a dog, and now it's too late! Someone has to do something. I will."

"If you dare hurt what's mine, you and your family will suffer the consequence," Silas warned. "Think long and hard before you cross me!"

Cam didn't answer. I wasn't sure why until I heard Mander calling for him, pleading for him to come back.

"Cam, stop walking!" Mander shouted. "Don't do this. Don't throw our friendship away!"

"You'd best decide whose *friend* you want to be, Mander— his or mine," Silas said grimly. "I'm finished with him. I'm going to talk to my father before Cam makes anything worse."

Grass crackled as Silas stomped off in a huff.

"Silas. Wait, I . . . Hell." Mander cursed in exasperation. I heard him hurl another glob of spit before stomping up the steps of his vardo, the door slamming behind him.

I rounded the corner, the swish of my skirts forcing the fog to swirl away from the ground, and spied his tobacco spit cup nestled in the grass beside his door. I paused. Laced with leaf or not, saliva had to be as good as hair for the purposes of ritual. It came from the body, and there was certainly plenty of it present.

I wrapped the red shawl around my fingers and collected the cup before lunging back into the fog and shadows, retracing my steps home. I paused at every new corner to listen for nearby people, afraid I'd encounter Silas or Cam. They were both threats to me, but for totally different reasons: Silas wanted me; Cam wanted to burn me alive.

Neither was welcome.

I let myself into Gran's vardo, the cup in my grip, the knife clean and ready to be put to rest.

"I washed the dishes myself. You do not need to return to the fire," Gran said in greeting, without turning from her task.

She was writing on our walls with white chalk, concentrating her efforts near the door and windows. She'd written letters above, below, and on either side of the frames to box them in. A line extended across the floor, too, as if she were creating a magical barrier.

"These are our words," she explained without turning around. "They're special—they beseech fire. We got them from the Scottish witches. If you learn to read one day, there are many books about the cultures beyond our own. The world is a very big place, Bethan. Our displacement exposes us to many people."

I left the spit cup on the table and put the knife in the bureau drawer, alongside the mirror that still held Martyn's image.

"Letters can help against fire?"

"It is the same as spellcraft—only useful if it helps me channel my will. In that, it will perform its function."

"I see," I said, more to myself than her. "I overheard the boys arguing outside Mander's vardo. Cam feels like his only chance against us is to go on the offensive. He's talking of burning us still."

Gran snorted. "He has no chance."

"I know that, and you know that. I think he knows it, too, but he's desperate." I nudged the cup across the table to her. Her curt nod was enough to tell me that the saliva was useful for our purposes, and I pulled off my scarf and shawl, my fingers slipping the pins from my hair. Some locks had come loose thanks to the wet fog, and I didn't like the way the ends felt brushing against my neck.

Gran put her chalk aside to finger the dwayberry cutting she'd taken down earlier, pinching one of its fruits between her thumb and forefinger. "It is best if we wait until tomorrow to make the dream. It is not complicated, but it requires much focus. You need sleep to be strong," she said.

I wasn't particularly tired, but if Mander struggled against me, I ought to be well rested.

While Gran put the herb back on its hook overhead and closed the shutters to block the night, I assembled my makeshift bed, doubling up on blankets so I wouldn't freeze. My gaze drifted to the patchwork shroud covering Martyn's still body. I'd been so addled after my assault and so exhausted after my first experiences with magic that it hadn't bothered me to sleep beside Martyn's body the last two nights. Now that I was more clear-headed, I was fully aware that Martyn was all but dead two feet away. If he had been truly dead, it would be unclean to be so near to him, and I wasn't sure if that made me afraid or disgusted.

I only knew that our magic had to succeed. If it didn't, surely a man who had died under such circumstances would return as an angry spirit.

I helped Gran into her bed and then climbed into my own nest. After a bit of twisting and turning, sleep came, but a loud clap woke me. I reared up in the darkness, clutching my blankets to my chest, listening as a series of smacks rattled the door.

I started to get up, but Gran growled, "Wait," and I went

185

still, my heart thudding in my throat. The shaking continued—something I quickly figured out was a hammer striking wood—and then someone pounded on our shutters. The wood groaned in strain, and there was another slam. The leftmost window exploded open under heavy impact.

I screeched as splinters of wood pelted me in the darkness, forcing me to huddle down and cover my head.

Torches sailed through the open window and my world went up in flames.

CHAPTER TWENTY-ONE

The torches struck the vardo floor with wet plops, the ends saturated with lantern oil. Flames spread like rippling orange water, the cold in the wagon consumed by a pulsing, searing heat. I could hardly bear it. I clambered to the wall, tangy smoke filling my nostrils and burning my eyes. One torch hit the table, one hit the floor, and another landed on the blanket covering Martyn.

Neither Gran nor I could do a thing for a body burned to ash.

I crawled toward the door, thinking to kick it out, but Gran's scream stopped me in the middle of the vardo. The sound was earsplitting and primal, and for a horrible moment I thought I was listening to her death throes, but then I saw her behind the flames, her hands raised to the roof, her eyes blazing gold like she, too, burned from the inside out.

She stooped low, her hands stretching for the fire gorging itself on Martyn's blanket. "Come," she said, and it leapt off Martyn to engulf her to her wrists. She should have been in agony; she should have been writhing and screaming and blistering; but no—she tilted her head back and laughed. I stumbled back. I was afraid of the fire, afraid of the woman wielding it with such obvious delight. Gran crooned to the flames like they were her beloved. She beckoned them, beseeched them to bend to her will. They were charmed, like snakes in a basket before a pipe player, and they flickered over her extended arms, no longer interested in consuming our modest home.

"The door, Bethan," she said. Fire snapped and hissed from her fingertips to her shoulders.

I scrambled across the floor to wriggle the latch and found the metal cool despite the heat surging around me. It didn't budge. Climbing to my feet, I shoved the wood with my shoulder, every collision of my body against the hard surface a small agony thanks to Mander's beating. Still it didn't move.

"Let me." Gran approached, her face serene, her arms blazing like torches. As soon as I stepped aside, she pressed her palms to the wood. The flames lashed out to steal an illicit taste, their golden hues brightening to star white. The door quivered and then it smoldered, new smoke billowing forth. I crouched low to avoid breathing it in, thrusting my arm across my mouth in an effort to protect my lungs. I didn't have to endure it for long; soon the door and the boards nailed to it crumbled to ash, the metal hinges and latch plummeting to the tall grass below. The smoke was sucked away on a passing breeze.

"My cane, Bethan," Gran commanded. "And I will need

your elbow. It is time to teach the boy his manners." I was about to ask how she'd manage an oak staff given her condition, but my question answered itself when the fire that had engulfed her shrank to a fraction of its size. A tiny flame no bigger than a candle head danced upon her palm. It flitted between her fingers, playful, like it couldn't wait for whatever fun she had planned next.

I helped her down the steps and onto the ground. She pointed behind us, at the fresh, gaping gash in the vardo front. "Bring your knife. You will need it. And Wen best have someone who can put up a door tonight. It is too cold to go without." I dashed inside, covering my hair with my scarf and retrieving both the knife and the red shawl. I snagged her a shawl, too, but she waved it off when I presented it. "I bear flame. I am plenty warm."

We pressed on to the bonfire, nearly colliding with the chieftain as we crested the benches. He looked startled to see us, as did Silas, who was on his father's heels. We were face to face for the first time since he had attacked me, and our gazes locked. With his hands stuffed casually into his pockets, Silas tilted his head to regard me, his oily smile making my skin crawl.

My anger was fast to rise. I stepped forward, already reaching for my knife, but Gran snagged the hem of my shawl and hauled me back.

"Silas said Cam meant trouble. He was concerned," the chieftain said, his big hand rubbing at his beard. His eyes swept from Silas to me and over to Gran. "We were coming to check on you."

Gran opened her hand to show off her flame, and let it grow

to a torch-sized fire on her palm. "Had we relied on your charity, we would have burned alive. Would that have worried you, Silas? It is your crime that saw us lit aflame in the first place, was it not? Tick tock. Tick tock. Your time runs short. If this fire were not aimed at its maker, I would enjoy burning you to cinders."

Silas scampered back, his backside smacking against a feasting table. At last he had proof of Gran's magic, and a tangible dread crept across his face, and I wanted to relish the rapid rise and fall of his chest, to revel in his fear, but I couldn't. My numbness was being consumed by anger, and there wasn't room for anything else, even satisfaction.

Silas glanced at his father like he expected him to intervene, but the chieftain just stared at his dull, scratched boots. Silas's confusion gave way to irritation, and he jerked his chin up, his nostrils flaring like a bull ready to charge. It was bravado—he couldn't look Gran in the eye and his pulse jumped in his throat—but he fought valiantly for the appearance of calm.

"I don't wish for there to be problems between our families, drabarni," Silas said. "I was extending a civility, from the chieftain's family to your own."

"'Civility,' he says. Do you want to see my civility, reptile?" Gran lifted her hand to her mouth and blew on the dancing flame. Fire snapped out like a molten whip, biting at Silas's face. He squawked and dove for the ground, and Gran blasted another fiery lash at his head. It scorched the grass beside his ear and dug a tiny smoking ravine in the hard-packed earth inches from his body.

Silas pushed himself up and ran off without another word, the night pulling him into its inky embrace. I could hear his boots pounding across the ground long after I could see his retreating back.

The chieftain looked after his son, and his left eye twitched with strain. Gran jabbed his leg with her cane. "Do not be stupid, Wen. He is Bethan's to do with as she pleases. There is nothing you can do that will not cost you. Now send somebody to repair my door while I am out. I have a firebug to catch." To illustrate her point, she waved the fire beneath his chin. The chieftain skittered back, his hand clutching the lapel of his green jacket defensively.

"Of course. Good night, Drina. Bethan." He lumbered off in the direction of his wayward son. I didn't need Gran's second sight to know he was still trying to figure out a way to save his boy, a way to buy our mercy.

But mercy was not an infinite resource, and for Silas, that well had long ago run dry.

Gran offered me her elbow, and I hooked my arm through hers. I wasn't sure where Cam lived—there were enough traveling with the clan that I couldn't keep track of everyone after the seasonal moves—but a cacophony from the east side beckoned us. We hurried along to the last row, where we discovered every lantern lit and every set of eyes peering out of their homes. All were watching a faded red vardo with open windows. Inside, I could see Cam's father, Marko, pacing back and forth. His fingers raked through the dark hair at his temples.

Behind him, Cam's mother and baby sister cried.

"I had to, Papa," I heard Cam say. "It was me or them, and I picked me."

That was his mistake. Had he simply come the day before, had he allowed me to take my due, he might have walked away with his life. It may not have been as happy, removed from the family as he would have been, but at least there would have been other sunrises to see.

That wasn't an option anymore.

"It is time, Cam!" Gran called, her voice carrying on the wind. "You baited your hook, and the fish are hungry."

Cam thrust the curtain aside. Seeing Gran there with fire on her palm and fog closing around her like she'd stepped out of a dream, he slammed the shutters closed. There was a thud, a crash, glass breaking, and a baby's cry. Panicked voices became panicked screams. Then the door swung open. Cam emerged with his tiny sister in his arms.

"No, Cam. NO!" Cam's mother, Myri, lurched after him, grabbing for his shirt, but Cam shoved her back inside, the squalling infant clutched to his chest. His father bumbled down the vardo steps after him, but he'd been injured. Blood streamed down his temple from a jagged wound that hadn't been there moments ago.

"She's your sister, Cam. Your sister," his mother sobbed, but Cam ignored her, too busy eyeballing Gran and me. He pulled a spring knife from his pocket, opening it and pointing the blade at the terrified baby's neck. She balled her fists in his shirt and wailed, not knowing why she'd been torn away from her mother.

"Back away, all of you, or I'll kill her. So help me, I will kill her." I wasn't sure if I believed him or not. He jostled the baby up and down to calm her—an oddly soothing gesture, given his threat.

Gran pointed her craggy finger in the baby's direction. "What is that child's name?" she asked me.

"Lillai," I croaked. "Her name is Lillai."

The baby bellowed again, and Cam shouted at her to shut up, bouncing her so hard that I thought she'd slip from his fingers.

"What's going on here?" I heard someone ask.

"Cam's threatening his sister!" someone else answered.

I looked around. Seeing Cam's knife pointed at the baby, the voyeurs' curiosity about the ruckus had turned to anger. People emerged from their tents and vardos in their nightclothes with gardening hoes, shovels, and smithing hammers to intervene. Voices called for Cam to do the right thing and put the baby down, but he only snarled like a rabid animal.

"Back, all of you. Back!" he screamed, and in his panic, the knife slipped. The baby shrieked, and a small splotch of blood appeared at the shoulder of her nightgown. Marko saw it, too, and he let out a roar as he charged his eldest child.

Cam scrambled back to avoid a tackle, but others were jabbing at his back with their makeshift weapons, condemning his atrocities. Cam slashed blindly at the air with the blade, and I could tell by the panic on his face that the situation would only worsen. Even if Cam hadn't actually wanted to hurt her, with so many people encroaching, the baby was well and truly in danger.

Gran must have come to the same conclusion. She raised her hand over her head, her fire surging to the night sky. "Back away from the boy!" she bellowed. Everyone listened, either because she was an elder and drabarni or because her power terrified them. The circle surrounding Cam widened, but the men still stood shoulder to shoulder facing him, their weapons at the ready, blocking any hope of escape.

"I'm going to go. I'll leave the caravan like Brishen. I'll leave Lillai at the fence. Just get away from me," he croaked.

"Lillai. Lillai. Lillai," Gran murmured, as if savoring the name on her tongue. "Lillai, child of Marko, is blessed by flame."

"What?" Cam pressed his sister's face into his neck, bouncing her again in a vain attempt to quiet her so he could hear Gran's words.

"It will embrace her as it has embraced me," Gran continued. "Lillai shall not burn, she shall have no fear of this fire, for it is friend to her and friend to me."

"I said I'm going to leave . . ."

Gran screeched to the heavens and the fire answered in kind, roaring as it leapt from her hand and onto Cam's body. I'd never seen anything like it. The flames were a savage beast, and they feasted on him—his clothes, his skin, his flesh. His once-fair skin puckered and turned black. His brows and lashes burned away, and his wolf-gray eyes seared shut forever. He thrashed, screaming in agony, staggering as if he could escape, but there was nowhere to go. The fire wanted him, and him alone, and it didn't stop rampaging until he fell to the ground, thudding like the torches he'd thrown onto our vardo floor.

My heart hammered in my chest. My blood raced through my veins. I was afraid, but of what? Gran? The magic? Both? The air stank of scorched meat and burned hair, and the black smoke was even thicker than the night's fog. Gran was close enough to me that I could see her beckoning, but it wasn't me she called, but her fire. It returned to her hand with a hiss, the blaze shrinking enough to shimmy upon her palm.

"Rest well, my old friend. Until we meet again," she whispered. The fire flared one last time, bright and brilliant like the sun, then winked away as if it'd never been there at all. Her eyes met mine over the coil of lingering smoke.

It was a challenge. It was a promise.

I wasn't ready for either.

CHAPTER TWENTY-TWO

Inside the billowing smoke, an infant whimpered. Lillai was alive despite the inferno, and her parents shrieked their relief. They'd lost a son already—an unfathomable cruelty. To have to burn the possessions of two children in their mourning would have been Hell itself.

A strange wind stirred, harsh and foreign on such a still, foggy night. I glanced Gran's way and noticed her whispering under her breath. She was calling the gales as she'd called them the night of the blood moon. Then it had been a tool to terrify. Now the wind revealed terror, but also mercy. With the smoke blown away, we could see one well child and one very dead one.

Cam looked like he'd been sculpted from soot. His body was blackened from head to toe, what was left of his face forever contorted in a scream. Clutched in his arms was a baby. Not only had Lillai been spared the worst of the flame, her white nightgown was free of ash. She was as whole as she'd been before the ordeal, save for Cam's nick to her shoulder.

Cam's parents collapsed beside their children. Myri pried Lillai from Cam's arms and clutched her to her chest as Marko wept over his son's body. Cam had been a murderous bastard—nearly twice so with the vardo fire—but at one time he'd been Marko's greatest joy. Eldest boys were prized among the clan.

Gran nudged me with her cane. "Take an ear and leave them to their grief."

"Now?" I looked around. Not only did we have an audience surrounding us, but Marko and Myri's grief was palpable. Desecrating Cam's corpse in front of them felt irreverent and wrong.

Gran didn't see it that way, or she just didn't care. She shoved me at them, her hand on the small of my back. I stumbled forward, but I stopped.

"I *can't*," I snarled at her over my shoulder. I never would have dared such insubordination before the blood moon, but I'd grown brazen since.

She didn't seem to care about that either, peering at me from beneath her brows, her hands resting comfortably on her cane. "Do not go soft, Bethan. We are too far along. A third piece of five brings us closer to your diddicoy's return."

The reminder of why I'd agreed to these horrors in the first place was enough to spur me on, though I resented her for it with my whole heart. I edged toward Marko, the knife at my side cocked and ready. He lifted his face to me, and I tried to ignore the tears running down his cheeks.

"One thing. A small thing, and then you can put him to

ground," I said. I leaned forward, poising the blade above Cam's black, shriveled ear. I kept expecting Marko to stop me, but he eased away to gather his weeping wife into his arms. The two of them turned their backs to me, shielding Lillai from my odious chore.

I knew then that they would likely never look upon me with kindness again. I was as good as dead to them, and forever unclean. They would not be the only ones, either; there were more than twenty pairs of eyes upon me. Still, no one uttered a word as I sawed the ear from Cam's head. I'd forgotten the gloves, so I had to touch it. The severed piece was a revolting texture, a cross between a gooey date and a piece of leather, and I wrapped it in my shawl as I hurried back to Gran's side.

For the first time since we'd started our dark business, I felt true fear. Fear that I'd damned myself for eternity, fear that my people would never accept me. But we'd come too far for me to abandon Martyn. We needed only two more tithes and he'd be restored. One more day and we could bring him back. I could hold it together until then.

I *had* to hold it together until then, for his sake.

Gran hooked her hand under my elbow and guided me away from the scene as our people floated to their homes like silent ghosts. We rounded our corner right as the elder Mikel was hammering an ill-fitting door onto the front of our vardo. Harvesting Cam hadn't taken very long, but the chieftain had wasted no time assisting us. He probably hoped it would buy him favor with Gran.

"Drabarni. Bethan," Mikel said, bowing his head in

respect, but his smile never reached his eyes. He'd probably heard about Cam.

Or Tomašis. Or Brishen.

"Mikel. God bless you for fixing our door."

"It's temporary, I'm afraid. There'll be a draft tonight, but I will send one of my sons over to right it in the morning." He gathered his tools and turned to go.

"No, not tomorrow. The day after," Gran called. "We will be too busy for distractions tomorrow."

Either Mikel didn't understand Gran's subtext or he chose to ignore it. He sketched a bow that would have done a courtly gentleman proud, his hammer cocked to the side like a royal scepter. "Of course. Good night, ladies." He retrieved his can of nails and strode off into the sweeping fog.

Gran waited for me to light the oil lantern and eyed the wooden frame. The door was crooked enough that I could wedge at least three fingers through the widest gap. "Of all the people to send, they send that one, the old buffoon."

She sighed and returned her cane to the bucket by the door. "Your diddicoy looks well, outside of some smoky feet. That is good. Now you must prepare Mander's cantrip so you can deliver the living dream before dawn. I thought we would have the full three days to complete our preparations, but I trust neither Wen nor the remaining boys. They will run. Of that, I am sure." Gran pulled the dwayberry sprig and the tangle of dream yarns from the ceiling. She slid them before me along with Thomson's straw pieces and Mander's spit cup. "Tether everything together with a nightmare-drenched thread. It will make strong magic."

She unwove a red yarn from the rainbow of colors, snapping two feet off and spooling it on the table. I glanced at the spit cup and frowned. It was black and sludgy with spent tobacco, and I didn't want to touch it. Sensing my reluctance, Gran tsked and offered me a bristle brush with a wooden handle.

"You are so squeamish. Tie the straw to the nightshade. When it is bundled, brush Mander's saliva over it. We will need one drop of blood to bind it to you so you may see what Mander sees, to share in his nightmare without suffering the affliction."

I assembled everything as she'd instructed, making sure to fashion a handle out of the excess yarn so I could carry the totem without having to touch any spit. "Will anyone else see it? Thomson, I mean?"

"No, only you and Mander. You must work hard for this, Bethan. Concentrate on the scarecrow's finer details—what it looked like, what it smelled like. The more Mander believes in the vision, the stronger it becomes. I knew a Welsh witch who conjured dreams so potent, they were tactile and had scents. She taught me that the key to this enchantment is strong imagination."

"If I'm concentrating on willing Thomson to life, how can I take my tithe from Mander? Won't my distraction weaken the vision?"

She grinned at me, wide enough that I could see the chipped canine on the right side of her mouth. "The beauty of this spell is that once you milk Mander for his terror, his fear fuels the effect. While he is crippled, you can will the scarecrow to do your bidding—to hold Mander still so you can work."

"I understand," I said, though I wasn't thrilled with the scenario. It felt like a lot could go wrong, like it was less certain than the roots. If the vision wasn't strong enough, Mander wouldn't be afraid, and if he wasn't afraid, he wouldn't hold still so I could harvest the fingers.

I glanced down at Martyn's still form.

What choice do I have?

I dipped the brush into the tobacco cup and coated the nightshade. I took my time with the berries and papery flowers, ensuring that every part was saturated. I painted the straw last, and lifted the charm off the table to inspect it. The bundle swayed back and forth like a pendulum. Gran took it from me to give it her own examination, flicking it with the tip of her long fingernail.

"Good." She nodded. "Now your blood." She reached for me and I braced for another brutal slice, but instead, she pulled a sewing needle from her basket and poked it into the side of my knuckle. It was gentle compared to my previous bleedings. "Just a drop," she said, rotating my finger and aiming the flow at the nightshade. Blood splashed down on the leaves before attaching to the fibrous yarn and staining it dark. "That is enough. If Silas's ritual requires blood price, I will provide it myself. I do not want to overtax your body."

She'd never alluded to the plan for Silas before, and I found myself hungry for details. I wanted to hurt him. The rest of the boys had been fodder—they'd been donors to the spell that would restore Martyn's life. Cam's loss was unfortunate, but we'd only reaped what he'd sown. With Silas, a sick part of me wanted to even the score. *"An eye for an eye and the whole world goes blind,"* Gran once said to me, but for Silas, I was willing to accept that consequence.

Perhaps hurting him would lessen my own hurt.

"What plans do we have for Silas?" I asked, leaning across the table.

"Mander first, Bethan. I do not want you distracted when you conjure the vision. For now, it is time for sleep. Dawn comes quick."

I sulked, but Gran paid me no heed. She put away our ritual supplies and hung the nightmare charm from a hook to let it dry. I crawled beneath my cold blankets, hoping my natural heat would be enough to keep the chill at bay. Behind me, Gran hung an afghan over the door and blew out the lantern. I could hear her shuffling back to her bed in the dark.

I fell asleep with chattering teeth, and when I woke hours later, it was even colder. Gran was awake already, humming. Her speaking voice was all rocks and razors, but her voice softened when she sang. It was still throaty, but there was a sweet trill to her high notes and a soothing vibrato to the low ones that made her pleasant to listen to.

It wasn't even close to dawn yet, but warm light spilled through the vardo from a half dozen beeswax candles she'd lit upon the table. Normally she preferred oil lamps, but by the placement of the honeycomb pillars and the wooden collection plates beneath them, I had to assume there was a reason for her choice, but I was too tired to ask what it might be.

I rubbed the sleep from my eyes and pushed myself to my feet. My gaze followed Gran, and I wondered if she'd slept at all. She looked no worse for the wear, though; she was hunched over a swath of dark fabric, her sewing needle flashing as she stitched something into it. A fresh bandage encased her hand, matching my own.

"There is fog still—good atmosphere for your visit with Mander. I have a chore for you along the way, though," she said. "It should be quick."

I danced around on one foot as I pulled on one of my boots. The previous night's smoke had polluted my hair, but there wasn't much I could do about it beyond rubbing in a sprinkle of Gran's talc. The stench of Cam's fire would linger until the vardo and I both had a good airing out. "What is it?"

"Wen's hat." Gran lifted it up to show me, giving it a good shake to puff out the top to a proper muffin shape. "Leave it on his vardo step on your way to see Mander." It hadn't occurred to me until then that the chieftain hadn't worn his hat since the blood moon. It was his favorite—he rarely took it off—and yet he'd been bareheaded for two days. I'd assumed he'd left it in the wheat field, where it had fallen off, but Gran must have snagged it. I wasn't sure why she had repaired it for him. They were friends, yes, but her courtesy went above and beyond the usual.

"Why did you—"

"That is my business," she said, cutting me off. Gran motioned at the stack of linen beside the washbasins. "Take one of the older aprons. Yesterday's is unsalvageable."

I chose a dark-blue apron that tied off around the neck and waist, faded flower embroidery decorating the neckline and the edging of the big pocket. It was far too festive for its business, but I didn't want to ruin one of the better ones. I snagged my cat fetish, the chieftain's hat, and the spit-covered totem with the strange tobacco odor. I was reaching for the knife when Gran motioned at me to wait. She pulled open the bureau drawer and rummaged around until she found a black steel hatchet. She offered it to me handle first.

"To take Mander's fingers. Two ought to do. Silas can be the nose when it is his turn."

"He has cut it off to spite his face enough," I said. "It seems apt."

Gran nodded and pushed herself up from the table to pull the afghan aside for me. "Be thorough. Be efficient. Most of all, be safe."

I dropped the hatchet into the apron pocket and pushed past her. Before I got down the steps, Gran clapped a hand on my shoulder. I glanced back at her, and she leaned toward me to wrap a shawl around my body.

"Do not forget to leave the hat, and when you get to Mander, lure him out of his vardo. His parents ought not to be involved. They will not be able to see what he sees, and it will confuse them. Also, destroy the bundle after you are finished with the nightmare. That is imperative."

"Why?"

"Because a nightmare is never a static thing. It is the same with all dreams, yes? It is their nature to change when you least expect them to. If you are not careful, the scarecrow could grow beyond your control. I would not have you a victim of your own conjuring."

I didn't want to consider what an unchecked Thomson could do. If destroying the totem meant I could spare myself that vision, I'd tear it into three thousand pieces. "I understand, Gran."

Gran looped an arm around my neck and pulled me down to press a dry kiss to the top of my head. "Of course you understand. You are mine. The secret to magic is not the words but the steel of your will. And you, my daughter, are proving to be ironclad."

CHAPTER TWENTY-THREE

Standing outside Mander's tent in the early dawn, fog swirling around me, a cat figurine clasped in one hand and a nightmare bundle in the other, I wished I had more of the steel Gran talked about. Many things depended on me getting the living dream right, but I had so little information. *"Strong imagination,"* Gran had said. I supposed it was simply another exercise in channeling my will, but her instructions were even vaguer than they'd been with the roots I used for Brishen.

I didn't like so much guessing.

I closed my eyes, sucking in the cold, wet air to quell my pounding heart. It was time to conjure a nightmare.

I lifted my hands and pressed my palms together, weaving my fingers. The yarn of the totem hung against the wood of the cat fetish. I breathed deeply, searching for that still place where magic was born.

The early-morning quiet made it easy to fall into the lull—the only sounds were the creaking of a shifting vardo, the gentle shiver of wind on Mander's window, and the trill of a hungry farm cat. I dropped my head, my chin touching my chest, and pictured Thomson as I'd first seen him. I remembered the grim, red-yarned mouth and the black-stitched eyes. Tufts of straw speared his floppy hat, and his burlap-sack head was tied off by a cord of fraying rope. Huge arms, huge legs, and patch-riddled overalls.

"Live for me. Be real, Thomson. Be real. I need you to be real," I whispered. It became a mantra, imploring the scarecrow to rise from the tattered straw pieces twined around the dwayberry.

"Come to me. Help me, Thomson; please be real," I pleaded.

My other spells built in intensity over time, but the living dream flared right away. The first thing I felt was a pulse beneath the skin. My eyes flew open as the flesh on my hands rippled, like something pushed at it from the inside. Then there was the heat. Warm became hot, and hot became agony. Blisters peppered my fingers and palms. A fat blister in the webbing between my thumb and forefinger burst open to seep fluid down my wrist. I gasped and clutched the cantrip, terrified dropping it would weaken the spell, but how it hurt! Tears rained down my cheeks as my skin boiled.

I was in so much pain that I almost didn't see the green cloud. It spawned some feet away, massive and quickly expanding, its center contracting to the rhythm of my slamming heart. I stumbled back, my fear rising as the cloud grew wider and taller. The initial shape was a mishmash of lumps and hills, but the longer I stared, the more defined it became, until I could discern a head, arms, and legs. There was the tilt of a hat, and a spray of straw fanning out around the neck like a lion's mane.

Thomson had come.

The magic flared hot one last time, and I groaned before it dulled to a more bearable thrum. The blisters receded into my flesh. The yarn stopped trying to burn its way through my palm.

I smelled freshly cut hay strong in the air. Thomson stood erect before me, his head slumped to the side, his arms straight out from his shoulders like he was still propped on poles. A part of me wanted to poke him to see how solid he was. The rest of me wanted to hide and not ever have to look upon his hideousness again. But there was work to be done.

"Th . . . Thomson?" I called.

The scarecrow jerked his face in my direction, Thomson's jagged yarn mouth curving into a smile, the stitches of his black-patched eyes fixing upon me as he awaited orders.

I glanced at Mander's family's tent. Gran had suggested bringing Mander out instead of sending Thomson in, but how would I do that? Shaking the tent was too brazen, and calling his name might send him running. The best idea I could come up with was to throw pebbles until someone came out to investigate. It was juvenile and unclever, but that didn't stop me from finding a few good-sized stones and tossing them. At first no one stirred, but after the second toss I heard dull, sleepy voices. I darted behind a nearby vardo to hide, watching Mander's door. I thought Thomson would follow me, but he stood in the same place where he'd been conjured, his head rotating all the way around on his shoulders to keep me in his sights.

"Here. To me," I whispered, and the dream lumbered my

way. His straw feet made his movements jerky and off-kilter, each step a lurching lunge propelling him forward. He was horrible to behold, and I forced my attention away so I wouldn't be tempted to flee my own creation.

The voices rose inside Mander's tent, people clearly awake. I hurled another stone. As fate would have it, Mander was the one to poke out his head. He looked exhausted, his hair standing on end as if he'd thrashed in his bed all night. He stifled a yawn and swiveled his head to investigate the disturbance. I lobbed more stones from behind the vardo, hoping he'd follow the sound back to find me.

At first he did nothing, and I thought maybe he expected a trap—a disturbance when there was still darkness to the sky on the heels of his friends' troubles was rather blatant. But apparently he was dumber than I thought, or he was not quite awake, because he bumbled outside a minute later. I tracked his movements by the swishing of his trousers.

Mander paused at the edge of the vardo I hid behind. "Who's there?" he demanded of the morning fog.

When the fog did not answer, he turned the corner. On a normal bright day, he'd have seen me there, crouching, my hand easing the hatchet from my apron, but it was dark and the mists were thick. There was a blanket between us. I pushed myself to my feet, my skirt rustling. He tensed, then stepped back—just one step—toward his tent.

He collided with a big, heavy body. I hadn't commanded Thomson to flank Mander from the other side, yet there he was. Worse, when the fog cleared enough to allow me a glimpse of him, his gloved hand was raised and holding a scythe.

I'd never envisioned Thomson holding a weapon when I'd

made the dream, but he was able and ready to strike Mander down if I wanted him to.

"*A nightmare is never a static thing.*"

This was what Gran had meant. He'd progressed on his own, without my commands, and that was scary.

Mander's face was whiter than porcelain when he turned around. Finding himself face to chest with the scarecrow, he took a step back, his bottom lip quivering like a terrified child's.

Thomson shifted his weight from one straw foot to the other, his stitched eyes rolling my way as if to ask "Now? May I hurt him now?"

Mander panted like an overheating dog. "How? *How are you here?*" he screeched, tripping over a stack of metal pails as he stumbled farther back.

Thomson tottered forward, closing the distance, holding the scythe's rusty curved blade at the ready. Mander lifted his hand as if to ward off a blow. I crept up closer, hatchet poised, hoping he'd put his hand against the vardo side so I could whack at his fingers and take my due, but he didn't comply.

"Thomson's mine," I said, emerging from the fog behind him. "He's here to help me."

Mander jerked his face my way, looking far more unnerved by my presence than that of the shambling scarecrow.

"You owe me, Mander. You owe the diddicoy. I watched you beat him to death," I said.

He opened his mouth to say something but then stopped, his tongue sweeping over his upper lip as he struggled with his words. Because I thought he was going to speak, I didn't anticipate him darting off, but Mander dropped his head and sprinted toward the fence that separated Cotter's Field from the road. I attempted to snag his shirt in my fist, but he was faster than me and twice as scared, and fear was a marvelous fuel. Thomson didn't need me to tell him to follow—the scarecrow tore off after Mander so fast, he was a blur. I lifted the hem of my skirt to give chase. I'd witnessed Thomson's ambling, jerky gait already, but he seemed to be skimming over the earth in his pursuit, as if the fog had become his personal ferry.

Mander vaulted the perimeter fencing, and I heard his boots skittering across the gravel road as he ran in the direction of Anwen's Crossing. Thomson slashed at the boy's back with his scythe, never quite making contact.

I wasn't sure if Mander *could* be hurt by the scarecrow's weapon. Thomson was made of ether and will, a creature born of fog, and though he looked dangerous, I didn't know if he could actually affect the world around him or if he was limited to his illusion state.

Time would tell.

I approached the fence. I'd fallen behind and the gap was increasing by the second. There was no way I could catch Mander on the main road, so I cut through the wheat fields to intersect him at the curve. I slithered over the top rung and then ran for the fence on the opposite side. The wheat field was slippery with dew and the stalks were high, but I forced my way through the crop, my hatchet hacking at anything barring my path.

The sky had brightened to a silvery blue, and a stripe of gold kissed the rim of the world. There was enough light now that I was able to avoid most of the rocky, uneven dips marring the field. My legs grew sore from pushing them hard, but I knew if I kept going, I could head Mander off at the pass.

Letting him escape into town wasn't an option—I wouldn't allow myself to fail so close to bringing Martyn back.

Not after what I'd been through. Not after what I'd done to my reputation with my clansmen.

I went deeper and deeper still into the field. I was nearing a farmhouse and could see its eaves against the skyline. I wondered if that was the Woodard homestead. Closer to the house, bales of hay lined the fencing, stacked neatly in twos, threes, and fours, and I had to search for a break in them to escape the property. It took a while, but with a little artful maneuvering, I was able to reach the road just in time for Mander to crest the curve ahead.

My breath came in short, cloudy gasps with the autumn chill. My body ached and my hair stuck to the sweat on my neck, but I'd beaten him. I saw Mander coming up the road, and I readied the hatchet and braced for confrontation. He was red-faced and scared, the veins in his temples and neck bulging with strain. Tears dripped down his cheeks and from his chin.

Thomson lunged at his back, scythe still slashing. I was unsettled to see that he'd morphed again in the minutes since I'd last seen him. Not only was he bigger in stature, but his yarn mouth had opened to reveal two rows of glinting fangs. And while before he'd been silent beyond the rustling of his hay, now he'd found his voice, and he crowed with insidious glee.

Mander glimpsed my looming shape against the fog, and his mouth opened in a silent scream.

He sees my true power.

I expected him to skid to a stop in the middle of the road, but with a single glance over his shoulder at the demonic scarecrow, Mander changed his course. He veered toward the wheat field through which I'd come. I ran after him, the hatchet held high above my head, Thomson mirroring my pose from the other side.

Mander climbed onto the top rung of the fence, crouching on his haunches to make a dive for one of the taller stacks of hay. "No!" I shouted, anger swelling in my gut at the possibility of him escaping. He shot me a quick glance, a smirk appearing, even now. He thought he'd outsmarted me, and his hubris overshadowed his fear for a tiny moment.

It would cost him.

He sailed toward the haystack. Thomson roared after him, still riding the fog, but then the strangest thing happened. Thomson stopped and took a step back, going as still as he'd been on the poles at the Woodards' farm. One moment he was a hideous creature intent on murder and destruction, the next he looked docile, cocking his head as if listening to the birds singing their morning songs.

It took me a moment to hear Mander's wet gurgles. He lay prone on top of the haystack, wheezy gasps sounding from his mouth like he was trying to breathe through water. His arms flapped and his eyelids fluttered. I eased toward the break in the wall of hay bales and slipped through to get a better look at him.

I dropped down into the field and turned the corner, only to stop dead. My eyes traveled over the twitching arms. The skewed legs. The lolling head. Some feet before me, beside the looming shape of the dream scarecrow, Mander was impaled on a pitchfork. Two of the prongs pierced his upper chest and arms, the tips thrust through and glinting ruby red.

CHAPTER TWENTY-FOUR

Mander wasn't going anywhere, impaled as he was, and by the labored rattle of his breaths and the gray-tinged pallor of his skin, I knew he was in peril of bleeding out if I didn't get him help. Gran always said fortune aimed to surprise us when we least expected it—I'd worked myself into a dither about having to capture him, and he'd captured himself in a most terrible way.

I left Mander gurgling on the prongs of the pitchfork and turned back to my monster. Thomson stood off to the side, his head at that odd angle, the scythe clenched in his fist. His unnatural gaze was fixed upon me, and his yarn mouth opened and closed as if he were smacking his straw lips together.

I lifted the bundle of dwayberry by its yarn. My earlier reluctance to touch Mander's spit seemed stupid in the face of hacking off his fingers. I gave the dream thread a tug to loosen it. Thomson rustled and sagged in response, his head dipping like he didn't want to watch what I was about to do. It made me inexplicably sad—I'd been scared of him not two minutes ago, yet there I was feeling guilty over a nightmare's ruin while a human boy writhed in pain nearby. I supposed it was because there'd be nothing left of Thomson when I was through. People you still had to account for.

"I'll have Martyn remake you. I promise." It was odd to talk to him. Odder still for him to nod as if he understood. Gran said Thomson would grow out of my control if I didn't finish him. And he'd transformed thrice over in a short time. I took a deep breath and destroyed the bundle.

The last bit of straw was caught in the rippling breeze. It was gentle and warm and more suited to August than October. I could smell hay and apples and freshly turned earth as it ushered the fog away, removing the creeping gray blanket from the ground. There was poetry to it in a way—Thomson was a thing of dreams and he had to end, so the fog ought to end with him. The scarecrow gave one last shimmer before he fell apart, his straw blades scattering like dandelion seeds.

I dropped the shredded cantrip and approached Mander's side. He was limp and quiet, his eyes imploring. Blood drenched the straw beneath him, a dribble of it spilling from the side of his mouth to run down his chin. His arms dangled uselessly at his sides. Most of his body was strewn across the top of the haystack, but the upper third was propped up by the pitchfork's metal prongs. I wasn't sure if pulling it out would do more harm than good, so I left it as it was for the moment.

I retrieved the cat fetish from my pocket, nicking my thumb on the hatchet's edge so I'd bleed. A small slice, barely deep enough to break the skin, but it was enough to smear the gold-painted eyes of my focus.

My blood to Gran's.

Blood calling to blood.

"Gran," I said to the wind, willing it to carry my voice home. "Send someone to the wheat field, near the farmhouse. Mander's had an accident. He'll need attention."

A heartbeat passed before her voice drifted to me on a gust, low and deep and musical. "They will come. Do as you must before they arrive."

I eyed Mander. Though I loathed him for what he'd done to Martyn, the fear on his face was pitiable. He looked young and scared, especially as I wielded the hatchet and reached for his hand.

"This is what you owe me and then it is done. Gran will see you righted, and you will go from the family. You won't come back," I said.

For the first time, I wondered if those words would be said to me one day for the things I'd done to right Silas's wrongs. Gran protected me, but she was old, and would not be around forever.

Are you and Mander so very different?

Do you even know anymore?

My resolve was wavering. As I pressed Mander's limp hand to the side of the hay bale, him too weak to fight, I started to feel sick with guilt. I lifted the hatchet, but self-reproach bubbled up inside me, threatening to shut me down before I harvested what I needed. Strangely, it was Mander's expression that gave me the strength to swing the small ax down.

It was pleading, wide-eyed innocence. The same expression that had been on Martyn's face the night of his beating. Mander had been the one to deliver that beating. It hadn't stirred Mander. Why would it stir me?

My ax connected with the knuckles on his pinky and ring finger and sliced straight through. Mander gurgled in pain as the digits fell from his hand to drop to the ground, into a nest of bloodied hay.

My apron was oddly clean despite the grim scene around me. I slipped it from my neck and wrapped Mander's bleeding stumps with the sash, trying to stifle the flow with a tight tourniquet. I was as Gran had been with Tomašis the night of his eye removal: the butcher, but also the savior.

Can I live with that?

Gran would have looked at Mander with a sense of accomplishment, knowing she'd save Martyn later, but was I enough like her? All I felt looking at him was disgust.

Not at the blood, but at my own actions.

My stomach roiled and clenched, my knees knocked together. What I'd done to Mander was not the act of a good person. What I'd done to Brishen, and the way I'd desecrated Cam's corpse—these were no better. Even if the victims were murderous wastes of human life, my deeds were hideous and punishable before my people. Before God.

For the first time since the attack in the field, I erupted into sobs. Standing in that same field now, holding Mander's limp, bloody hand, tears poured out of me. Every ounce of sadness and anger, every frustration and hurt pummeled me. I mourned Martyn; I mourned my loss of innocence; I mourned having to become the type of person I'd become. I was a catastrophic jumble of emotion. My world crashed around me, and I cried until I was blind and light-headed with the need to breathe. Openly weeping, I collapsed to the ground.

I'd pushed away emotion for so long, now I felt it all.

CHAPTER TWENTY-FIVE

A wind ripped through the field, not gentle like Thomson's summer breeze, but ferocious and angry and holding the bite of winter. I lifted my face to it, letting its strong gusts dry the tears on my cheeks. "Come home, Bethan," it commanded. "The men will collect him."

After I'd composed myself enough to gather Mander's severed fingers in my shawl for transport, I eyed the suffering young man. His breathing was shallow, his skin clammy-looking. I reached out to cup his cheek, patting it as gently as I could, and his eyes flew open. His pupils were enormous inside his irises.

"They're coming for you, to bring you back for healing," I said. It was likely no comfort at all, but it was the best I could offer. I left him there and ambled toward home, keeping to the wheat so I wouldn't encounter any of the Romani. As tired and achy as I was, the field seemed to go on for days, but I pressed on until I came to the fence railing on the other side of Cotter's Field. I passed camp, not pausing to look at the fire to see who might be milling about. My only concern was getting back to Gran and delivering my fleshy burdens.

Arriving at our vardo, I pulled open our ill-fitting door. Inside, Gran had an array of mystical oddities spread out on the table. On one side was the cauldron awaiting Mander's parts. Next to it was the mirror with Martyn's breath trapped inside, and next to that was a black basin filled to the brim with water. Gran sat in her chair on the opposite side of the table, her fingers kneading and pinching at a white blob of wax. She must have collected the drippings from the candles on the table that morning.

"I am sorry to summon you home, but we are short on time. Put the fingers in the pot. I will take care of them when I am done with this." She paused her kneading to look up at me. "Are you faring any better than you were?"

"Barely, but yes." I dropped Mander's digits into the iron cauldron before approaching the washbasins. Lye took care of most of the blood, though my nail beds were stained rusty red. I threw the pink water out the window and changed out the bowl.

When I turned back to Gran, she lifted what she'd been working on from the table so I could see. It was another fetish—this time a skeletal structure of twigs fleshed out by layer upon layer of molded wax. Two legs, two arms, a head—there was even a dangling part to signify maleness, which made me blush. The only incomplete portion was a gap in the middle of its chest where there should have been a heart.

"That's for Silas?" I asked.

"Yes," Gran said. "With it, you can control his body—bring him harm. But we need to get his essence as quickly as possible."

"Why?"

Gran gestured at the black bowl of water, where a faint image danced across the surface. I could see the inside of a vardo, and a young man's back as he hunched over a bed. He was stuffing clothes into a bag, and someone standing behind him was handing him his personal effects. *Silas,* I thought, recognizing his lean, muscular build, though I couldn't discern his face. Which meant the helpful hands were those of his father.

"I sewed a hawk feather to the chieftain's cap. I knew he would try to save his son. We have no time. You must get Silas's hair, his blood, his spit—anything—and when we have it, we will put it inside the chest—"

"We already have his essence," I interrupted. Gran looked quizzical, and I motioned at the heap of clothes from the blood moon. We'd plucked them free of straw, but it seemed they would serve yet another purpose before their fiery demise. "When he . . . After he . . . was done with me . . ." I took a deep breath, feeling my face flush hot at what I was about to say. "His seed is on the skirt. We have his essence."

CHAPTER TWENTY-SIX

Gran shredded the skirt. I tried to do it myself, but the moment my fingers grazed the wool, I started to shake. That dirty, wrinkled heap of clothing was a stark reminder of the worst day of my life. Looking at it spread across the table made my tears well a second time, but Gran laid a hand on my shoulder and gently pushed me aside. She took her shears to it, dismantling it into thin strips with brutal efficiency.

"What is happening in the water?" she asked.

I peered at the scrying bowl, thankful for the distraction. Across the rippling surface, I watched the chieftain pull coins from his pocket and motion at the vardo door. Silas darted around to shove his clothing into a brown sack. "The chieftain has given Silas money. Silas is getting ready to leave."

"Wen is sending him to the Crossing. If the dog makes it

there, he will be on a boat by the afternoon. I need more time to finish this spell."

Anwen's Crossing was a port town, so ships docked at all hours of the day. With full pockets, Silas could find himself a ride to anywhere before the next moonrise. There should have been consolation in knowing that he wanted to leave, but banishment was supposed to come after his punishment, not before. First I needed his nose.

I spared a glance at Martyn's mirror. His image had grown so faint that it was difficult to even see him in the glass anymore. "He's fading. What happens if Silas leaves?"

"That is not an option. He must be delayed until I finish the fetish." She held up a piece of skirt, and I could see the dry, flaky remains of Silas's spend on it. My teeth clenched around my tongue, and I jerked my gaze away.

"What would you suggest I do to keep him here? Tie him to a tree?"

"No. Silas is stronger than you, and you have been worked hard these past few days. Get Tomašis to help you. A strong boy is an asset."

It hadn't occurred to me to involve him, but there was merit to the idea. He was a sheaf of skin over bones, yes, but Tomašis was still hardy with all his lean muscle. I knew firsthand what it was like to try to escape his iron grasp.

Gran lifted the fetish to examine it, and a deep crease furrowed her brow. "Send Tomašis for Silas and then come back to me. Be clear with your instructions so Tomašis cannot wiggle out of doing his duty. I ought to have the charm finished by the time you return. I will have to attend to Mander after, but . . . we will persevere. Do you understand?"

"Yes, Gran. I understand."

"Then go, and be quick."

I wasted no time, the broken vardo door slamming shut behind me. I didn't have the luxury of creeping and skittering my way to Tomašis's tent. Instead, I brazenly strode past the great fire, my head high despite everything I'd done. At least a dozen people were gathered for breakfast, and I could feel the weight of their stares. Some murmured, while others blessed themselves as if warding off evil.

I didn't acknowledge any of them. Within minutes, I was bearing down on Tomašis's tent. Through the open flap, I saw Florica bent over a pile of sewing, her needle flashing in the morning light. I called her name, and she poked her head outside, her expression darkening upon seeing me.

"Bethan."

"I need Tomašis," I said, not bothering with pleasantries. Florica didn't hesitate like she had the last time. She climbed from her tent to meander toward the river, calling her son's name. Tomašis appeared a moment later, looking rumpled from sleep. His hair was mussed, and the top button of his pants was undone. Bare feet, suspenders, a sleeveless white shirt, and a fresh black eye patch completed his morning presentation.

"What do you want?" he barked in greeting.

"You."

"For what?"

"To get Silas for me. To hold him until I'm ready for him."

"No." He turned on his heel like that was the end of the discussion.

The denial surprised me. Here was the boy who'd wept and begged for his life not two days before, yet he had the nerve to openly defy me. I had to wonder if it was loyalty to his friend that made him act that way or the mistaken belief that my ire was preferable to Silas's.

"Tomašis, stop." He ignored me and ducked into his tent, probably to hide behind his fretting mother.

Before he got too far in, I lifted my hand. Gran had said a few times that magic was nothing more than the ability to turn will into action. I'd paid the blood price to bind Tomašis to me, and I had my cat fetish with me, so by all accounts, wanting to punish him for insolence should have been enough to make it happen. I curled my fingers into claws, picturing myself catching Tomašis by the neck and jerking him from the tent. Immediately, my hand throbbed with mystical heat—the spell had caught quickly.

Tomašis bolted upright like I'd nailed a stick to his spine. He squawked as he stumbled from the tent, falling to his knees before me and gasping for air. Florica cried out behind him, but I kept my concentration fixed on her thrashing son. Tomašis's fingers clawed at his neck to try to peel away my grip.

"I need a nose to finish the ritual, Tomašis. You have two choices: stop Silas for me, or donate yours in his place. I know which option I prefer. It should be the one you prefer, too." Tomašis's face washed red as I choked the air from him, but he still managed a frantic nod. I dropped my arm and let the magic wither, giving him a moment to collect himself.

He coughed and staggered to his feet, swaying back and forth. When he looked at me, hatred made his ugly features uglier, but how he felt didn't matter to me. I needed him; he was mine—our relationship did not need to be friendly, just efficient.

"How?" was all he asked. "Where is he?"

"Heading toward Anwen's Crossing. I don't want you to kill him. Find a way to hold him until I can get there."

I looked at the clutter surrounding Florica's tent, hoping to find something Tomašis could use as a makeshift weapon. There was a pair of buckets for laundry, a broken vardo wheel, and a small pile of lumber stacked beside a half-crafted wheelbarrow. Leaning against the pile of lumber was a board about two feet long with a nasty spray of nails sticking out from the tip. I picked it up, hoisting it in my palm to feel the weight. It was heavy, but not cripplingly so, and I offered it to Tomašis nail-side first. He eyed it and then me before taking it in hand, his expression glum.

"Fine. I need boots."

"Hurry up. He's leaving now. And when you have him, figure out a way to restrain him. You're quite good at that, as I recall."

His face twitched at the reminder of the part he'd played in my attack. "Where am I bringing him?"

I considered the question for a moment. Too near camp and Silas could call on his father's support. Too far away, and he'd attract people going in and out of Anwen's Crossing. The last thing I needed was to have to fend off well-intentioned gadjos for the privilege of harvesting the boy who assaulted me.

"Take him back to the scarecrow's posts. You remember where that is, right? Where you dragged me and Martyn to be attacked and crucified?"

Tomašis averted his eyes, a flush creeping over his cheeks. "Fine."

"There's no room for failure, Tomašis. Have him there or—"

"I'll get him there." That was the last he said of it, pulling on his boots and loping toward camp, the board clutched in his fist. I wanted to follow so I could supervise, to ensure that he went after Silas as promised, but I needed to get back to Gran.

Florica prayed behind me. I couldn't be sure if it was for her son's soul or mine.

I turned on my heel to hurry home, hoping Gran had completed the wax doll so I could finish my bloody ordeal. Growing up, I'd dreamed of following in Gran's footsteps—I thought the worst I'd do was treat sick children, deliver babies, or curse someone who behaved poorly. The things Gran had taught me over the last few days proved how ignorant I'd been. I'd maimed and dissected in the name of my craft. I was bloodied to the point I barely recognized myself anymore.

Perhaps seeing Martyn alive again would soothe my conscience. Perhaps his smile would remind me that the violence was retribution, and retribution facilitated the return of a life. . . .

I doubted it, though. I knew in my gut that I no longer wanted to succeed Gran. She'd said I had a talent for magic, and maybe that was true, but if the only way to nurture that talent was to leave a river of mothers' tears in my wake, it wasn't worth it.

I ran all the way to the vardo, my breath coming in short pants, my cheeks burning with exertion. Gran sat at the table with her eyes closed. Her skin looked pale and more leathery than usual, and she swayed like she might collapse. I rushed to her side and knelt, reaching up to her brow to feel for fever. She started like I'd torn her from sleep.

"Are you going to be all right?" I asked, turning her wrist to look at her injuries.

She pulled away with a scowl. "I will be fine. I have to be, as the men are almost here with Mander and he must be doctored. I'm afraid you are on your own with Silas, Bethan."

"But your arm . . ."

"If it still bleeds true when you have taken the last tithe, perhaps I will have you stitch me, but for now you must go."

"But, Gran, I think—"

"I do not care what you think, annoying girl. Go now, before my sacrifice is for nothing." She reached into the pocket of her apron to withdraw the new fetish. She'd sealed the form's chest closed while I was gone, but the wax was translucent enough that I could see through it. There was a piece of my skirt bundled at the center, but Gran had bled on it so much that the gray fabric had turned a muddy brown. The twig skeleton was also much darker than it had been before I'd left, because she'd filled all the hollow space inside the doll with her blood.

"Gran, you shouldn't have. This is too much."

She tutted and lifted her good hand to cup my chin in her palm. Her skin was a little too cold, and her fingers trembled with strain. I'd never seen her so weak.

It scared me, but looking into her face provided some comfort. The cold, calculating gleam in her eyes was as ferocious as ever. Her body quaked like the last autumn leaf on the branch, but I knew the strength inside her would sustain her through the trauma. Gran was simply too hard-willed to die on me yet.

"Want it enough, Bethan," was all she said to me, but I knew the weight behind her words. If I wanted it more than anything, Martyn would live again because I willed it.

It was time.

CHAPTER TWENTY-SEVEN

I ran all the way to the Woodards' field, the knife in one hand, the blood-filled wax doll in the other. I'd rolled the cat figurine and leather gloves into the waistband of my skirt. Between Mander's living dream and the mad race to catch Silas before he could escape, I'd run more that day than I had in years.

By the time I reached the fence outside Thomson's posts, I was breathing so heavily I almost didn't hear the nearby voices. There was a groan, an angry grunt, and a roar from behind the wheat stalks. I scaled the top of the fence to investigate. The moment my feet touched Woodard land, my muscles furled, tension flowing through my body like a river.

"Whoreson!" Silas's voice echoed from the field.

Hearing his voice in this place—the place where *it* had happened—made fear shred my insides. But I was determined to finish what I'd started.

Silas is last. Silas is the hardest yet.

I must persevere.

I pressed on, passing Thomson's deserted posts, tromping through bits of discarded, muddied hay. Wheat rose tall in every direction, but I pushed it aside, forcing it to bend before me.

To my left, I heard the thud and rustle of a struggle. I raised my knife toward it, approaching slowly—I didn't want to leap into anything sight unseen. I was not so naïve that I didn't put it past Tomašis and Silas to hatch an elaborate scheme in my absence—they'd done it before. Tomašis was in my thrall, but the chieftain was indebted to Gran, and he'd betrayed her. It wasn't so far-fetched to think Tomašis would turn on me as well, given the opportunity.

I spotted the spatters of blood first—ruby speckles shining on the wheat like a gruesome trail of breadcrumbs for me to follow. The ground around me was littered with snapped stalks. If it was a setup, it was an elaborate one, and I sincerely doubted either of them could come up with something so clever.

I'd never attributed Silas or Tomašis with much in the way of brains.

I followed the carnage another twenty feet to discover Silas's brown sack abandoned on the ground, his sundries tossed about like rubbish. Tomašis's board was there, too, the nails at the end smeared with blood. The wood was also splattered, so I had to assume Tomašis had managed to hit Silas.

I heard heavy breathing and pushed a cluster of stalks aside, peeking through to see Silas sitting astride Tomašis and glaring down at him. Silas had gouges in his cheek like he'd been raked by a bear. His gray shirt had a plate-sized circle of blood near his shoulder, the tears in the fabric showing the ravaged spot on his upper back where he'd been struck.

Tomašis had wounds of his own. There was a long gouge across his cheek, bisecting the one I'd made to mark his face. A flap of skin dangled from his jawline like he'd been peeled below his ear. He was sticky and red from neck to arms, his suspenders torn off, and a slash in his shirt revealed a series of nasty cuts across his ribs and stomach. The eye patch was gone, too, exposing the angry, swollen gap where his eye used to be.

The two of them wrestled for the dominating stance. Tomašis's hands wrapped around Silas's wrists, the muscles of his arms straining as he squeezed. It took seeing Silas's pocket-knife flashing in the sunlight for me to piece the scene together. Tomašis had struck Silas with the board, and Silas had whirled on him with the knife. Tomašis should have had the upper hand, but somehow Silas managed to turn it around on him. Silas wasn't *as* strong, but he was fast and wily.

"I'll take your other eye for this. You serve a woman now? Is that it?" Silas shouted, lunging down at the boy beneath him. Tomašis groaned and shoved back, but Silas had the advantage—his knee was wedged between Tomašis's legs, pressing hard. The pain of it had turned Tomašis's face purple. Sweat beaded on his temple, and his lips pursed together so tightly that they looked like pasty white worms above his chin.

Silas was so consumed with toppling his opponent that he didn't see me standing there with my wax doll. I fumbled with the knife, putting it in my waistband so I could retrieve the cat fetish. Gran hadn't told me how the doll worked, but I was learning. I needed to call my magic first, to make will into reality, and so I pressed the cat to the wax, imploring both to lend me their power. I pictured Silas's face on the little molded head, and imagined myself controlling his body using the doll.

I expected my hands to go hot as they had with every other spell, but that time there was nothing. It wasn't working. Gran had bled for it and *it wasn't working.*

I peered down at the artifacts in desperation. I wanted sovereignty over Silas—Gran's one instruction had been to *"want it enough,"* and I certainly wanted him to suffer for hurting me. I shook my hands as if I could force the familiar burn to come, but there was no trace of the heat I associated with calling power.

My flailing attracted attention. Both boys jerked their gazes to me. Tomašis looked relieved to see me, but Silas was furious. He rolled off Tomašis with another one of his doglike snarls, his lip curling up to reveal his teeth. He jerked the switchblade out to his side as he advanced on me. I nearly tripped over my own feet to get away from him, still trying to keep my eyes fixed on the doll in my hands.

Work! Work!

Had Gran forgotten something important? I shook it and pictured Silas's face on it again, but it remained dormant, unwilling to bequeath to me its gifts.

Silas stalked my way. He swooped down to grab Tomašis's bloody nail board as he passed it, swinging it back and forth threateningly. I gave the doll another squeeze, but it slept.

Why, why? I asked it, but there was no glimmer of magic.

Silas was too near for comfort, and without my tricks, I wasn't strong enough to fight him off. Physically, I was no match. Before he got close enough to strike me, I fled into the field, my heart slamming against my ribs. This time, the wheat snagged the hem of my skirt like clutching fingers, and some of the tallest stalks were so strong on their roots that they snapped back at me when I pushed against them.

This wasn't how it was supposed to go. I wasn't supposed to be at Silas's mercy again. Tomašis was supposed to have him ready and waiting for me. The magic was supposed to grant me an easy harvest. The only thing that had gone right was that Tomašis had managed to get Silas into the field in the first place. The rest was disastrous.

"Bethan! Come back here. Perhaps we can *work something out.* Bethan, my love!" He singsonged the endearment, so close by.

I hated that he managed to sound like he wanted to kill me and kiss me at the same time. It made my skin crawl, and I swallowed a sob. Focusing only on getting away from Silas, I hadn't kept track of my path. I plunged past one row of wheat only to stumble into another, and now I was lost in a maze, unsure which direction was which. I spun around, my head cocked as I listened for the sound of Silas's footsteps and the rustling of crops to indicate his position, but the wheat formed walls that hid him from my sight.

The wind let out a scream, making the plants around me quiver, and I wanted to hush it. I couldn't hear Silas coming with the rustling, and he'd stopped calling my name. Not knowing his location unnerved me. I pulled the knife from my waistband and tried to sneak along one of the alleys, but each of my steps was echoed by a faint crackling as fallen leaves snapped beneath. The summer was over, the cold had come, and that meant growing things were dying. There was no place I could go where I wouldn't make some kind of noise.

Hopelessly lost, I decided to walk toward the sun. Sooner or later I'd get to a fence. I sidled by another line of crops just as a breeze whizzed past my ear. But it *wasn't* the wind. Silas had been waiting for me on the other side of the row—he'd swung the board at my head and just missed my cheek. I had no idea if it was a scare tactic or if he'd gotten unlucky with his strike, but I wasn't willing to wait to find out. I took off running as fast as my tired legs would carry me.

"Come back here, Bethan. I just want to talk!" Silas shouted behind me. He took another swing at me with the board, a horrible laugh bubbling from his throat.

"No. NO!" I wished Gran were with me then, even under the guise of the wind, but she'd been so weak from crafting the wax doll, and she still had to attend to Mander. She couldn't be in two places at once, nor could she bleed herself into her grave.

It was just me with Silas on my heels, and he clearly enjoyed having me to himself.

"I'm afraid you are on your own."

"Did the others lie down and let you carve them? Did you think I would?"

He swung the nail board again. The nails tangled in the wool of my skirt, and he jerked on it, destroying my balance. I sailed forward, striking the cold earth hard enough that my teeth clenched down on my tongue. I tasted coppery blood in my mouth, some of it slipping past my lips to dribble down my chin. The impact forced me to drop everything I'd been carrying as well: the knife, the cat fetish, and the wax doll scattered to the ground around me.

I wailed as Silas's weight landed on my back, pinning me. I tried to crawl out from under him, but his hand found my hair and he jerked my head back as he had the night of the blood moon. I clawed at the dirt under me until my fingernails broke. I bucked and snarled, feeling more animal than human in my desperation to get away from him. When Silas flashed his shiny pocketknife by my eye, all I could do was writhe. I sobbed and heard the sound echoing through the wheat.

"Feel familiar, Bethan? Are you remembering now that you belong to me?" He ground himself against me to emphasize my vulnerable position.

When I stretched for one of the wheat stalks for purchase, Silas swung his knife down. The blade penetrated skin and fat and muscle, passing through the gap between my arm bones and digging into the hard earth below, staking me to the ground. The pain was excruciating. I screamed over and over, hysteria blinding to anything except the awful burn ransacking me from wrist to shoulder. I reached over, trying to tear the knife from my forearm, but Silas grunted and slapped me upside the ear.

"I don't think so. Maybe I'll use your knife on the other arm. That ought to keep you out of trouble long enough."

His hips undulated lewdly, making it clear what he meant to happen after I was splayed. I let out another scream, and Silas clamped his hand over my mouth to silence me, the other reaching for my abandoned knife.

My bladder twinged with fear. He'd pin me to the ground, use me, and kill me. He'd leave me for the crows, just as he'd promised to do to Martyn.

Martyn. I'd failed him.

It is over. It is done.

A howl blasted from the wheat beside us.

I jerked my head up in time to see Tomašis throwing

himself at Silas. Tomašis hadn't run. He hadn't abandoned me to yet another bout of Silas's cruelty. He'd found us in the field, and he'd followed my screams. He'd come for me without being told he had to.

Tomašis wrestled Silas onto his back and pinned his shoulders to the ground. Freed, I tried to slide the pocketknife from my arm, but it didn't come easily, and I left it alone for fear of opening a wound that wouldn't clot. I clapped my hand over it as best I could to stop it spewing, bright crimson oozing out from between my fingers to cascade over my skin.

The boys rolled around like furious cats beside me, dirt and fallen leaves glued to their clothes. I looked around for my knife, worried that Silas had it still and that he'd use it on Tomašis. For all that Tomašis had wronged me before, he'd come to my aid when he hadn't been asked. He didn't deserve a stab to the gut for learning his lesson.

I crawled across the ground to get to the fallen cat fetish and doll. The magic had been good to me throughout my ordeal, and I wanted to try to invoke it one last time, to see if I could get it to come when I needed it most. If it didn't, Silas would surely come for me when he was done with Tomašis, and weak as I was from my wounds, I didn't stand a chance. The fingers of my right hand were slick with blood from the knife impaled in my wrist, so I had a hard time gripping the smooth wax of Gran's creation. It fumbled from my hand to strike the ground.

Behind me, a snarl, a series of thuds, and another bellow.

I didn't see how Silas had escaped Tomašis. I only felt Silas's weight as he landed on me yet again to drag me down, back to Hell. I collapsed to my knees first, and then, as he wrapped his arms around me in a bear hug, I fell forward, onto my chest, leaving me prone, Gran's wax doll trapped beneath my body. Silas scrambled to get a better hold on me, trying to crawl atop me, but a lucky kick that connected with his chest allowed me to flip over onto my back for the moments he reared away.

It didn't last long. He lunged again.

"Enough of you, witch. Enough of this!" he shouted. I raised my hands to ward him off, protecting my face, and he grabbed the pocketknife in my arm, giving it a hard jerk. The pain bowed my back from the ground and my vision exploded. The wound oozed, drenching me and my clothes and the ground beneath me. I bucked up at him, I rolled and kicked, but no matter where I went, he was there—pinching, scratching, hitting, hurting.

"I'll kill you. I'll kill you!" His fingers manacled my good wrist and pinned it down. I wriggled again, screaming for Tomašis, but it was just me and Silas, alone, and I was losing the fight, especially as Silas reached for the pocketknife again and tore it from my wrist. The bubbling torrent was so dark it looked black.

I was certain I was doomed to fall to the boy who'd ravaged me, who'd stripped me of my innocence and forced me to do heinous things in the name of righting his wrongs, but then something remarkable happened. My blood touched the wax doll. I'd bled so much, it had pooled beneath me, and one touch, one single drop against the wax fetish, quickened the spell. Fire exploded beneath me, a blaze that seared my skin and felt like it would burn me up and leave me a pile of cinder in the wheat.

Of course. Gran's blood, Silas's seed. I needed to tie myself to the ritual somehow. I needed to bleed for it.

And now it's mine.

Ecstatic fury sizzled through my body, a mix of pleasure and pain I'd never before experienced. The burning engulfed me from head to toe. The hand not touched by my birthmark glowed like moonlight. The other was as dark as a starless sky. It was so intense, I screamed—a raw, primal scream, like Gran's at the caravan fire.

Hearing it, Silas lifted his head to stare at me, awe crossing his face. His distracted state allowed me to buck him off, my flailing digging the wax doll into the dirt.

There was a crunch above me and Silas screamed.

I didn't understand at first—Where was the pain coming from? Why was he grunting and swearing and shivering?—but then I noticed that his grip on me had gone slack because one of his arms bent at a wrong angle, like invisible hands had gripped it and snapped it in half. Blood seeped through his shirt, the tear in the fabric above the elbow exposing a raw, jutting bone with jagged edges.

"How? How!" he demanded, his free hand reaching up for my throat and squeezing—but without a second hand, he didn't have the strength to choke me. I wiggled again, bucking and kicking in an effort to force him off me, and there was another snap that promptly birthed another howl.

It's the doll. It's crushed beneath me and it's crushing him.

"Stop. Stop!" Silas shouted, his spittle splashing my face. *Like his spit in the field,* I thought, and it infuriated me. I put both of my hands against his shoulders and shoved as hard as I could, despite the pain in my forearm. He gasped, his pupils stretching big enough to swallow the brown irises. He increased the pressure on my throat, his thumb digging into the soft column and adding another bruise to my museum of injuries.

"No. NO! You will not hurt me anymore," I rasped, flopping down on the doll beneath me, on purpose for the first time. Silas bellowed just before the third crack sounded, his screech ending on a muffled wail. Something was wrong with his face—it looked like a foot pressed down on it, his lips and cheeks spreading as if under a great weight.

His skin reddened. His eyes bulged.

The pressure is mounting.

"Get off me!" I tried to shove him aside, but Silas either didn't listen or *couldn't* listen. He wheezed for air the doll denied him, his red skin darkening to purple. He was suffocating, and with no fight left in him, he grew heavier atop me, his body a dead weight that I was too weak to move by myself.

"You're killing yourself, you fool!"

Is that bad?

Silas was a threat to me. He'd beaten me, he'd assaulted me, and not a minute ago, he had every intention of killing me. If I managed to escape him, take the tip of his nose, and banish him, I couldn't trust that he'd stay away. He wanted me, claimed me as an object that was his, and he would come for me again and again.

Gran had taken Cam's life for far less than Silas's crimes. Could I do the same? Could I simply wait for Silas to be the architect of his own demise? Could I lie there and let the pressure of our bodies steal his last breath?

Yes. Yes, I can.

I was more like Gran than I ever realized.

I peered up into Silas's face and went slack, allowing our

combined weight to finish what he'd started. He trembled. He sweated. I watched the whites of his eyes go red. I watched him twitch and drool, his mouth snapping at the air like a dog hunting bees. He gasped for breath that wasn't there before he shuddered one last time. Silas's panicked gaze met mine. We shared a look—mine dispassionate, his accusing and desperate—before he collapsed atop me, never to move again.

CHAPTER TWENTY-EIGHT

Taking the tip of Silas's nose was easier than I anticipated. Gory, yes, but quick. My knife bit through the soft flesh and severed it with efficiency. I didn't bother with gloves; I already looked like I'd drowned in blood. I'd go downstream and dunk myself and pretend that I wasn't forever mochadi.

Finished, I glanced over at Tomašis. He pushed himself up from the ground, his movements measured and communicating hurt. He'd watched me wriggle out from under Silas's body and then take my tithe, never saying a word. Silas had punched him in the ear during their struggle. It had swelled to an impressive cauliflower already, and would likely be twice as big by morning. It explained how Silas had gotten away from him to attack me again—Tomašis was too disoriented to intervene a second time.

"Did he stab you?" I demanded.

"I . . . I'm fine. No stabbing."

"Good. Then go home and get yourself attended." Tomašis wobbled on his feet, casting a last glance at Silas's form before shambling down the wheat path and out of my sight. He was injured, but it was nothing life-threatening—his mother would be able to patch him up easily enough.

I looked back at Silas's corpse. I willed myself to find some satisfaction in what I'd done. I'd ensured Martyn's revival, and I never had to fear Silas or his cronies again. Silas's things would be burned so his spirit couldn't haunt me. My life was about to improve in many ways. The piece of flesh between my fingers was the physical evidence that I had overcome all of my obstacles.

But there was only despair.

Silas had shattered a part of me that I wasn't sure I'd ever be able to rebuild. Killing him hadn't changed that. I'd spent so much time focusing on Gran's magic over the previous days, I hadn't allowed myself to consider what the assault truly meant. . . .

No, not assault. *Rape.*

I couldn't say such a word aloud. I'd feared censure, feared shame. I'd feared so much for so long. But I had to be honest with myself in my head and my heart. With Silas gone and only Martyn's ritual left to finish, there were no distractions left to protect me from the hideous reality of what had been done to me.

Once more, I thought of what would happen when I returned. For the first time since we'd concocted our bloody vengeance, I was forced to ask myself what I'd do about Martyn if and when he came back to life. I didn't want him touching me—now, or maybe ever. Gran stroking my hair had been enough to make me shudder, and Martyn had always been affectionate and bold. Now, such attentions would turn my stomach.

That didn't mean I wouldn't see him brought back, of course, but it did mean I didn't want his flirtation. I had scrubbed Silas from my body, but I wasn't sure how or when I'd scrub the terrors he wrought from my memory. There were some parts of me the river would never reach.

I have to give myself time.

I pushed myself to my feet, leaving Silas's body to cool upon the ground. It was possible Mr. Woodard would tromp through that particular wheat field on that particular day, but the likelihood was that someone from my clan would collect Silas long before then. The chieftain wouldn't leave his youngest's corpse for the carrion birds. There'd be a good and proper funeral. Silas didn't deserve it, but I wouldn't deny any family their grief.

Not wanting any passing gadjos to see my bloodied condition, I cut over the fence to walk through the middle of the caravan. I didn't have the knife out, but people still gawked at me like I was armed. I stopped to look at them, tired and miserable and achy from the top of my head to the tips of my toes.

"It's over," I said to those who'd listen. "I never want to have to do anything like this again. I don't want to hurt anyone. I just want to restore the diddicoy. Then I can go back to being me . . . to being the Bethan you know." So much had changed that I didn't know if that was even possible, but saying the words—admitting that the magic was not a burden I was willing to bear—lifted a tiny bit of the weight from my shoulders.

I wanted to live a life free of blood prices and pain, and making that decision afforded me a small, weary smile. I would not be drabarni—at least, not that kind. Maybe there would be a place for my healing medicine one day.

"Maybe one day you'll forgive me," I told my people. "Maybe one day, when I am healed, I can be a healer as well."

Some people acknowledged my words with a slight nod. Others did not. I couldn't win all of them over. All magic had a cost, after all. Perhaps their fear was my tithe. I had Gran to support me, and as long as she lived, she'd be my loyal champion.

I skirted the feasting tables and started toward home. Approaching the vardo clearing, I spotted the chieftain speaking to two of his advisers by the southern paths, their heads bowed together, their voices low. I wondered about them for the first time—the three elders had been old friends, together and talking since I could remember. Were they, perhaps, the same boys who had run my father into the river so many years ago? Were Mikel and Niku the Brishen and Mander to Wen's Silas?

The chieftain lifted his head and glanced my way. He saw me standing there, covered in blood and clasping something in my fist, and fear and horror crossed his face before settling on crushing sadness.

He knows.

"The scarecrow's field. I don't know where, but he's in there. Perhaps Tomašis can show you."

Despite the chieftain's scheming, despite his having betrayed the pledge he'd made to serve Gran for life, I'd prevailed, but as the older man ran a weathered hand down his face, struggling to hide his grief, I didn't feel victorious. I just felt tired.

I walked past the men to climb the vardo steps, my hand hovering over the latch. I glanced behind me, raising my voice so it would reach their ears. "Gran saw everything in the scrying bowl. Expect to see her soon."

Wen's agony over losing his son was replaced by the same terror I'd seen on Silas's face right before he'd died. He backed away from me, then started to run.

I opened the door and stepped inside, depositing the cat fetish, the knife, and the wax doll on the bureau. Gran was busy cleaning, scraps of bloody bandages heaped in with the tattered remains of my skirt, all ready for the fire. Perhaps the catharsis I longed for was found not in the river, but in the purging flames that would rid us of so much soil.

"I am proud of you," she said.

"I'm not."

"I know, and that makes me sad for you."

She looked better than when I'd left her. The bandage on her arm was new, pristine and white. The color had returned to her face, her weathered cheeks sporting a red flush. This brought me relief, at least.

"Mander will live. He lost much blood, but given time and rest, he will prevail. The family asked if he could remain for the duration of his recovery. I said that was fine, but that he has been banished for his crimes and must leave when I deem him well enough to travel. They agreed to the terms." She glanced at me and flinched, motioning me over to the iron pot where we'd burned the rest of the offerings. "Leave the nose and go to the river. I will burn it while you wash, and then we will wake your yellow-haired man."

245

"He is not mine, but thank you."

"No, not yet, but he will be yours one day."

I was reaching for the towel and soap, and that stopped me cold. I looked at her, but she kept scrubbing the table, grunting with exertion. I could see her profile, though, and she wore a tight smile.

"What?"

"His thread is woven into your tapestry. I have seen it, and it is beautiful. Not now, perhaps, but one day, when you are recovered. He is patient, as all good love is patient. It pleases me."

I looked from her to the huge swaddled form on my mattress. I had no idea how to feel about her proclamation. I had no idea how it changed me, or him, or what would truly happen, so I shoved it off, retrieving my things and a fresh linen for my arm and bustling to the river.

"One day."

"One day."

"One day."

As far downstream as I dared, near a large tree at the river bend, I stripped to my shift. I waded hip deep into the frigid running water. I scrubbed hard, rinsing my hair a half dozen times to ensure no dirt remained, and I felt the blood and sweat washing away with the current. I was freezing when I climbed to the banks, the long locks of my hair dripping icy water over my shoulders, but it was worth the modicum of comfort it gave me. I dressed in the last of my unbloodied clothes, covered my hair with a scarf, and bundled the ruined garments for the fire. My arm looked surprisingly good considering the violence of Silas's stabbing, and I wound the bandage tight, thinking Gran might not need to take a needle to it after all.

I walked back to camp, my fingers working through the mess of my hair to loosen the snags and tangles. As soon as I neared our vardo, I smelled a strange odor, and I knew Gran had reduced Silas's nose to ash while I was gone. I walked inside right as she was using a wooden spoon to scoop chalky-looking dust from the bottom of the pot, collecting the five boys' burned offerings into a single jar.

Gran nodded at the blighted wardrobe and bandages and then pointed toward a wooden bucket.

"Burn all of it. Bucket, too. Then wash your hands."

I practically ran to the great fire so I could cast it all away. My eyes were as hungry as the flames devouring the clothes that had seen so much unpleasantness. The bucket would linger in the depths, but the fabric was consumed within minutes, and that, as much as the river, made me feel better.

I turned to go home, expecting the people around me to meet me with the same fear and distrust I'd seen earlier, but one of the women—an elder matron named Eldra—approached me, her hand reaching for my elbow.

"I am sorry," she said quietly, "for what happened to you. It sometimes takes a woman to know that particular suffering. Sit, sit."

She gestured to one of the benches where our meals were taken, and a moment later, I felt a comb streaking through my long hair. I spared a glance at the other women doing the cooking for breakfast. Most eyed us suspiciously, but because Eldra had dared to offer me kindness despite my deeds, one of the younger wives, Sophia, smiled my way, too.

It would not be easy, but perhaps it wouldn't always be terrible, either.

Eldra wrung the excess water from my hair and adjusted my shawl around my shoulders. "There. You can fashion it at home. Give my regards to the drabarni."

"I will, thank you."

I hustled home, the cold air brutal on my wet head. It was better in the vardo, but because of our drafty door, I added a second shawl to the first. I went to the basin to wash my hands as Gran fussed with supplies she'd laid out on a mat on the table.

"Did you bring the wax fetish home with you?" she asked.

I nodded and pointed at the things I'd left on the bureau. Gran rooted through the small pile to retrieve the doll, clearly not caring that the blood smearing it might transfer to her hands.

She twisted the head from its shoulders and turned it upside down to pour the contained blood into the ash. "We will reuse what we have already given," she said. Gran shook the jar to mix it, and a revolting sludge formed inside. The tarlike consistency reminded me of spring moors.

"Bring the mirror and your focus here," she said, hobbling to Martyn's side. Her joints creaked as she lowered herself to the floor.

I held them in the bell of my skirt so I could sit beside her. As soon as she rolled the blanket away from Martyn's bruised and broken face, my pulse pounded in my ears.

He's for me?

He's mine?

I just . . .

Gran tapped his waxy forehead with one of her talons. Satisfied with whatever she was looking for, she selected a small paintbrush from her supplies and dipped it into the ash jar to paint his forehead and cheeks with words I couldn't read.

It took her an hour to prepare the words. Martyn had letters over his eyes, and a letter each on his nose and mouth. There were some painted on his scalp, and others on his chest over his heart. The work was painstaking and detailed, and Gran was squinting by the time she put the finishing flourishes on him.

"I had thought one day that I would teach you all I knew," she said after a time. "This language is an old one, dead before my mother's mother and her mother's mother before her, but there is power to it still. But that is no longer your path, is it, Bethan?"

I hadn't expected her to broach the subject with me, especially not with Martyn on the floor ready for his ritual, but if this was when she wanted to discuss it, so be it.

"No, but I'd like to learn to read—Welsh first, and then maybe English."

Gran capped the ash jar and pushed it aside. "I think that is a good idea. Some of our people claim our language loses power when it is trapped upon the page, but I am not so convinced. Reading has proven useful to me as a healer over the years."

My eyes cascaded over Martyn's face, and I thought of his offer to teach me to read. Perhaps, after some time, when I was more comfortable with being in a man's presence, I could ask him to help me.

"You will heal. He will help you," Gran said quietly, likely reading my thoughts.

I nodded and sighed, my head dipping low. "I will. I'm sorry that I don't want to do magic. I'm not as strong as you."

"I disagree," she said forcefully. "Strength comes in many

guises, Bethan. Knowing yourself, your limitations—knowing what you will and will not do, following your heart—*that* is strength. Enduring what you endured and still being merciful and hopeful? Also strength. I will teach you what you would like to know of herbcraft. You can still be drabarni if you choose, without magic or just without dark magic, but your happiness will be elsewhere, I think. Clarity will come with time." She took my hand in her own, and I felt the coin she used as her focus pressed between us. She gave my fingers a squeeze, and I lifted my chin to look at her. "I am proud of you no matter your choices. All I would ask is that you weigh your happiness and the happiness of those you love before embarking on any path. Think not only of yourself, but of them, too. It was my failing long ago. Learn from my mistakes."

Her acceptance was a mercy. For years, I'd nagged her to teach me her trade. Only three days into my lessons, I was telling her I couldn't handle it, but instead of casting me out, she treated me with respect. It made my chest go tight and my eyes sting.

Gran tsked at me and gave my fingers another squeeze, much harder than the last time. Sometimes, when she wanted to make a point, her hands felt like hawks' claws. "You don't have to be a witch. But *daughters of witches* do not weep over foolish things. I will not have a soggy girl in my company. Now. Help me summon the young man. Put the mirror over his face, glass side down, so his breath can slide back in."

It was just like Gran to ruin a soft moment with scathing criticism, but I smiled in spite of it.

Balancing the mirror against Martyn's forehead and nose, I tapped my fingers along the frame to make sure it wouldn't fall. When it was as secure as it could get, I put the cat fetish in my palm and locked my hand to Gran's. She dipped her head and murmured spell words to herself. She didn't have to tell me what she wanted of me; after three days of intense ritual and spellcraft, I knew what I had to do to help Martyn—I had to want him back.

No, I had to want him back *enough*.

The slow burn of magic danced across my fingertips as I thought about Martyn behind his vegetable counter smoking, joking, and flirting. I thought about how he had stood up for me against Garth and Silas and the others. I thought about his drawings and how he'd taken the time to make me a sign for my table. I thought about the shade of his blue, blue eyes, and the richness of his laughter.

Come back to me.

Please, come back.

A warm, intense wind careened through the vardo. I opened my eyes to welcome the magic Gran and I had created. White light flickered around our joined fingers, escaping through the gaps to make starbursts on the wall. The words written on Martyn twinkled like stars before sinking into his skin and disappearing, illuminating his body from the inside.

Gran pulled our joined hands to the back of the mirror and pressed down. "Live. Live, boy," she commanded. Our power flooded the mirror, swirling from the frame to the front of the glass, honey-colored sparkles raining down on Martyn's face. It was not the cold, sludgy last breath I'd pulled from him on the poles, but an inviting sliver of sunlight that cast him in gold.

Gran dropped my hand so she could lift the glass from Martyn's face. The differences between what he'd looked like minutes ago and what he looked like now were breathtaking. The ashen quality to his skin was gone, and the bumps and bruises he'd suffered during the beating had all but disappeared. Martyn Woodard had returned to himself. Gran hovered her fingers over his mouth to feel for breath.

"Breathe, diddicoy," she barked, her brow wrinkled in consternation.

I licked my lips. "Is he . . . What's . . ."

"Be still," she said, moving in close to stare in Martyn's face. Her hair dropped down to form a stringy gray veil around his cheeks, and she touched the tip of her nose to his. Her fingertips dug into the sides of his jaw as she tilted his head back and forth to better gauge his progress. Unfortunately, that was precisely the moment Martyn decided to wake from his three-day sojourn. His eyes flew open, and as soon as he found himself face to face with a white-eyed, grizzled old hag, he screamed at the top of his lungs and bucked up from my bed.

CHAPTER TWENTY-NINE

It was not how I'd envisioned our reunion. Martyn hollered into Gran's face, Gran hollered back, and I bellowed at the top of my lungs in an effort to silence them both.

"Martyn, stop. Martyn . . . it's fine. I'm here. It's Bet." He jerked his panicked eyes my way, and I reached for his tattered sleeve, giving it a hard pull. "Stop. I'm here. It's fine. *Please.*"

His shouts diminished to mewls, and he slammed his eyes closed to take a long, deep breath. Gran muttered an unladylike oath and held her hands out to me for help. I braced under her elbows and lifted her to her feet.

"If this is the thanks I get for helping your diddicoy, Bethan, I am not sure I will leap to do it again." She reached for her cane, her hands clenching the top knob as she loomed over Martyn. "Silly boy."

"I'm sorry." Martyn's voice was raspy from disuse, and he

turned his head away from us to cough. "I'm sorry. Where am I? Bet, hello. Hi."

"In my house. My vardo," I explained.

He nodded and forced a smile, his hands going to either side of his body so he could sit up. It took him a minute to get his bearings, but after a few good head tosses and a rub of his eyes, he looked steadier. Calmer.

"Who's she?" he asked, nodding at Gran. The motion seemed to upset his equilibrium; his hands swept up to his temples and he wobbled back and forth like he might fall back onto the mattress. "Feel like I got kicked in the head by a horse. What happened?"

I was about to answer, about to explain everything, but Gran stopped me with a poke to my side. I craned my neck to peer at her, and she shook her head, letting me know without words that I ought to hold my tongue. I didn't like the idea of lying by omission, but I could see the merit in keeping my peace. Maybe one day, when I was sure he wouldn't forswear me for the foul things I'd done, I could share the whole of it.

Not yet, though.

"Silas and his boys beat you," I said. "We brought you here from the field to treat you. Gran . . ." My voice trailed off as Martyn pushed himself to stand, ducking his head so he wouldn't smack it against the ceiling beams. He reached for the thickest beam at the center and used it to right himself as he tested his legs. When I was sure he wouldn't tumble over, I continued. "This woman is my mother, but I call her Gran. She saved you."

"Oh. Oh, no. I was rude to yell. I'm so sorry." He turned to Gran and lowered his eyes, offering her a respectful bow of his head. "I'm sorry, ma'am. I didn't mean to be so thankless. You startled me, is all. You're so . . . so . . ."

"Ugly," Gran said, finishing the sentence for him.

"No! That's not what I meant!" Martyn's eyes darted my way, and he looked horribly embarrassed, but Gran snickered and jabbed at his foot with her cane.

"I am an ancient, diddicoy. But there are certain privileges that come with age. One is that we can be ugly and everyone else must suffer it."

She turned on her heel toward the vardo door, then thrust it open to let in the cold air. Her hand braced against the frame as she took the first step down, going slow to ensure she didn't misstep. Before I could rush over to help her, Martyn was there, lending her an arm and getting her steadily to the ground.

Gran patted him like he was a puppy who'd pleased her. "Good boy," she said, adding salt to the wound. I winced, hoping Martyn didn't take exception to the condescension.

"Where are you going? Do you need help?" I ran after her, but her snort stopped me in my tracks.

"I have unfinished business with Wen, and I thought you might wish to walk the yellow-haired man home before the screaming begins. You may begin your reading lessons with him whenever you are so inclined, so long as they are done here—with my supervision, during daylight hours." The fanged grin she flashed over her shoulder was more for Martyn's benefit than mine. He smiled back, likely assuming she was jesting about the screaming, but I knew better. The chieftain had broken her trust, and for it he would suffer. There was no mercy for those who betrayed her, not even for grieving fathers.

I watched Gran amble toward the great fire, ready to bolt after her at the slightest sign that she needed me, but she turned the corner with no issue.

I ducked back inside to retrieve my comb, ripping it through my hair to rid myself of any remaining snarls. Martyn watched, saying nothing, but as soon as I reached for the first hairpin, he gasped. He knew what it meant. The tradition of virgin girls being the only ones allowed to wear their hair down must have carried over to his family, too.

"How badly did he hurt you?" he croaked.

"Badly." I wanted to act like I was all right, like I was strong and resilient and nothing Silas did to me in that field could break my spirit, but the truth was, I was fragile. Martyn had proved himself a good man, and yet a part of me was too keenly aware of his presence. I noted how he looked at me, how close he was to me, where he was in relation to the door. His maleness made me view him as a threat when I knew, logically, that he deserved so much better.

I must have worn my consternation, because he retreated to put the vardo wall to his back, providing ample distance between us. The action suggested that he understood—that he cared.

"He will be yours one day," Gran had said.

Maybe.

"Thank you," I said quietly.

"No. No, I'm sorry. I wish I could have stopped it for your sake. If he comes near you again . . ."

"Don't, Martyn." The bite in my voice was softened by the strained smile on my face. He couldn't know, but unless he was interested in wrestling a ghost, there was nothing for him to defend me against anymore. "There was nothing you could do. He likely ruined me for a good marriage, but I'll be quite content helping Gran with her herbs for the rest of her years."

Martyn tossed his head, reminding me of an angry horse pulling against its reins. "Any man who wouldn't have you because of that is an idiot. It's not your fault, and damn him for hurting you."

"Oh, he is damned. Of that I have no doubt."

I finished putting up my hair, pinning the last fat lock into place near my crown. I reached for yet another fresh scarf to put over my hair, adjusting it before stepping outside. It was midday, with plenty of sunlight left, and though the wind held winter's nasty nip, the sky was blue and clear.

Together we circled the fence of Cotter's Field to find the road. Martyn fell into step beside me, keeping a respectful distance so I wouldn't know unnecessary fear. His hands explored the rips and bloodstains marring his clothes in wonderment. His shirt was so tattered that it was in danger of falling off his body, and the hooks had left gouges along the inner thighs of his pants. I wished I'd had some kind of clothing to offer him, but he was large like his father, and many of our men were short and slight. Many of us also didn't have clothing to spare, even for a good cause.

"How long have I been here? It must have been bad if I look like this. Is this blood?" he asked.

"Three days."

I stopped in the middle of the road to peer at him, my eyes traveling over his face. He paused with me, his brows lifted as he waited for me to speak. It took me a moment to collect my thoughts. I didn't want to admit that we'd lied to Mr. Woodard, but I hoped that, given the circumstances, Martyn would understand.

"My people were responsible for your injuries, and Gran was the only one who could save your life in the aftermath. She knows healing. We took you to our home, but we knew your father would be looking for you, so our chieftain told him you and I had run away to get married. He said it to buy us a few days, but I assume your father has been looking for you since. He knew we'd had trouble in Anwen's Crossing. You can tell him whatever you'd like now, but I thought you should know what was said."

Martyn reached for my unbandaged wrist, but stopped himself from making actual contact. He swept his fingers through the sides of his hair instead, taming only a few of the wheat-colored locks. "There's a problem," he said quietly.

"I'm sorry. We thought the lie was necessary."

"Don't apologize. I don't care about that. But if I were to run away with you, why would I be stupid enough to come home unmarried? He ought to wallop me."

He turned back to the road, leaving me standing there stupefied. Something stirred in my gut then—something foreign that I hadn't felt in days. *Hope.* His kindness had broken through the emptiness, fear, and self-loathing to give me a glimmer of something good.

Maybe Gran is right after all.

I'd climbed a mountain for the privilege of speaking to Martyn Woodard again. I didn't know what would happen between us. Our lives were different—he among the gadjos,

I with my people. He was a farmer, while I was a drabarni's apprentice. I had a long, hard journey ahead of me to heal my heart.

But maybe, with enough time and patience, I'd see the beautiful tapestry Gran had promised.

I picked up my skirt and hurried after him so I could walk by his side.

ACKNOWLEDGMENTS

The Hollow Girl has been a labor of love, from inception to drafting and all the way through edits. It's claimed brain real estate for well over ten years now. I remember sitting in my grandmother's apartment, listening to her talk about the story she wanted to write with the two Romani sisters, one who stayed with her people and one who moved on. Sadly, she died before she could pen it, but years later, when I followed in her footsteps as a professional, I swore I'd write something just for her. While I didn't duplicate all aspects of her tale for the reasons outlined in my foreword, I tackled the ones I felt I could do justice.

And so my biggest and most obvious thanks go to my grandmother Dorothy. She was strong and funny. She was quick and sharp and brooked no stupidity. She was proud—so proud—and never let anything keep her down for long despite odds that would have crushed others. Without her, I would not be Hillary. She was one set of hands that shaped me into the quasi-capable adult I have become. I miss her every day. I'm crying while I write this. Her loss is always with me, a wound that will never completely heal.

There are others who helped get this book onto shelves, too, and I'd be remiss not to mention them. My immediate family. My adopted family of Dave, Becky, Ethan, Lauren, Greg, and Eric. My extended family. My extended friends. I love you all. *The Hollow Girl* wouldn't have been possible without Sarah Johnson's eye—as a biracial Romani woman, her feedback was invaluable. My beta readers, including Evie Nelson, are always in my corner, and I adore them for that. T. S. Ferguson is as much a fan of me as I am of him, and he always gets me through the crazy publishing days. Thank you, love, for being there for me time and time again.

Special thanks go to Miriam Kriss, agent extraordinaire and part-time Hillary therapist, for putting up with me. My editor, Kate Sullivan, gets equal props. I remember hearing that Kate loved and hated this book in equal measure, so she had to have it, and I knew then that she'd be perfect for it—this is a book designed to make you feel, and those feelings aren't always good. She got the work and what I was trying to do with it; she gets me. Kate, you and the Delacorte team are fantastic. Thank you for everything.

ΛBOUT THE ΛUTHOR

Hillary Monahan lives in Massachusetts with her husband, hounds, and cats. She loves horror, humor, feminism, and makeup. Her YA book *Mary: The Summoning* hit the *New York Times* ebook bestseller list, and she is currently working on more dark things for the YA market.